KU-325-804

THE HEAT OF WINTER

THE HEAT OF WINTER

HOWARD HIRT

WEIDENFELD AND NICOLSON LONDON

First published in Great Britain in 1984 by
George Weidenfeld & Nicolson Limited
91 Clapham High Street, London SW4 7TA

Author's note: This is a work of fiction, and all the events recounted herein are my own creation. The personal characteristics, words, and actions of historical figures as portrayed in the book are also products of my imagination, as are the town of Ramgarh and the activities of the political parties.

ISBN 0 297 78483 8

Printed in Great Britain by
Redwood Burn Limited
Trowbridge

For Muriel Hirt, Arthur Edelstein,
and J. William Fulbright
Jai Hind

RAMGARH

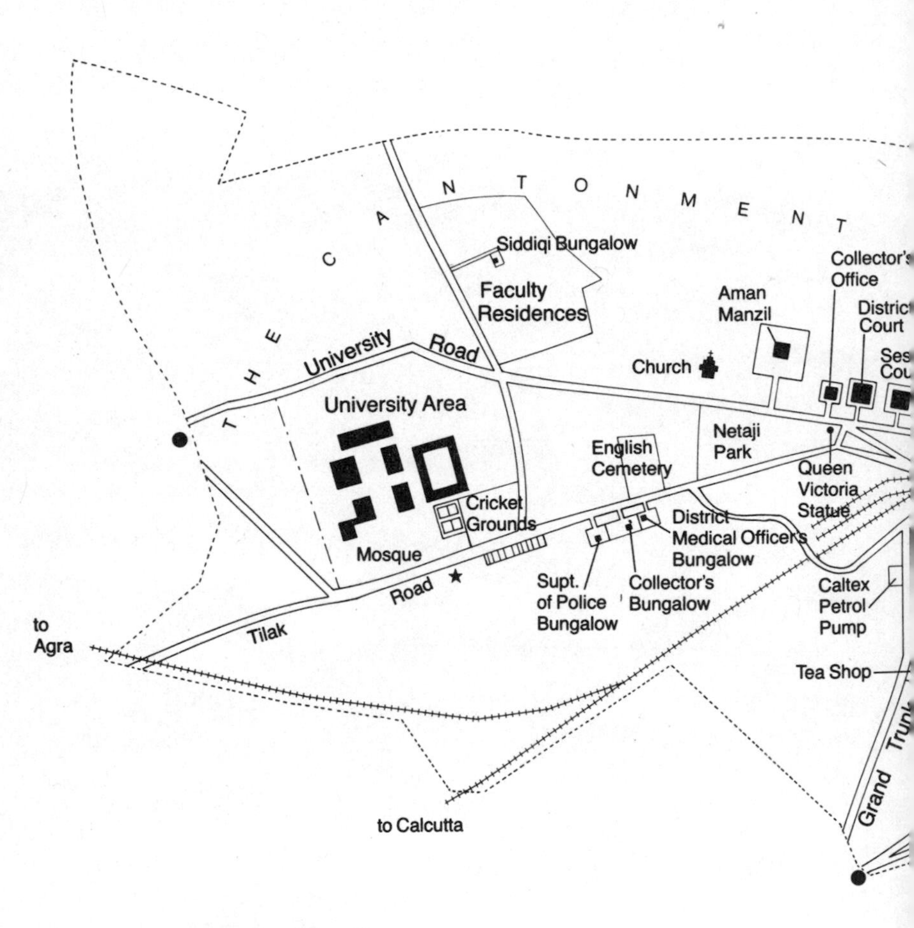

★ Police Chauki
✪ Police Headquarters
● Octroi Post
Ancient City Wall
The Old City

Scale
0 1/4

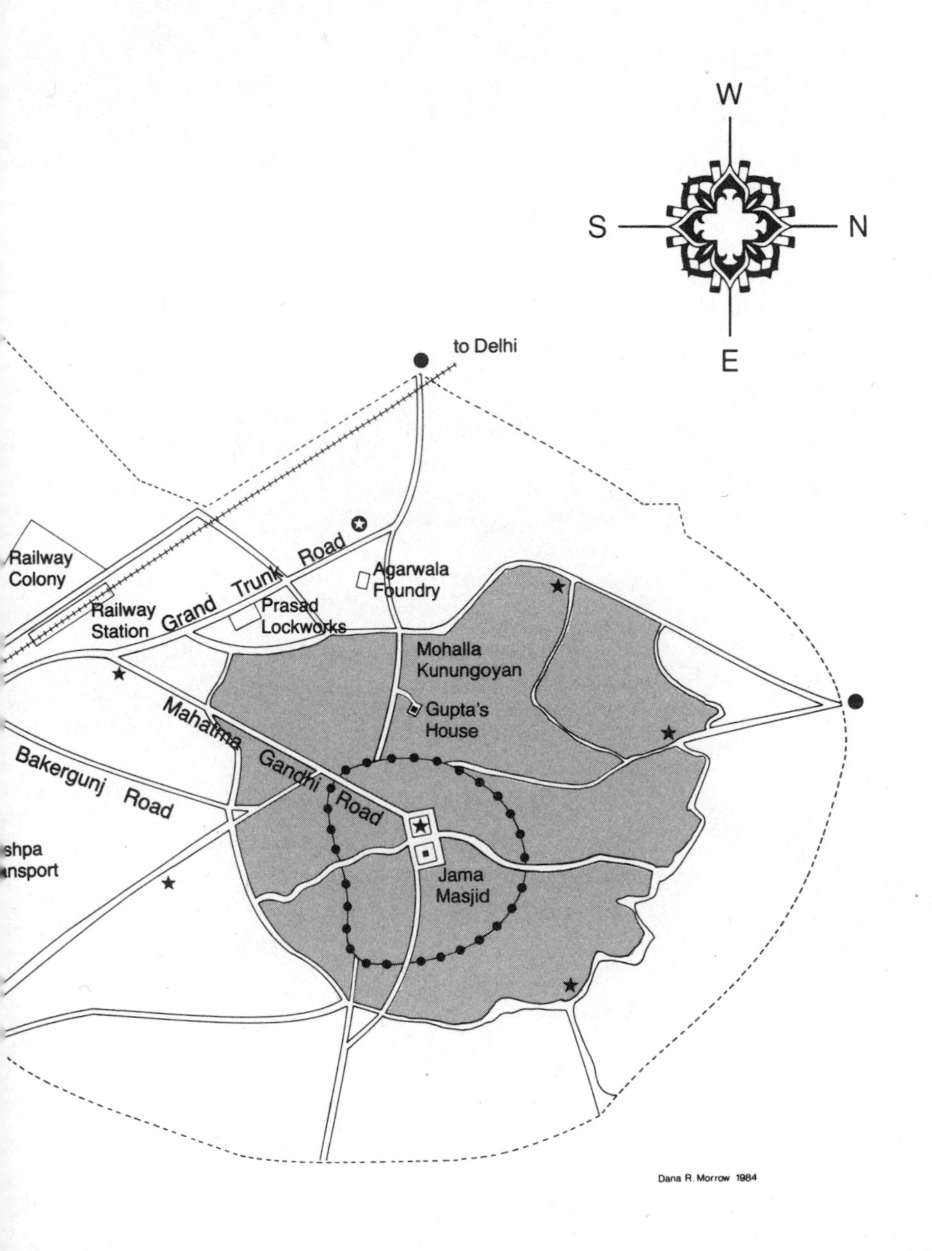

Dana R. Morrow 1984

THE HEAT OF WINTER

1

Saturday, February 9, 1952

At first only the khaki-colored dust could be seen in the distance. The dust cloud hovered in the ancient trees bordering the Grand Trunk Road southeast of Delhi. On either side of the tree line, fields of wheat—green and gold as the winter crop season neared its end—lapped at the edge of the busy thoroughfare. The north wind, streaming fitfully down from the Himalayan slopes, brushed the wheat and blew the dust into the fields lying south of the road.

As the dust cloud drew closer, the siren could be heard. Then a police jeep came into view, the first of two that shepherded the black Buick sedan. Four khaki-clad armed policemen rode in each jeep, scarves wrapped around their noses and mouths against the dust. From a small staff fixed to the Buick's hood ornament an Indian flag fluttered, its green, white, and orange stripes emblazoned with the gold *chakra* wheel of Emperor Asoka.

The road was wide enough for two lanes of traffic, but it was congested. There were ancient rusty bicycles with riders whose flowing homespun garments constantly threatened to get tangled in the sprockets. There were pedestrians of all ages and carts of all kinds—bullock carts, camel carts, and horse carts, or *tongas*. There were darting herds of goats and lumbering lines of cows and water buffaloes, none of them holding either to the left or to the right. The driver of the leading jeep jammed his foot on the brake when an old man suddenly dashed across the road in front of the motorcade as if he hoped some closely following demon would be killed by the vehicles. The officer sitting next to the driver stood up and violently thrashed his swagger stick, shouting unheeded curses.

The black sedan was driven with its windows closed—a bubble of quiet order insulated from the dust and turmoil of the road. Three men could be seen inside the car. The driver was a burly Sikh policeman with a black beard, oiled and tightly curled around a cord that passed below his jowl and was tied on top of his head under his khaki turban. The thin, clerkish-looking man next to him was physically overshadowed by the driver, but his well-cut suit, horn-rimmed glasses, and the leather dispatch box on his lap gave him the look of bureaucratic authority. Periodically he took documents and briefs from the box and passed them over his shoulder to the man in the back seat.

The passenger in the back studied each document carefully, occasionally speaking to the rider in the front while making a notation on each one before returning it. He was a man of medium build, perhaps sixty years old, with gray hair visible under his white Congress cap. His face was clean-shaven and very fair—what the Indian matrimonial advertisements describe as a "wheat" complexion. His eyes, somewhat hidden by reading glasses, had dark circles under them. His appearance was patrician; indeed, it was more European than Indian, although his expression lacked the cold detachment so characteristic of Europeans long resident in India. He wore tight white jodhpurs and a brown woolen Indian *achkan* coat with standing collar. A small red rose was fixed in the third buttonhole from the top.

The Grand Trunk Road was the ancient caravan and invasion route from the Khyber Pass to Delhi, passing from there down the valley of the Ganges to Bengal and the sea. Even in the time of Gautama the Buddha, two and a half millennia ago, it had been provided with milestones and travelers' rest houses. Now British milestones and furlong stones marked the distances, each one regularly whitewashed by the Public Works Department. The P.W.D. had also carved numbers into the trunks of the bordering trees to establish them as government property. But this did not deter the goatherds, who continued to lop off the branches with their long pruning hooks and feed the brittle leaves to their goats. The goatherds stared in sullen silence as the Buick rushed past and the dust settled on their ragged clothes.

In each town the motorcade entered, the open road became a noisy business street. Dealers in grains and spices had ranked their burlap bags in rows along the road at the front of their wooden stalls. Other businesses displayed their wares at streetside as well: rope, plows and cart wheels, timber, and clay pots. They all needed large amounts of space for their goods, and each fought to maintain access to the lorries and carts parked haphazardly both on and alongside the road, waiting to be hired.

At midmorning the motorcade stopped briefly for the policemen to moisten their dusty throats at one of the restaurants and tea stalls clustered near the town bus stand. The travelers and shoppers from rural villages sat on benches outside the stalls and slurped milky tea from saucers. Cups of tea were brought out to the policemen from a restaurant whose gaudy red and yellow signboard proclaimed in English, "Shri Nivas Vegetarian Hotel—Cheapest and Best!"

A small crowd immediately gathered, the men staring in silence and the boys giggling and pushing each other. The passengers in the Buick closed the privacy curtains fitted to the side and rear windows and drank their tea from a thermos flask. After a few minutes the senior police officer shouted a command and the motorcade moved on.

Animals and people, crowded together by the bustle of commerce, were even greater obstacles to the motorcade in town than on the highway. Women, who padded along the road holding babies on their hips and, with their free hand, carefully shielded their faces from view with the ends of their *saris*, were barely able to see the moving vehicles. Blowing their horns continuously and weaving from side to side through the towns, the motorcade managed to reach Nawabganj, the last town before Ramgarh.

The lead jeep slowed as it entered the town. Nawabganj seemed to differ little from other towns they had passed through. But here the shops were closed and the road, although narrow, was clear of traffic. The route took them closer than usual to the center of town, and there was a sharp ninety-degree turn where the road avoided an ancient shrine. The lead jeep's driver, tense and tired, rounded the turn, swerved to avoid a woman, and collided with a lorry that was blocking the road. Another lorry lurched out from an alley and pulled up behind the Buick. The motorcade was trapped. And, in a small room whose window overlooked the street, the waiting gunman drew back the hammer of his revolver.

2

Tuesday, January 1, 1952

Superintendent Mohammed Abdul Karim Khan, B.A., B.L., Indian Police Service, groaned wearily, lifted himself onto one elbow, and peered into the darkness of his second-class compartment on the Raipur–Delhi Night Passenger train. For the fourth time the old steam engine and its six ancient cars had lurched to a stop. Karim groped for the handle, raised the dusty steel shutter a few inches, and scanned the flat landscape of the Upper Ganges Valley. The full moon, hanging in the clear winter sky, delicately sculptured the flat-roofed mud and brick buildings of a nearby village. From the other side of the train he could hear the hoarse, agonized shouts of watchmen in the fields, who were vainly trying to frighten the monkeys away from the ripening wheat crop. From the crowded third-class carriages forward, and from the ticketless travelers riding the roofs, came animated conversation, punctuated by frequent laughter and song.

A railwayman plodded by, deeply inhaling from a brown *bidi* cigarette held in his cupped right hand.

"*Arrey bhai,*" called Karim. "What's the matter now?"

"The Calcutta Mail, sahib. We must wait until it goes by." The railwayman coughed, the wheeze reverberating through his chest, and spat onto the gravel roadbed.

"How long must we wait?"

"Coming just now, sahib."

With a sigh, Karim reached into the deep side pocket of the khaki police jacket hanging from a hook above his head and pulled out a packet of Sepoy cigarettes and a box of matches. He knew that "Coming just now" meant that the wait might be twenty minutes or two hours. Shifting his lean body under his blanket, Karim struck a match; its flare illuminated the timeworn walls and fittings of the carriage and the picture of a soldier on the cigarette packet. He lighted his cigarette, rubbed his mustache, and lay back.

"So you are in a hurry to get to Ramgarh, sahib?" observed a man who lay in his bedroll on the opposite side of the compartment. "Even though I live there, I am in no hurry to go back." Karim switched on the light, which revealed a Sikh with a grizzled beard and hair gathered in a bun at the top of his head.

"Why not, sardarji?" Karim asked, using the respectful form of address.

"Why yes, sahib! It's not a good place. I belong to Lahore. I came to Ramgarh at Partition time in 1947," he said. So the old Sikh was going to tell his life story. Well, there were worse ways to pass the time. "My wife and my three children were killed in the riots. With my wife's gold bangles I bought a share of a Caltex petrol station on the Grand Trunk Road. I'm a good motor mechanic, sahib." The Sikh sat up in his bedroll, rubbed his bearded face, arranged his blanket over his shoulders, and made himself comfortable. "And what about you, sahib?"

"I am posted to Ramgarh as superintendent of police. What is your name, sardarji?"

"Harbans Singh, sahib. And yours?"

On hearing Karim's name, Harbans Singh fell silent. There it was again. That silence when they learned you were a Muslim. These refugees. Would they ever forget? He sat up and folded his arms over his chest, one hand covering two round scars in his upper left arm.

"I am not one of your Pakistanis, sardarji," Karim said after a moment. "I belong to Lucknow, and my family has been Indian for five hundred years. I am sworn to uphold the law, sardarji, and I don't care if a man is Muslim, Hindu, Sikh, or Christian. Now tell me, why don't you like it in Ramgarh?"

Harbans Singh's mouth fell open and he leaned back against the compartment wall as if to deflect Karim's intensity. He stared at Karim. After a moment he bent forward, his brow knitted and his hands clasped in front of his chest.

"Ramgarh is not a happy place, Superintendent Sahib," he said in a low tone. "It reminds me too much of Lahore before the Partition. There is the smell of riot in the air." He paused. "Last week, when I was in a tea shop near my petrol pump, I heard some men talking about going out to the university and setting fire to some of the buildings."

"Why would they do that?"

"Well, sahib, the university is all Muslim, as you must know. And they say that most of the teachers and students are more loyal to Pakistan than to India."

"Who are 'they'?"

"The Hindu Mahasabha and the R.S.S., sahib. They're very strong in Ramgarh City, and they say that the university is full of Communists and Muslim Leaguers."

Harbans Singh's words were almost drowned out as the Calcutta Mail, its whistle shrieking a warning, rushed by on the main track at fifty miles an hour. In response, the Raipur–Delhi Night Passenger sounded a weary, plaintive whistle to gather up its passengers and trundled slowly onto the main line to continue its interrupted journey.

Karim reached again into his jacket pocket and pulled out another cigarette. As he fumbled with the matchbox he glanced over at Harbans Singh. An expression of mild distaste had come over the Sikh's round, tough-looking face, with its nose like an apricot. Karim put away the cigarettes and matches.

"Smoking may be against our religion, Superintendent Sahib, but smoke if you want to. This is a railway bogie, not a *gurudwara*." The train lurched and the old army overcoat hanging on a hook over his bench brushed against the Sikh's face. "No, sahib," Harbans Singh chuckled. "Definitely not a Sikh temple."

Karim took a deep breath and rubbed his hooked nose and his narrow cheeks. He could stop smoking for a few hours to avoid offending this cordial Sikh. "How long did you serve in the army, sardarji?" he asked.

"The army? Ah, Superintendent Sahib," the Sikh chuckled, "you are a true policeman. My coat is the evidence, isn't it? Five years, sahib. Good years they were, even though I was in Egypt, far from my village. I was trained as a motor mechanic."

"The army was a good schoolmaster, eh, sardarji? If you did your job and didn't complain, it treated you like the top boy in school. If you got into trouble, it could make the worst caning seem like a tickle."

"That's the truth, sahib. The real truth. Were you in the army too?" Harbans Singh rummaged in his kit bag and pulled out a *chapati*.

"I was only in the military police, sardarji. Before the war I was a new assistant subinspector in Bharatpur Town. Meerut District. You know it? No excitement in Bharatpur.

Very peaceful, very law abiding. Not the kind of place for a policeman to make a good record. I'd still be an assistant subinspector if I'd stayed in Bharatpur."

"Well, sahib," Harbans Singh broke in, "if countries did not go to war there would be no need for generals." He tore off a piece of the *chapati* and offered the flatbread to Karim.

"Sad but true, sardarji. Well," Karim continued, shaking his head to decline the offer, "I used to visit Meerut Cantonment on my days off. I met a friend there from law college. He was a sublieutenant in the military police. It seemed like an exciting life with good pay and lots of time for sports. So when the war came I became a sublieutenant also."

"Did you serve in the Western Desert, sahib?" A bit of *chapati* clung to the Sikh's beard.

"No, sardarji. No glory in my army career." Karim sighed. "I spent my six years catching deserters and stealers of military supplies. Just an ordinary police job with different badges on my uniform. I guess I wasn't bad at it, though," he said with a smile. "They made me a major before the war was over."

"*Shabbash!*" Harbans Singh said approvingly. "Bravo!"

The man seemed more relaxed now, Karim thought. Maybe he could probe a little deeper.

"Tell me, sardarji, as one old soldier to another, which do you think is stronger in Ramgarh, the Hindu Mahasabha or the R.S.S.?"

Harbans Singh hesitated. He kept his eyes on Karim as he chewed and swallowed the last bit of *chapati* and then wiped his beard with his hand. There was a sudden jolt as the brakes squealed and the train came to a quivering stop. Karim's jacket and Singh's overcoat swung back and forth on their hooks. After a few seconds the train moved forward again, accompanied by the shrieks of its whistle.

"Superintendent Sahib, they are both strong," the Sikh said carefully. "But the R.S.S. is more dangerous."

"More dangerous? Why, sardarji?"

"They have arms, sahib. I don't know where they get them, but they have pistols and they hold target practice out in the jungly land by the Black River. Some take shotguns and say they're hunting birds, but others go with pistols and practice shooting. I go out to the villages once a week with paraffin for the farmers' lamps, and I've heard them and talked with the farmers about them. I'm a soldier, sahib, and I can tell the difference between the sound of a shotgun and a pistol."

"Who is the chief of the R.S.S. in Ramgarh, sardarji?"

"I'm not sure, sahib. Some say it's Surendra Gupta. He's an advocate in the city."

"And who is the leader of the Mahasabha?"

"That is well known, sahib. Ram Lal Prasad, the president of the Municipal Committee. He became head last year when his father died. Shiva Prasad, the lock merchant. Very rich man."

Harbans Singh yawned and stretched his arms. "I think I'll try to get some sleep. Busy day tomorrow."

Karim lay down, pulled the blanket over his shoulders, and turned out the compartment light. New Year's Day, 1952 had already arrived. With any luck he also might get a few hours sleep before the train arrived at Ramgarh in the early morning. Time enough to get cleaned up and ready to inspect the welcoming party that would be waiting at the railway station. He lay with his eyes open, listening to the click of the steel wheels, thinking about what Harbans Singh had said.

The Raipur–Delhi Night Passenger rattled south toward Ramgarh, its decrepit engine puffing and hissing faster now as the line gradually descended to the Ganges River. The moon revealed a more rugged landscape as the train entered the eroded, ravine-laced northern fringe of the river. In this jungle of nearly impenetrable brush and trees, there were few villages or fields. The land was too poor and gullied for cultivation, but it was ideal for *dacoits*, bandits like the one who had shot Karim in the arm.

After several miles the slope flattened, but the engineer and the fireman struggled to keep the train at top speed to help it up the ramp of the Ganges Bridge. There were excited cries from the Hindu passengers as the train rumbled onto the bridge and the Holy Ganges, shining under the moonlight, came into view. At the exact center of the river, almost in unison, they gave a great shout: "*Mata Ganga-ji ki Jai!*" Hail to Mother Ganges!

Mohammed Abdul Karim was asleep.

3

Prime Minister Jawaharlal Nehru stood isolated and remote from the fifty thousand people gathered on the grassy *maidan* below the Lahore Gate of the Red Fort in Delhi. But to them the white-clad figure on the parapet was the designated successor to their saintly assassinated leader, Mahatma Gandhi. Nehru was their father and their mother. Their happiness, their welfare, even their lives were in his strong, competent hands.

The prime minister finished his speech in English, celebrating the second anniversary of India's adoption of a republican constitution, which ended her formal status as a dominion within the British Empire. Some of the people thronging the field understood him, but most were there mainly to receive *darshan,* or blessing, from his presence. They cheered as the prime minister, with a warm smile on his patrician features and a red rose in his buttonhole, joined his palms together and accepted their ovation.

Nehru turned, stepped down from the podium, and shook hands with the ministers who had sat behind him during his speech. Then he made his way down the steps leading to the vaulted arcade behind the massive wooden gate. Followed by his military aide and his ministers, the prime minister passed by the souvenir and jewelry shops lining the arcade and entered the outer court of the palace of the Moghul Emperor Shah Jahan. There they turned left and crossed the carefully trimmed lawn toward a large striped tent in which refreshments had been set out on tables.

The prime minister was frowning. The Republic Day reception, the principal event of the year for the foreign diplomatic corps, was about to begin. He walked slowly along the open side of the tent, checking the trays full of crisply fried *samosas* stuffed with spiced vegetables and meat, the piles of cucumber sandwiches and biscuits, the mounds of sweet *halva* covered with tissue-thin sheets of beaten silver foil, and the teapots kept warm under their cozies. Everything seemed ready. His instructions had been followed to the letter. He smiled gratefully at the white-turbaned servants who stood behind the tables and bowed as he passed.

The prime minister turned away from the tent and looked out at the crowd. Everyone seemed to be on hand. The ambassadors, high commissioners, bemedaled military attachés, and their wives were sitting on lawn chairs or standing around chatting and looking at their fellow guests. Probably, he thought, they were mentally appraising each other's finery. Even the Soviet ambassador had turned up in a white diplomatic uniform with lots of gold braid, rather than in his usual baggy blue suit. The colorful scene reminded him of the Shalimar Garden in his ancestral Kashmir.

The president of India rose to greet the prime minister as he approached. He had been seated in a cushioned wicker chair near the tent listening to the prime minister's speech broadcast over a loudspeaker. The president was about six feet tall, with a ruddy complexion and a trimmed gray beard. His black *shervani* coat and gray karakul cap identified him as a Muslim, one of the few senior Muslim politicians who had rejected Mohammed Ali Jinnah's call for a theocratic state of Pakistan. He had cast his lot with a democratic, secular India in which all religions would be equal. The ruling Congress Party had elected him to his largely ceremonial office to show their gratitude for his support, to display to the world India's secular constitution, and to bind India's fifty million Muslims to the party.

The president stepped away from the gold-braided military aides surrounding him and greeted the prime minister with a handshake.

"Congratulations, old friend," he said. "A fine speech. You have said what needed to be said. India must not let its conflicts with Pakistan poison the relations between the Hindu and Muslim communities in this country."

"Thank you, Khan Sahib. I know that the Pakistanis would like nothing better than a full-fledged communal riot to damage us in the eyes of the world and weaken our claim to Kashmir."

The president laid his hand on Nehru's shoulder and looked down at him with a wistful smile. "Now that I've given the speech my official blessing, Panditji, I must tell you that you're still a spellbinder. I would give anything to move an audience like you do."

"Thank you again, Khan Sahib. But let's not keep our guests waiting any longer for their tea."

The president and the prime minister went over to the tables and were served their cups of tea. Now the diplomatic guests could be served. The British high commissioner and his wife, given precedence by protocol, made their way to the table and took cups of tea surrounded by several *samosas* on each saucer. They came over to Nehru, who was circulating among the guests urging them to try the Indian snacks.

"I couldn't agree with you more, Prime Minister," Sir David White said with a chuckle. "My wife has been looking for a year for a good cook for English dishes and she's finally given up. We serve our guests mainly Indian food now." Sir David took a large bite of his *samosa*. Bits of flaky crust fell onto his dark blue jacket. "Oops! I'm making a mess of this one," he said, brushing crumbs from his gray military mustache.

"David, you're getting yourself all dirty! I've told you to lean forward when you eat!" Eve White flicked the handkerchief in her white-gloved hand over her husband's jacket and sent some of the crumbs flying onto the prime minister's spotless white *achkan*.

"Oh, my gracious, Prime Minister, I'm awfully sorry! Here, let me get those crumbs off your coat." Eve White was a full head taller than the prime minister. The sight of a large, bleached-blonde Englishwoman in a flowered print dress flicking and whipping her handkerchief up and down the prime minister's chest created a certain amount of amused interest among the bystanders.

"I see the Pommies have developed a new technique of diplomatic intercourse—flogging with the kerchief of nine tails," cracked the Australian military attaché.

With a wry smile, Nehru stoically endured his punishment, anxious to let the incident pass without further embarrassing his guest.

"Thank you, Lady White," he said gently. "Have you tried any of our South Indian food, Sir David?"

"Not yet, sir. My consul in Madras tells me it's mostly vegetarian."

"Two weeks from today, when I return from Ramgarh, I would like you and Lady White to come to my house for a real South Indian dinner. I'll borrow a cook from Doctor Chettiar, my physician. We'll have some *masala dosa*, *idli*, rice, *sambar*, vegetable curries on a banana leaf, and real South Indian coffee. Can you eat with your fingers like an Indian?"

"We'll be delighted to try, Prime Minister. And I'll be sure to lean forward when I eat. May I ask what takes you to Ramgarh?"

"India has two universities that are administered by the central government, Sir David. Banaras Hindu University and Ramgarh Muslim University. I'm driving down there to install the new vice chancellor, Doctor Ibrahim Shamir Khan Gilani. He's distantly related to our president, you know."

"Is he the Doctor Gilani who tried to save Mahatma Gandhi when he was assassinated?"

"Yes, he is. He's also a good educationist. He's the principal of Delhi Medical College. And he's written some excellent poetry in Urdu and English. I hope he'll be a stabilizing influence at Ramgarh."

"Perhaps I'd better not take up any more of your time, Prime Minister. My wife and I will be looking forward to our dinner at your bungalow."

Shadows had begun to lengthen across the garden. Noting that his guests were eating, drinking, and chatting, Nehru felt he could slip away and get back to work. But first he had to take leave of the president, who was talking with the Soviet ambassador. He sent his aide to the president's aide, who whispered a message into the president's ear. Gracefully concluding the conversation, the president turned toward the prime minister, who came to him with his palms joined together.

"It's time for me to leave, Khan Sahib. Please give my *salaams* to your good wife. You and the guests will enjoy the fireworks this evening. There are chairs set up on top of the wall overlooking the river. It should be very fine. *Namaste*," he concluded, using the Hindu greeting.

"*Adab Arz*, sahib," said the president, raising his right hand to his forehead in the Muslim greeting. "It's been good to see you looking so fit. And that speech. Marvelous! I'll call you when I return from my visit to the South."

Signaling to his aide to follow him, Nehru left the garden by the little used Delhi Gate in the southern wall. There his black Buick sedan and jeep escort were waiting for him. The car moved slowly out of the fort onto Elgin Road, turned south, and entered Faiz Bazaar Road. Crowds of celebrants were leaving the *maidan*, many of them headed for the riverbank to see the fireworks. The Buick had to slow considerably to avoid hitting pedestrians. Cheers arose when it became known whose car it was. People crowded closer to look.

As the sedan reached the Delhi Gate of the Old City and turned right onto Circular Road, an old sandal flew out of the crowd and landed on the roof of the prime minister's car. The road seemed clear ahead so the jeep speeded up, its siren wailing. But suddenly the Buick was all but surrounded by two dozen young men on bicycles, who tried to slow its progress. Every cyclist had an old sandal in one hand. Shouting the slogan "*Hindu Raj! Hindu Raj!*" they rode close to the car and pounded with their sandals on its roof and windows. The Sikh driver, shocked at this insult, raced his engine and roared out of the crowd, knocking over one of the bicyclists. The young rider quickly picked himself up and, with his fellow demonstrators, disappeared into the crowd.

4

The Raipur–Delhi Night Passenger arrived at Ramgarh Junction at 5:07 A.M., thirty-two minutes late. The train clanked and hissed slowly through the dark railway yard, feeling for the switches that would move it onto the main line to Delhi and into the station. As usual, the second-class sleeper bogie in which Karim and the Sikh were riding was detached and shunted onto a spur so that its passengers could detrain at a later, more convenient time. The remaining five bogies, all third class, discharged passengers and picked up new ones with the customary tumult of shouts and haggling with the platform coolies. After about thirty minutes the train guard blew his whistle and the ancient engine sputtered and rattled out of the station in the direction of Delhi, pulling its bogies like ducklings behind it.

Karim and Harbans Singh were both awakened by the noise and jerking of the shunting process. Karim raised the steel shutter slightly. Morning twilight had just begun, and the shapes of low buildings with flat roofs were just emerging from the darkness. Karim noticed a coolie, dressed in the traditional smock and turban and carrying a lantern, walking along the track toward his bogie and stepping cautiously on each tie as if in an unfamiliar environment. The coolie carefully circled the bogie, holding up his lantern to peer at the names of the passengers written on paper reservation slips pasted alongside the compartment door. Ramgarh was indeed an exceptional place, Karim thought. Here was a platform coolie who could read English.

The coolie did not notice Karim. After looking under the bogie for a moment, he moved away, continuing to step carefully along the tracks.

"It's a cold morning, Superintendent Sahib," Harbans Singh said from under his blanket. "A hot cup of tea would be very nice, but there's no chance of getting one until we're pushed in to the platform at seven."

"I can wait, sardarji."

Harbans Singh sat up and stroked his beard. "I have a suggestion, sahib. Let's leave our baggage in the bogie and go over to my petrol station. It's only a short distance from here on the Grand Trunk Road. You come with me there. I'll make some tea and toast and an omelet with chilies. My nephew will heat some water so we can have hot baths. Then we can come back to the station and get our trunks and bedding when they push the bogie in."

Karim thought for a moment about the Sikh's invitation. His arrival in Ramgarh would be expected, of course. Saxena would be meeting him with a delegation on the platform. It was an important part of the ritual of his taking charge of the district. Yet Harbans Singh's suggestion was intriguing. It would cement a relationship with a knowledgeable local citizen. And with no one to raise an eyebrow. Once he had taken charge, his chances of meeting anyone informally would be limited.

"Good idea, sardarji. I'll be happy to come with you. But maybe I'd better visit you in mufti. I'll wear my civilian coat." Karim extracted from his steel trunk his brown tweed jacket with the leather elbow patches, purchased from a departing English officer in 1947. He folded his uniform jacket carefully and locked it in the trunk—first, however, removing his service revolver and putting it in the inside pocket of his English jacket. "Let's go, sardarji. I need that bath."

The two men opened the compartment door and backed down the steps to the ground. The sky was light now but it was still very cold. Harbans Singh led the way across the tracks to a barbed wire fence. After helping each other through the fence, they stepped carefully down a narrow, fetid alley. Dogs barked as they passed. Karim wrinkled his nose and held his breath at the smell of excrement. Then they emerged onto the Grand Trunk Road. Turning right, away from the city, they walked on the concrete pavement for a quarter of a mile to the Caltex sign.

The petrol station was closed and dark. It consisted of a pump, a small, white cement building, and an open grease pit.

Harbans Singh rapped on the door. "Tej Pal Singh, wake up!" he called softly and rapped again. "It is I, Harbans Singh."

There was a rattle of bolts being drawn and the door opened, at first slightly, then wide. "*Sat Sri Akal*, uncleji," said a young Sikh boy in a sleepy voice. "I didn't expect you until later."

"*Sat Sri Akal*, Teja. Now listen. This is a friend of mine who will have a bath and breakfast with me. Now I want you to light the pressure stove and heat up a bucket of water. While it is heating you can boil water on the charcoal stove and make us tea."

Tej Pal Singh could not have been more than fifteen years old, and looked twelve. Without his turban his hair reached to his waist. Only his wispy beard gave a hint of his approaching manhood. He quickly gathered his hair into a bun on top of his head and secured it with a wooden comb. "I'll heat the water for the tea first on the pressure stove, uncle. We have no charcoal left. The kettle will boil quickly."

While his hosts were getting things ready, Karim took in the room. The place looked as if the two men were camping there, ready to move out at a moment's notice. Two *charpoy* beds made of wood and rope, steel trunks, clothes hanging from hooks on the wall, a place to bathe, a few pots and pans, a picture of Guru Govind Singh. At one end of the room were an iron safe, a table with some ledgers, a few tools. Not much to make a decent living with.

"I think I'll go outside for a moment while the water is heating, sardarji," Karim said. He needed a smoke. The road still lay in the shadows of early morning and the street lights were on. Karim lighted a Sepoy and inhaled deeply. As he exhaled, he heard a dull boom as from a muffled explosion. Looking toward the source of the sound, he saw a tower of yellow and red flames shoot up in the direction of the railway yard.

"Harbans Singh, come out here for one moment, please."

"Coming, sahib." The Sikh emerged from the building energetically mixing egg and chili mixture in a cracked china bowl.

"Look over there. Where do you think that fire is burning?"

"It looks like it's in the railway yard, sahib. What can it be?"

"Put down the bowl and lead me over there, sardarji. It may be an emergency of some sort."

"Yes, Superintendent Sahib." Harbans Singh went back into the building and came out wearing his military overcoat and carrying a five-foot, steel-tipped bamboo *lathi*. "Just in case, sahib."

The two men hurried in the direction of the flames, retracing their path of thirty minutes before. They went back through the same noisome alley to the barbed wire fence. Then they stopped and looked through the fence at the flames.

"Our bogie is on fire, sahib," Harbans Singh said in a voice trembling with wonder and shock. The ancient wooden railway carriage was completely engulfed in flames. Its steel framework glowed with heat, while the steel shutters barely concealed the inferno within. Karim heard pistol shots and he remembered that he had left a box of .38 caliber rounds in his trunk. He felt in his pocket to be sure that his pistol was safe. But his clothing . . . his papers . . . everything else . . . !

The two men squeezed through the fence for a closer look. The heat forced them to shield their faces with their hands. Crouching down and thrusting his *lathi* forward, Harbans Singh poked at the door of the burning bogie.

"Sahib, look there!"

Karim peered at the door but was unable to make out what the Sikh was pointing to. "What is it, sardarji?"

Harbans Singh turned to Karim. He looked bewildered. "A lock, sahib. A lock on the outside. The door was locked from the outside!"

Karim looked at him with narrowed eyes. Then over Singh's shoulder he saw a small group of men moving toward them. Some of the men seemed to be carrying *lathis*.

"Come, sardarji, let's get back to your petrol pump. We can't save our baggage. We're lucky to have saved our lives. There's nothing we can do at the moment."

Karim's heart was pounding and a dull ache knotted his stomach as he followed Harbans Singh back through the fence and out to the Grand Trunk Road.

"Superintendent Sahib, I think this fire was no accident."

"We shall look for evidence, sardarji. The police will take care of it. Now let's see how Teja is doing with the bath water."

5

"So now we are to have a Muslim pig for a superintendent of police!" Surendra Gupta spat out the words as he sat in his sparsely furnished office in *Mohalla* Kanungoyan, the ancient lawyers' quarter. His left heel was pulled up to rest on the seat of his chair, while his fingers busily explored between the toes that stuck out from beneath the folds of his clean white *dhoti*.

Govind, Gupta's peon, looked down at the handwritten note that Gupta had crumpled and thrown onto his desk among the green file folders and week-old newspapers that covered it. He reached for the note and his gnarled brown hand knocked one of Gupta's brass paperweights onto the tile floor. Squatting down in front of the desk, he picked up the paperweight, replaced it, and took a box of matches from his jacket pocket. He struck a match, which broke; struck another, which fizzled out; and finally lighted one and set fire to the message. He dropped the paper on the rust-colored tiles and watched it burn to ash. Govind then extracted a packet of *bidi* cigarettes from his pocket, lit one with similar difficulty, and retreated to the corner of the room. Puffing and coughing, he waited in a squatting position for his employer's instructions.

Gupta removed his steel-rimmed eyeglasses and rubbed his eyes. His knuckles pressed into his eye sockets, driving his anger deep into his skull. Replacing the glasses, he pushed himself up from his chair, adjusted his sweater and brown tweed jacket, and went over to the mirror on the grimy, fly-specked wall. Its dusty, blotched surface tried to reflect the gaudy image of Ganesh, the Elephant God of Wisdom and Success, the Remover of Obstacles, that bedizened a calendar hanging on the opposite wall. The calendar proclaimed the virtues of Shiva Prasad and Son (Private) Ltd., Lock Merchants and Manufacturers.

Gupta wiped the mirror with his sleeve and stared at his image. He was a thin, ascetic-looking man. His head, shaved except for a small tuft in the back, was covered with gray stubble. In this respect it resembled his face, for he had not been to the barber for several days. A totally ordinary face, he thought. It could pass unnoticed in any crowd in North India. Perhaps he should get new glasses and grow a mustache. That might look more distinctive. His lips were getting red from betel leaf. He would definitely have to stop chewing so much *paan*.

Gupta turned away from the mirror and went over to the front door. He opened it and stood on the threshold, looking up the narrow alley toward a busy street fifty yards away.

"What time did Ram Lal Prasad say he would come to see me?" he asked over his shoulder.

"At four o'clock, sahib," Govind answered.

"Then go upstairs to the kitchen. Tell my wife to prepare tea and sweets for four o'clock. Tell her that my guest has a good appetite."

While Govind circled around the desk and past a large steel safe to the rear door of the office, Gupta lingered in the doorway. He looked down the nameless alley toward another lawyer's house—*Mohalla* Kanungoyan was still occupied by many poor advocates—and noted with satisfaction that the man's porch, which he had illegally extended into the narrow street, had been damaged by a passing bullock cart. The December sun was warming the paving stones briefly before the alley returned to its usual shadow. Flies, enlivened by the heat, buzzed along the open drains that ran down each side. A dollop of human excrement was flushed from one of the many pipes that emerged from the bases of the narrow old buildings lining the alley. Gupta wrinkled his nose at the smell.

Returning to his desk, Gupta pondered his situation. The R.S.S. The Rashtriya Swayamsevak Sangh. The police knew he was the leader of the R.S.S. in Ramgarh. It was a banned organization, since those hotheads had shot Mahatma Gandhi in '48. It wasn't fair! It was stupid! They weren't even members of the R.S.S. Why should the R.S.S. suffer?

The R.S.S. had a record to be proud of. Who else had gotten revenge for the killing of Hindus by the Muslims in Pakistan? Who else had shown those Muslim pigs that killing refugees was a game that Hindus could play as well?

But that was the past. It was the future that was the decisive question. *Hindu Rashtra!* That would be the future for India. *Hindu Rashtra!* Once again India would be a Hindu realm, where the ancient gods and the ancient virtues would again be supreme and Hindus would rule. Gupta turned his head and looked at the picture of Ganesh, whose three eyes contemplated the office with unfocused benevolence. The god would grant me success, Gupta thought, in spite of the temporary victory of those Muslim lovers.

Gupta picked up his copy of *The Statesman* and began to read the political columns once again. Their parliamentary correspondent was analyzing Prime Minister Nehru's latest speech to the House of the People. Socialism, equality, and respect for the different traditions of India's diverse peoples. Gupta's teeth clenched, his hands trembled. He read on. Nehru wanted peaceful relations with India's neighbors. Settlement of the Kashmir dispute with Pakistan. Pakistan! Gupta's fist hammered the desk in frustration. If it hadn't been for Nehru and Gandhi and that Congress crowd, there would never have been a Pakistan! A thousand years of Muslim and British rule had failed to eliminate the Hindu religion. If it hadn't been for Nehru and Gandhi, *Hindu Rashtra* would have been achieved in 1947 when the British pulled out!

A fly buzzed into the room and settled on Gupta's head. He waved his arm abruptly and the fly landed on the desk. Gupta slapped and swatted at the fly, but it nimbly evaded his hand. He sat back in his chair and contemplated the fly, cleaning itself with its two front feet. Then he slowly stretched his arms and clapped his hands together about three inches above the fly. Success! The fly had jumped up and been trapped in Gupta's palms. Gupta smiled. Planning and stealth could achieve what sheer violence could not.

He turned to his other newspaper, the *Times of India*. An article on Mao Tze-tung and the Chinese Revolution. Power comes from the barrel of a gun, the quotation read. Smart fellow, that Mao. A humble peasant's son, unknown, yet now he ruled a quarter of the human race.

Ahmedabad. Riots down in Ahmedabad, he read. Muslims and Hindus fighting. The Muslims objected to a Hindu procession using one of the streets in their *mohalla*. The police had opened fire to disperse the rioters. Guns. That was how the government enforced its rule. Mao was right.

Guns were power. To control India you only needed a few guns in the right places at the right time.

Gupta sat back in his chair, rubbing the stubble on his cheeks. He looked around the room with distaste, taking in the grimy walls, the decrepit chairs, the bookcase with the broken glass door and the aged, leatherbound books on contracts, torts, and the Code of Criminal Procedure filling its sagging shelves. A nobody, that's what he was. An unknown lawyer in a nameless street in an obscure town. Well, it wouldn't be for much longer.

What a pity old Shiva Prasad was no longer here. What a man he had been! What an appetite, for power as well as food. The fattest and the most feared politican in Ramgarh. The leader of the Hindu Mahasabha, the political party that controlled Ramgarh, much to the annoyance of the Congress Party. Oh, he had known how to get things done. If you got on the wrong side of Shiva Prasad, you risked having your head bashed in or your shop vandalized by the tough *goondas* who hung around the Mahasabha's headquarters on Mahatma Gandhi Road.

But a man of culture too. Those monthly concerts in his home. Anyone in Ramgarh who wanted to enter the inner circle of power and wealth prayed for an invitation to one of Shiva Prasad's cultural evenings. Gupta had prayed in vain.

He returned to his desk. Poor old Shiva Prasad. The lock business and the leadership of the Hindu Mahasabha had passed to his son, Ram Lal. The young man had spent all of his thirty-eight years in his father's massive shadow. The opposite of his father. Where Shiva Prasad gained ten pounds by merely thinking about food, Ram Lal gorged on sweets and remained slender. Where Shiva Prasad had bought up the local supplies of steel sheets when he learned of a furnace breakdown at the Jamshedpur steel mills and had made a killing selling them to other lock manufacturers, Ram Lal was known in the bazaars as a donkey who would buy without bargaining down the dealers' asking price. Where Shiva Prasad had ruthlessly sought power, Ram Lal had been content to be his father's mouthpiece as president of the Municipal Committee, using that position to make certain that the city inspectors turned a blind eye to his father's violations of the child labor laws, his tampering with electric meters, and his storing of merchandise and raw materials on public land without payment of fees. Ram Lal found the outlet for his energies in the whorehouses in *Mohalla* Tavaif. They referred to him in the tea shops as a man who would make a worthy successor to his father if only his backbone were as stiff as his penis.

Sitting at his desk in the failing light of the winter afternoon, Gupta wrinkled his brow and stared unseeingly at the opposite wall. How had Ram Lal managed to hold on to the leadership of the Mahasabha without challenge for the past year? How peculiar it was that Shiva Prasad's tough henchmen had quietly acquiesced while Ram Lal assumed the authority that his father had been loath to share with anyone. Gupta pulled at his earlobe, pondering the strange passivity of the Mahasabha.

Could Ram Lal be a secret Congress supporter? Had he signaled to the Congress bosses that he could be bought with a promise of a seat in the Legislative Assembly, perhaps even a deputy ministry in some trivial department like Small Industries? Gupta's right heel began to tap with a nervous rhythm on the tile floor. How far could Ram Lal be trusted? How to find out where his loyalties were? How much control did he have over the Mahasabha organization? How far would the members follow Ram Lal?

Gupta's ruminations were cut short by the sound of loud

conversation coming from the alley. He looked at his watch and saw that it was twenty minutes after four. He smiled. Ram Lal was establishing his position. To be twenty minutes late for an appointment was to demonstrate that you were superior to the other person, but not overly superior. That would be signified by being at least an hour late and not sending your peon with a note. Twenty minutes meant that you respected the other person's position but that he was clearly your inferior. To be prompt was to demonstrate your own inferiority. To be early meant that you wanted something that was likely to be withheld.

Gupta folded the newspapers, opened a file folder on his desk, took a pen from the brass inkstand, and waited for Ram Lal to knock. When the knock came he tapped the bell on his desk and waited. Soon Govind shuffled down the back stairs and into the office.

"Sahib?"

"See who is at the door." Gupta pretended to make notes in the file. Govind opened the door and stood aside as Ram Lal Prasad stepped out of his sandals and bustled into the room.

"*Namaste*, Prasadji," Gupta said, rising from his chair. "I'm delighted that you could come. Govind! Go upstairs! Bring the tea and sweets! Come, my friend, take your seat." Gupta took out his handkerchief and flipped it twice over the tattered cane seat of one of the two chairs that faced his desk.

"I would have been here earlier, Guptaji, but something came up at the Municipal Office and I had to take care of it right away." Ram Lal was establishing himself as a man of affairs. More likely he had been for a visit to one of his favorite girls in *Mohalla* Tavaif.

"No mention, my friend. You have given my wife more

time to prepare your favorite sweets. Sit down and tell me how you have been keeping."

Ram Lal Prasad lifted the fold of his fine white cotton *dhoti*, adjusted his shirttail, and sat down with his right heel resting on the edge of his seat. He leaned his head back, opened the top buttons of his sleeveless black waistcoat, and sighed with relief as the constricting collar was loosened. The seat creaked as he moved. Then he removed his black cloth cap and revealed a thick head of black hair, a suitable complement to his cleanshaven, youthful face. The only visible effect of his years of subservience was in his eyes, which moved warily from Gupta's face to his desk and back again. Ram Lal sighed again.

"It has not been easy, Guptaji. My father carried many of his business records in his head. It's been a nightmare getting all of his accounts sorted out. He seems to have had a different arrangement with each one of the contractors who supplied us with lock parts. Now they are all saying he cheated them." He took a folded white handkerchief from his pocket and patted his neck. "They have probably been cheating us for many years, holding out steel and brass and making locks to sell on their own. But I've hired a firm of chartered accountants and they're working things out. We'll have a proper set of books when they are finished."

"Your father did not manufacture his locks from the beginning itself? I didn't know that, Prasadji."

"It's very complicated, Guptaji. First of all, there are two kinds of locks made in Ramgarh, spring locks and lever locks." Ram Lal's face brightened as he prepared to begin his lecture on the lock business. Just then Govind appeared from behind the safe with a large tray containing a teapot, cups, sugar, hot milk, and plates of *gulab jamun* and carrot *halva*, the only two things that had been known to deflect

Ram Lal from his course on the way to the whorehouse. The *gulab jamun* were oval balls of fried milk solids swimming in syrup, and the *halva* was a sweet mound of carroty confection covered with a sheet of finely beaten silver foil.

"Your wife knows my weakness, Guptaji," the young man said with his mouth full of *halva*. "This is absolutely superb!"

"You shall take some home with you, Ram Lal. Govind! Ask my wife to pack up some sweets for my guest to take home with him. Prasadji," Gupta continued, "you should get married. Your wife will make you all the sweets you can eat."

"My mother is looking, Guptaji, my mother is looking. Maybe she'll find someone suitable for me." Prasad poured some milky tea from his cup into the saucer and slurped it. "Meanwhile, let me continue about the lock business."

Half an hour later Ram Lal Prasad had finished both his description of the lock business and the plates of sweets. With his stomach full, he exuded warmth and friendliness.

"Words cannot do justice to this interesting business, Guptaji. Let me show you my factory tomorrow and you'll see the whole process. Come to the office at two o'clock."

"*Achcha*, Prasadji. I will be there. In all the years I knew your father I never had the opportunity to visit the factory. By the way, speaking of something else, I was quite surprised when I got your message about the new superintendent of police. How did you find out that he was coming?"

"I have my sources, Guptaji. I keep my ears open at all times. When I hear anything useful I see that it gets to the right people. They are grateful. In exchange, they keep me informed from time to time. It works out well for all concerned."

"Who is this Mohammed Abdul Karim?" demanded

Gupta. "What have you heard about him? What is his background? How good is he? Why has Ramgarh been given a Muslim when there are so many good Hindu superintendents?"

"*Chup, chup*, Guptaji! One thing at a time. All I know about him is that he was deputy superintendent in Raipur District, he has a brother serving in the Pakistan Army, and he comes from a family of landowners in Lucknow. Beyond this, I don't know."

"The Pakistan Army?" Gupta was aghast. "The Pakistan Army? Is the Congress infiltrating the police with Muslim spies and traitors now? My God! What will be next?" He pounded his fist on the desk. Prasad leaned back in alarm. After a moment Gupta removed his glasses, rubbed his eyes, and wiped the glasses with his shirttail. He seemed lost in thought. "Tell me, Prasadji," he said, "what will the attitude of the Hindu Mahasabha be?"

"To what?"

"To a Muslim S.P."

"Should we have an attitude, Guptaji?" Ram Lal sounded wary.

"Do you not think that the appointment of a Muslim S.P. in Ramgarh is a flagrant challenge to the Mahasabha by the Congress government?" Gupta demanded, leaning forward over the desk as if examining a recalcitrant witness.

Prasad turned away from Gupta's intense stare. "How are we to know that it's not just a normal transfer? After all, these things are decided by the inspector-general in Lucknow, not by the Chief Minister. These are internal police matters."

"I suppose you're right, Prasadji." Gupta sat back in his chair. Ram Lal's answer had been evasive. Was it his reluctance to make any statement until he saw where his own interests lay? Or was he trying to give Gupta a signal to lay off and acquiesce in the Muslim's appointment? At any rate, if Prasad really thought that the appointment of a district superintendent of police was merely an internal police matter, he was certainly naive. The stink of political conniving could be detected in the appointment of even the lowest village constable.

"Well then, I must make a move. Tell your good wife how much I enjoyed her sweets."

"The sweets!" Gupta cried out in dismay. "Govind! Oh Govind! Bring the package of sweets for Prasadji!" Govind reappeared from behind the safe with a package wrapped in newspaper. He went to the door and held it open for Prasad.

"Run and fetch a cycle rickshaw for Prasadji," Gupta ordered.

"Not necessary, my friend. I will enjoy the evening walk. I may stop off at the temple for a few minutes on my way home."

"*Namaste*, then, Prasadji. See you tomorrow at two." Gupta wondered if "temple" was the proper word for the place where he expected Prasad to stop off on his way home.

At last he was gone, Gupta thought. Another ten minutes with that spineless simpleton and he would probably have thrown a paperweight at him. He rose from his chair and went over to the calendar. Lord Ganesh, with his broken tusk and his fat paunch, smiled down on him. Gupta gazed at the image and felt better. Yes, the God Who Overcomes Obstacles would help him to succeed.

6

The enameled steel sign proclaimed to Surendra Gupta that he was about to enter the premises of Shiva Prasad and Son (Private) Ltd., Lock Merchants and Manufacturers. The cement plaster on the modern two-story building already was beginning to crack and fall off, exposing crudely mortared bricks underneath.

Gupta entered the building and climbed a grimy staircase decorated with splashes of red spittle. Reaching the top, he turned, opened a heavy wooden door, and was puzzled by what he saw. Instead of the expected chaos of clerks, mounds of papers tied with colored ribbons, and an accumulation of decrepit furniture, he found himself in a carpeted reception room under the scrutiny of the bold black eyes of an Anglo-Indian stenographer—a girl in her early twenties wearing a cardigan over a flowered cotton dress—who was filing her fingernails. Gupta's sudden appearance did not make her miss a stroke.

"State your name and business!" she ordered in high-pitched singsong English as if Gupta were a peddler of cheap trinkets. He winced.

"Surendra Gupta. To see Ram Lal Prasad." The girl pressed a buzzer and picked up the telephone next to her typewriter. A door opened behind her desk.

"Welcome, Guptaji! Come in. Come in. Miss Campbell, send my peon for tea and *samosas*. We'll want them in about half an hour." When the stenographer had flounced off on her errand, Prasad turned to Gupta and said with boyish pride, "I'm the first lock merchant in Ramgarh to have a telephone and a secretary. For years I tried to convince my father to do this, but he was too old-fashioned." He held up his index finger. "I'm going to be the biggest lock maker in India, Guptaji, and I want to be ready."

Prasad ushered Gupta into his private office, a corner room overlooking the walled compound of the factory. He had Gupta sit in one of two chairs that faced his massive chrome and plastic desk. Then he lowered his slim body into his large leather-covered swivel chair and began carefully to straighten the objects on the desk: a fountain pen in its alabaster stand, a covered silver box, a telephone, a pad of note paper printed with his name. His eyes shifted uneasily from the desk to Gupta's face to the window and back to Gupta's face.

"Well then, Guptaji. What do you think?"

Gupta removed his glasses. With an elaborate show of concern he breathed on the lenses, wiped them with his handkerchief, held them up to the light, wiped them again, and replaced them on his nose. Prasad waited expectantly for his approval.

"Very handsome, Prasadji. I can see that you're a progressive businessman." He looked around the room, taking in the steel bookcase with only a dictionary and a copy of the *Illustrated Weekly of India* behind its glass doors, the familiar Shiva Prasad and Son calendar, and the framed pictures on the walls. He nodded his head approvingly. "Very handsome indeed! Your father's portrait looks very fine in that silver frame. Very fine. Yes, very progressive. A fine office, a telephone, and a secretary. Tell me," he added, sliding his hand over the smooth plastic surface of the desk, "what does Miss Campbell do for her wages? Not many other businessmen in Ramgarh have a telephone, do they? Your father had no real need of one, did he?"

"Ah, my friend, you are very wise to ask. Miss Campbell, you see, is the stationmaster's daughter. There aren't many jobs in Ramgarh for Anglo-Indian girls. Most of us feel uncomfortable with these Anglo-Indians, and . . ."

"Uncomfortable?" Gupta exploded. "Uncomfortable? The very sight of them makes me want to take a bath and purify myself!"

"I know, I know, Guptaji. But don't blame them if they can't change their ancestry. Look at it this way. Without this job Miss Campbell would have to leave her family and look for work in some big foreign firm in Bombay or Calcutta. She types for me and she can answer the telephone if it rings, but more important," Prasad leaned across the desk and said in a confidential tone, "having her in my office means that my raw materials and my locks get priority treatment at the railway goods shed. When there is a shortage of wagons on the railway, this can be crucial for business. To me, Penelope is a good insurance policy."

Gupta rubbed his freshly shaved chin. "Very clever, Prasadji. Very clever. I don't suppose little Penelope provides other services as well?" Gupta winked. "You know what they say about Anglo-Indian girls."

Prasad smiled. "That wouldn't be businesslike, would it, Guptaji. Come on. Let me show you around." He ushered Gupta into a large hall that occupied the remainder of the upper floor. Here was the main office, the real Shiva Prasad and Son, behind the modern façade. Here were the chaos, the clerks, the decrepit furniture. As they passed through, the grizzled clerks rose and bowed behind desks piled with file folders, their palms pressed together in a servile *namaste*.

The two men descended another staircase and emerged at the rear of the building. "Here is my factory, Guptaji," Prasad proclaimed, stretching his arms out with pride. Gupta saw a walled enclosure covering about a quarter acre, with a series of open sheds around the perimeter. There was a wooden gate, wide enough to admit a bullock cart or even a small lorry. His ears were assailed by the rasp of files and grinding wheels, the whir of electric motors, and the rhythmic clank of metal on metal.

Ram Lal pointed to the nearest shed. "This is where we stamp out the spring lock parts," he shouted into Gupta's ear. Two barefoot men were feeding sheets of metal into stamping machines. From the other end came correctly formed halves of lock cases. Jagged scraps of metal littered the ground. A workman, whose hand lacked two fingers, reached into the running machine to clear away accumulated slivers of steel.

"That looks like dangerous work, Prasadji," Gupta yelled, holding his hands over his ears. "Can't you protect these men against accidents?"

"There are some new machines with safety devices. We'll get them when these machines wear out. Don't worry. I take care of my men if they get injured. Come on. Let's take a look at the nickel-plating vats."

Holding up his *dhoti* to keep it out of the dirt, Gupta followed Prasad as he explained the activities in each shed. But the image of the mutilated workman kept coming into his mind, distracting him from Prasad's detailed descriptions. And another image appeared also. It was puzzling. The outline was unclear, imperfect. But he sensed that it was made of metal.

In front of the polishing shed Gupta paused to wipe his

glasses. When he replaced them, his eyes met those of a preadolescent boy, staring at him between eyelashes white with polishing powder. The boy coughed white spittle onto the ground.

"Isn't that unhealthy work for those polishing boys, Prasadji? With all that dust in the air?"

Prasad turned and looked warily at Gupta. "Nobody complains," he answered. "They wear those kerchiefs over their noses and mouths. When they get big enough to do heavy work, we hire some of them for other jobs. Come over to the assembly shed. There's less dust."

Gupta followed, thinking about the man with two fingers missing and the boys breathing polishing powder into their lungs. Was this the future that Nehru and his Five-Year Plan were offering to India? Mutilation and lung disease?

"This is the assembly shed, Guptaji. These men take the finished parts and put them together to make a lock. Then we inspect it, stamp it with our trademark, and pack it for shipment to the customer. Here, have a look," he said, offering Gupta a shiny but flimsy padlock.

"It doesn't seem very strong, Prasadji."

"It's not supposed to be strong. It's only a cheap *kutcha* lock that sells in the bazaar for less than a rupee. If you want a good strong *pukka* lock you need a lever lock or a cylinder lock. We make lever locks and I want to import the machinery to make cylinder locks."

"Ah, yes. As you said yesterday, the lever locks are made by contractors." Gupta covered his ears as a screeching sound cut through the din made by the machinery and the hammers.

"Not made, Guptaji, only cast." Prasad held up his index finger and wiggled it from side to side. "The parts are cast by the contractors in their own workshops. Then we finish and assemble them. Here, have a look at this one."

Gupta hefted the brass lock he was handed. It weighed at least two pounds. It was strongly constructed and on its face he saw stamped, "SPL Gov't Grade I—6 levers."

"The more levers, the better the lock. Do you know that there are some manufacturers," Prasad said with mock loathing, "who will stamp '10 levers' on a lock but only put two levers inside?"

"Heaven forbid!" Gupta gasped, joining in the joke.

"But you must see the casting, Guptaji. Bahadur Singh! Come here!" A young man in his twenties—tall, broad shouldered, and cleanshaven—left off packing crates and approached Prasad, an inquiring look on his face. "Run over to Agarwala's and tell him that you will bring Shri Surendra Gupta, a personal friend of mine, to visit his workshop in half an hour. He should show him the casting of locks. Then come back here to my office."

"*Achcha*, sahib." Bahadur Singh gave Gupta an appraising glance and trotted off toward the gate.

"That's a fine young man, Guptaji. Very intelligent. I've had him do a few things for the Mahasabha. Even knows some English, although he's had only a few years of schooling. I'm thinking of getting him some private tuition so he can take the secondary school examination." Prasad looked at his gold watch. "Well then. Our tea and *samosas* should have arrived by now."

Prasad led the way back to the office, where a teapot, cups, and a plate of crisp, warm *samosas* were waiting on the desk. As the two men sat down, Miss Campbell appeared and began to pour the tea. Gupta noticed that she brushed her chest against Ram Lal's shoulder when she leaned over to fill his cup.

They had barely finished their refreshments when Miss Campbell returned and announced in her singsong English that Bahadur Singh was waiting in the reception room.

"Well then, Prasadji," Gupta said, rising from his chair, "it has been a very instructive visit. If your father could see how you're running the business he would be proud of you."

"You're most kind, Guptaji." Prasad leaned back and rocked in his oversized chair. "By the way, I'm continuing one of the traditions that my father loved. You know? Those cultural evenings? Two weeks from Thursday *Ustad* Bashiruddin Khan will play the sitar and some of my friends will be coming. You come too. You're free?"

Gupta's eyes blinked behind his steel-rimmed glasses as he fought back tears. Never had Shiva Prasad invited him to one of his cultural evenings. He nervously wiped his mouth with the back of his hand. "I would be happy to come, Prasadji," he said. "Now then, I must make a move. Shri Agarwala will be waiting, and I would like to get home before evening. *Namaste.* You've been extremely kind."

Gupta turned and followed Bahadur Singh down the staircase. As they emerged onto the Grand Trunk Road, he thought he heard a peal of high-pitched feminine laughter.

Bahadur Singh strode off down the Grand Trunk Road. Gupta had to stretch his legs to keep up. "Not so fast, Bahadur Singh," he called, puffing and wheezing.

"I'm sorry, sahib. But you should have told me to go slowly before you became so breathless."

Gupta stood panting with his hand on Bahadur Singh's shoulder. "No matter. I'm not breathless any more. Let's move on." He wiped his face with his handkerchief. "Bahadur Singh, Shri Prasad told me that you had done some work for the Mahasabha. What work was that?"

"Nothing much, sahib." Bahadur Singh looked down and scraped a pattern of lines in the dust with his sandal. "It wasn't political work in the usual sense."

"What do you mean?"

"Nothing, sahib," the young man replied, still scraping his sandal. He looked directly at Gupta. "It's not the kind of work I prefer to talk about. My father would be angry with me if he knew what I had done."

Mystified, Gupta decided not to press him further. "Who is your father, Bahadur Singh?"

The young man hesitated. Tears filled his eyes. "My parents are both dead, sahib. Killed in the riots in the Punjab. I had two younger sisters. Carried . . . carried off. The Muslims. Five years. Not a word in five years." He covered his eyes with one hand.

Gupta was silent. It was too much! Thousands of Hindu girls stolen from their families, forcibly converted to Islam, and taken as wives, concubines, or worse. And Nehru had done nothing about it. Gupta put his arm around Bahadur Singh's shoulders.

"I'm not looking for sympathy, sahib," Bahadur Singh said in a strangely soft voice. "I'm looking for revenge. If I ever have the chance to even the score, I won't let it pass me by." He turned away but Gupta could see his clenched fists.

"Let's move on, Bahadur Singh," Gupta said gently. He would wait until the young man calmed down before asking any more questions.

They had now left the Grand Trunk Road and entered an area of low, mud-walled houses with flat roofs.

"We turn here, sahib." Bahadur Singh led the way into a narrow alley between the blank mud walls. Gupta smelled coal smoke and heard the sound of hammers beating on metal. There it was again. That indistinct metal image.

Bahadur Singh rapped on a wooden door whose paint had been eroded by time. "Bahadur Singh," he called out in response to a muffled query. The door opened and the two men stepped into a large open space surrounded by mud-walled rooms. A cow was tethered in the corner, munching on chopped straw.

"Welcome to my foundry, Shri Gupta. I am Jagdish Narain Agarwala." A short, middle-aged man greeted them with his palms pressed together. His white cap and homespun clothing were sooty and sweat stained. "You're just in time to see my last castings of the day. Wait one moment and I'll see if everything is ready." Agarwala went to the center of the compound where a teenage boy was pumping a leather bellows at a coal fire. He looked into a ceramic crucible suspended over the coals.

While waiting, Gupta decided to renew his questioning of Bahadur Singh. "How did you happen to come to Ramgarh, Bahadur Singh?" he asked.

"My father was an agent in Sialkot for hardware. He used to sell the locks made by the Prasad factory." Bahadur Singh smiled. "Not cheap *kutcha* locks. Only the good *pukka* locks like they're making here. No real Punjabi would put a cheap lock on anything. Not like these Ramgarh people." He spat in the dust. "Well, one time Shiva Prasad himself came to visit my father to sell his locks. He gave sweets to us children. I remembered this when I was in the refugee camp and I wrote to him. There was no one else I knew in India." He swallowed and kicked the dirt. "Shiva Prasad was a good man. He took me in and gave me a job. He let me sleep on a *charpoy* in the factory. He was a good man. And his son Ram Lal has been good to me also."

Gupta wiped the coal dust from his glasses. So, the old pirate Shiva Prasad had some milk of human kindness in him after all. This strong young man, with his intelligence and his need for revenge, could be a useful ally.

"Come over and have a look, Shri Gupta," Agarwala

called. "The metal is nearly ready to be poured." Gupta peered into the crucible, where he could see brass bars melting into liquid. "We melt enough for one or two dozen locks. We can use iron or steel, as well as brass, depending on the customer's order. Let's go over there, Shri Gupta."

Agarwala led him to a corner of the compound where three men were packing fine dark sand into pairs of wooden boxes, each about eighteen inches square and six inches deep. "This is a molding box, Shri Gupta. The founder will take the various pieces of a model lock and arrange them in the sand. There, you see? When he's finished there will be cavities connected by channels to the top of the box. It's like a tree, Shri Gupta. When the brass is melted they will pour it into the hole in the top, and the metal will flow through the channels to the cavities. Ram Gopal," Agarwala said to the founder, "if the brass is ready, pour this one so our guest can see the results."

"All ready now, sahib," Ram Gopal said. His two assistants lifted the crucible from the fire with an iron implement and carried it over to the molding box. They tipped it slightly and poured the molten brass into the hole. Within three seconds excess brass started to spill out of the hole. They tipped up the crucible and returned it to the fire.

"Now we wait ten minutes for the new pieces to cool down a little," Agarwala said. "I've had some tea prepared. We can have it now while we're waiting." He clapped his hands and a little girl emerged from one of the rooms carrying two glasses of milky tea. With her lips pressed together and her brow knit, she carefully handed the glasses to Gupta and Bahadur Singh. "This is my youngest child, Asha. Asha, make *namaste* to the sahib." The little girl pressed her palms together, then clapped them over her smiling mouth and scurried back into the room, her pigtails waving behind her.

"Do you also have your home in this foundry, Agarwalaji?"

"Most foundry contractors are poor, so we fix up a place to live where we have our work. It's not bad. We have some privacy and we can use the leftover coal to cook our food." He wiped his face with a sweat-stained sleeve. "My wife has been living with me here for twenty years. Although she has complained enough, it hasn't been about where we live. Come," Agarwala said, "let's open up the molding box and see what has been made." Gesturing to one of the workmen to open the box, Agarwala crouched down and, using a screwdriver, gently lifted the brass casting from the sand. There were the parts of a lock, all joined together by branches of brass. That image, that metal image, came into Gupta's mind again. "When the casting has cooled down some more, we'll cut the pieces apart and put them in a bag and send them to the factory to be polished and fitted together. This rough finish you see now will be smoothed off and the lock will shine."

"It's amazing, Agarwalaji! So simple, yet so effective."

"You could make many things by this method, Guptaji." Agarwala's eyes flashed with enthusiasm. "Bigger pieces than these, more complicated shapes, and when we use steel we can make the pieces very hard or very strong. I'm told that up on the Northwest Frontier there are Pathans who even make copies of the British Army rifle by this method."

"Rifles, did you say? Are they good rifles?" Gupta's eyes widened. His heart pounded. He wiped his mouth with his handkerchief, struggling to conceal his excitement. "Can they actually shoot with these homemade rifles?"

"Oh yes, so I'm told. Of course, they won't be as good as foreign-made rifles, but the Pathans use them for hunting and in their family feuds." Bahadur Singh nodded in agreement.

"Agarwalaji, do you know if these Pathans also make pistols by this method?" Gupta jammed his hands into his jacket pockets so Agarwala wouldn't notice how they were trembling.

"Pistols? I'm not sure." Agarwala frowned. Then he brightened. "But why not? It wouldn't be difficult once you had a model. No gunstock to worry about. Sure, you could make a pistol. It would be easy."

7

Deputy Superintendent of Police Mohan Saxena was in a sour mood. Not that this was in any way unusual. Saxena had good reason to be feeling sorry for himself and for making his subordinates suffer the consequences.

Saxena sat with his feet on the desk in his office at police headquarters. His unshaven face mirrored his sour mood. It was not the type of face to inspire confidence in either superiors or subordinates. The narrow space between his upper lip and his broad flat nose was filled with a black mustache. The marks of childhood smallpox were scattered across his cheeks. But his most memorable feature was the pronounced bags beneath his eyes—pouches into which had been poured the accumulated licentiousness of his life. Saxena's muscular frame made the desk chair squeak as he rocked back and forth.

Mohan Saxena was in disgrace. His posting to Ramgarh had been punishment for misconduct in his last station, Lucknow, the capital of the state and the most desirable assignment for an ambitious police officer. If he played his cards right, an officer could meet important people, get himself known to influential political circles, and get the most rapid advancement to higher rank.

But Saxena had made a mess of things. He had been put in charge of a subdistrict police station in a Muslim *mohalla* of the city. It was unusual for a deputy superintendent to have charge of a city police station. But *Mohalla* Rahimganj was critical for the Congress Party in the forthcoming elections. It was to be the showpiece that would demonstrate to Muslims everywhere that their political future lay with the Congress. The assignment demanded shrewdness and sensitivity of a high order.

Saxena had been the wrong man for the job. His hatred and contempt for the Muslims had led him to terrorize them, rather than to seek their respect and cooperation. He and his men had been brutal. As a consequence, he had faced departmental charges of "mistreatment of prisoners" and "failure to take care the prisoners in his custody were not mistreated." In addition, he had been known as a frequenter of houses of prostitution.

These were serious charges, enough to cause his dismissal after a departmental investigation by the inspector general's office. But Saxena was an officer in the Hindu Police Officer's Association, an influential group with important friends in the Home Ministry. So, after the Congress won the election by a wide margin, even in *Mohalla* Rahimganj, Saxena was merely sent to Ramgarh with a notation on his record.

After coming off duty the previous evening, Saxena had hoped for a bit of pleasure and some sleep before taking the welcoming party down to the station to receive the new superintendent. The first part of the night had gone well. With eyes closed and head tilted back, he mused now about Aijana Bibi, his favorite girl at Zakia Begum's house. Ah, those Muslim girls. So fair skinned, so shapely. He pictured Aijana Bibi in his mind's eye. Only sixteen, yet so well developed. Such an accomplished girl. She was a musician, creating sensual *ragas* on his body. Never had he found a girl so delicate, so sensitive to his moods and feelings. She knew when to caress him and when to be caressed, when to make love and when to let him sleep.

But things had gone bad later in the night. Returning to his bungalow next to the police compound at three in the morning, he had fallen asleep in his clothes. Moments later, or so it seemed, he had been shaken awake by a constable with news of an explosion and fire at the railway station. Now he was waiting at his desk for Subinspector Om Prakash to report on what had happened.

The jangle of the telephone shook Saxena out of his reverie. His duty head constable, dozing at a desk in the corner, answered the phone and listened intently. After a moment he turned to Saxena and said, "Sahib, Subinspector Om Prakash."

Saxena picked up the telephone on his desk. "What happened, Prakash?" Saxena's voice was harsh. "How did it happen? Where was the bogie? Was anyone inside? My God! How do you know it was the Raipur–Ramgarh bogie? Who was the stationmaster on duty? Have you questioned him? *Thik hai.* All right. I'll be down there in fifteen minutes."

Saxena leaned back in his chair. "My God!"

"What's wrong, sahib?"

"Misra, it seems that our new superintendent of police has just been burned up in a fire. The Raipur–Ramgarh sleeper bogie has caught fire and burned to ashes." Saxena looked wildly around the room. "I can't believe it!"

"Misra, my jeep, *ek dum*! At once, I said! And wake up Inspector Hafiz-ur-Rehman. Tell him I want every available man with rifles at the railway station at once. Take them down by lorry. *Achcha?* Take this down. I want four men around the burned bogie. No one is to go near it without my personal authorization. I want the railway station sealed off. No one is to enter or leave the station. No passengers, no coolies, no employees. Dammit man, don't sit there! Write these orders down! Hafiz-ur-Rehman is to take some of his men and go into the *mohallas* near the station and ask questions. Find out if anyone saw anything suspicious or anyone moving about before or after the explosion. Send a message to Subinspector Sharma to come down here and take over the duty. Now, get me that scum of a stationmaster on the telephone. Get moving, you dolt!"

Misra frantically spun the handle of his telephone box. "This is a police call. Get me the stationmaster, Ramgarh Junction, at once. Deputy Superintendent Saxena is calling. Ring back 100 when you have him on the line."

Five minutes later the telephone jangled again. "The stationmaster, sahib."

"What's happening down there, Campbell?" Saxena demanded of the Anglo-Indian stationmaster. He listened intently for a few moments. "*Achcha*! I'm sending my men down to the station to seal it off. I want no one to enter or leave, understand? No one! One more thing. Telegraph all stations up and down the line. All trains must stop outside of Ramgarh Junction to pick up or discharge passengers. No train will be allowed to stop inside the station area. Goods trains must be shunted to a siding. What? Of course, you idiot! This is a police emergency! I'll be down there myself in a few minutes." Saxena slammed down the receiver.

"Misra, get me Lucknow. Quickly, man!" Misra rang the special telephone line to state police headquarters in Lucknow and asked for the superintendent on duty. Saxena took the phone and informed him what had happened and what steps he had taken to deal with the situation. He rang off, stood up, and buttoned his uniform jacket. Taking his service revolver from the desk drawer, he barked, "Where's that jeep, Misra?"

"Waiting outside, sahib."

Now they would see what good police work looked like, Saxena thought. Swift, decisive action, that's what it took. Now maybe he'd be able to get promoted to superintendent or at least get a civilized posting somewhere. How in God's name did that damned bogie catch fire? Well, at least there was one less Muslim to worry about.

Saxena jumped into his jeep and tore off to the railway station.

8

The sun was above the horizon when Karim left Harbans Singh's Caltex petrol pump to walk down the Grand Trunk Road to the railway station. He had enjoyed a refreshing bath, and later, when he heard the call to morning prayer from a nearby mosque, he had borrowed a mat from Singh and prayed and given thanks for his deliverance. Now, reinvigorated by hot tea and an omelet with toast, he was ready to take on his new responsibilities.

Karim looked about him as he walked, taking in his first daylight view of his new post. To his left, somewhat obscured by the morning haze and the acrid smoke of cow dung cooking fires in the servants' quarters, he could see the straight roads, official buildings, and substantial bungalows of Ramgarh's cantonment area. To his right, beyond the railway line and the rows of wooden stalls and open-air workshops that bordered the Grand Trunk Road, he could make out the rising tiers of old brick buildings that crowded into the ancient walled city of Ramgarth. Quite a contrast, Karim thought. In those old houses the women and girls of the family were preparing *chapatis* and tea for the men and boys. In the cantonment the male cooks were making porridge and frying eggs while the memsahibs slept late.

The white domes of the *Jama Masjid*—the great Friday mosque—appeared to float above the city like three large white turbans.

As Karim approached the railway station, he noticed that there were no *tongas* or bicycle rickshaws, which normally waited in line for passengers leaving the station. Saxena must have sent them away. No one would be permitted to leave the station for a while.

The station did not impress him. He had seen many of its conventional counterparts, as alike as if they had been made from the same mold: a one-story brick building parallel to the tracks, with a central entrance hall and two wings. The door and window openings were arched in late Moghul style. Karim knew that after entering the main door he would see the hall, with the black wood-rimmed chalkboard for announcements, and the ticket booking office, with one wicket for third-class tickets and one for the upper classes. There would be a folding steel barricade at the end of the entrance hall, the opening guarded by a white-uniformed ticket inspector.

When he had passed through the barrier onto the platform, Karim would see on one side the three refreshment rooms: vegetarian Indian style, nonvegetarian Indian style, and European style. The waiting rooms for first- , second- , and intermediate-class passengers would be there also. The waiting third-class passengers squatted on the platform. On the other side he would see the offices of the stationmaster and his assistants, the telegraph office, the parcel room, and the left-luggage office. A corrugated iron roof would keep the platform dry in the rainy season and ensure that it would be an inferno in the hot season. Coolies in red smocks and red turbans would be squatting on the platform, puffing *bidis* and waiting for the next train. The vendors of hot snacks would be fanning their charcoal fires and readying the trays to be hawked to passengers at the train windows.

Across the two main line tracks would be a similar structure but with only an exit barrier—no wickets, no offices, no refreshment rooms. Passengers unfortunate enough to have to board a train on the opposite platform had to cross the tracks outside the railway yard, enter the station at the main entrance, purchase their tickets, and then cross to the other platform on a pedestrian overpass.

The tracks themselves were in a dark pit, a gloomy battleground smelling of stale urine. Here the pye dogs—half-starved, mangy creatures resembling large rats—skirmished with each other and with real rats for bits of food that fell from the platform.

Karim turned into the station driveway only to stop short at a warning shouted by a head constable, one of three armed policemen leaning against a lorry parked in front of the entrance.

"I am Superintendent Mohammed Abdul Karim Khan, your new superintendent of police," Karim called back to the head constable.

The head constable, a beefy man with a bushy, upturned mustache, froze for a moment, then pulled back his rifle bolt, rammed a round into the chamber, and pointed the rifle at Karim. "Stand where you are!" he shouted. Then he turned to the two other policemen and ordered them to bring Karim over to the lorry. Holding him roughly with his arms pinned behind his back, they marched Karim over to the head constable.

"The superintendent of police is dead. Who are you? Identify yourself. Search this man," he ordered the constables.

While one constable held his arms behind his back, the

other rapidly and thoroughly frisked Karim.

"He's carrying a pistol, Vermaji!"

"Put handcuffs on him! Quickly!" the head constable ordered. Karim's captors threw him face down on the macadam pavement and roughly fastened his wrists together behind his back with a pair of heavy manacles. "Now, search his pockets! I want to see who this bastard really is."

"Here is his billfold, Vermaji."

The head constable placed his boot on Karim's neck and began to examine the documents in his wallet. He suddenly stepped back when he came upon Karim's official photo identity card.

"Where did you get this, you murdering swine?" The head constable reached down and pulled Karim's head back by the hair. Karim cried out in pain as his neck was twisted.

"Call Superintendent Saxena! He knows who I am."

"Shut your mouth, you swine, or I'll shove my boot into it! You men stay here. Give me the pistol. Get up, you bastard! We're going in to find Deputy Superintendent Saxena."

The head constable pulled Karim to his feet and pushed him toward the station entrance. Karim's coat and trousers were soiled with dirt and coal dust. They passed the barrier and emerged onto the platform. Saxena was not there. Subinspector Om Prakash, the only officer present, was sitting alongside Stationmaster Campbell at a table on the platform. A coolie was standing in front of the table, abjectly pleading for something. A line of coolies, railway employees, and various other people stretched down the platform guarded by armed police. Prakash appeared to be recording information on a sheet of paper and examining the coolies' hands and arms. Meanwhile, a constable was bodily searching them and sniffing their clothing. Good procedure, Karim thought. But would the smell of petrol be able to cut through the normal coolie stink of sweat, tobacco, and unwashed flesh?

"Subinspector Sahib, may I speak with you for one moment, please?" the head constable called. Om Prakash looked toward him, muttered something to the stationmaster, and walked over.

"What is the matter with you, Verma? Don't you know enough not to bother me when I am interviewing witnesses? Who is this man?"

"Sahib, this man claims to be the superintendent of police who was killed in the fire. He had the superintendent's papers and pistol. He may have taken them after he killed him and then set fire to the bogie."

"Show me the papers and the pistol." Prakash looked carefully at the identity card and at Karim. The resemblance was strong but the picture was not recent. There were thousands of Muslims with hooked noses and thin lips. "Who *are* you?" he demanded.

"I am Mohammed Abdul Karim Khan, your new superintendent of police. I was not killed last night because I left the bogie before the fire. Now take me to Deputy Superintendent Saxena, who knows me and will identify me correctly."

"Wait here," Prakash said and went to the stationmaster's office. Through the sooty window Karim could see him sitting at the stationmaster's desk speaking into the telephone and then listening intently. He read something aloud from Karim's papers and glanced back at him as if to verify his impression. Finally he rang off and came out to the platform.

"Deputy Superintendent Saxena is sending his jeep to take you to headquarters. Meanwhile, you will wait outside the station with Head Constable Verma. Until positive identification is made you must remain handcuffed. I'm sorry."

"Very well," said Karim. "Tell me, subinspector, has a party been organized to search the railway yard for any evidence?"

"We are sending all of these people out of the station as soon as we have interviewed them. By that time the haze will have lifted and the constables will be sent out to search for physical evidence. The bogie is still very hot and we have not been able to get into it." He paused for a moment and then he said, "I am Subinspector Om Prakash."

"One more thing, Prakash. When you interview the coolies, find out the names of those who can read English script, like the names on reservation slips."

Prakash, a young man with a smooth, cleanshaven face, knitted his brows and stared at Karim. Would Prakash tell him to mind his own business, Karim wondered? Or would he accept the suggestion on the chance that he really was the superintendent of police?

"I will take care of it. Meanwhile, please wait outside the station with Head Constable Verma. The jeep will be here shortly. Verma!"

"Sir!"

"Fix the man's handcuffs in front of him and give him a cigarette if he wants one. Help him to get it lighted. I've got to get back to work."

Verma was gentle with Karim as he guided him out to the station entrance. "Do you want to smoke, sahib?" he asked.

"I would like very much to smoke, Verma. I had a packet of Sepoys in my coat pocket, but I suspect that your men took them."

Sure enough, the two constables were smoking cigarettes instead of their usual *bidis*.

"Here, you two!" demanded Verma. "Give those cigarettes back to the sahib." Verma removed a cigarette from the packet, put it between Karim's lips, and lighted it with one of his own matches. "I'm sorry about them, sahib. They didn't think they were doing wrong."

The sound of a siren prevented Karim from pursuing the matter. A police jeep skidded into the station driveway and came to a stop with its brakes squealing in protest. A tall, thin, cleanshaven police officer got out of the passenger's seat, adjusted his uniform, came over to Karim, and saluted.

"I'm Inspector Hafiz-ur-Rehman, sir. Please come with me. Take the front seat in the jeep. I am sorry that it will be necessary to keep the handcuffs on you until positive identification is made. Where are the sahib's identification papers and pistol, Verma?"

"I left them with Subinspector Om Prakash, sahib."

"Then go into the station and bring them to me." Hafiz-ur-Rehman guided Karim to the jeep and helped him to get seated, and then he nimbly jumped into the rear seat. "This is a shocking business, sir. But we may have found the culprit. My men picked up a man who was seen leaving the scene of the fire this morning. His hair and beard were singed. If he knows anything, Deputy Superintendent Saxena will get it out of him."

"What sort of man is this suspect?" Karim asked.

"He certainly had access to inflammable substances. He's a Sikh who runs the Caltex petrol station on the Grand Trunk Road."

Inspector Hafiz-ur-Rehman's jeep hurtled down the crowded Grand Trunk Road, scattering dust over the goods piled in front of the shops and over the people walking on the edge of the pavement. The siren screamed and pye dogs danced out of the way as the driver spun the steering wheel ferociously from side to side, careering the jeep around bullock carts and lorries.

Karim clung to the windscreen frame with his manacled hands. He dreaded to think what could be happening to his friend Harbans Singh at police headquarters. He knew of Saxena's reputation for wringing confessions from suspects. The bastinado on the soles of the feet and the cane on the buttocks were just the beginning of the shortcuts he—and others too—were known to use to avoid the painstaking gathering of evidence.

The jeep reached the stuccoed brick wall of the police compound, startled the sentry to attention, and squealed through the gate to stop in front of the duty office. Karim jumped out of the jeep and ran up the steps to the veranda, followed closely by Hafiz-ur-Rehman.

"Saxena! Superintendent Saxena! Where are you?"

"Who is calling me?" Saxena's voice came, not from the duty office, but from next door, from a small square building with steel latticed windows—the jail. Karim turned and ran to the jail, meeting Saxena as the deputy superintendent came out. Saxena's unshaven face was dripping with sweat. His sleeves were rolled up, revealing muscular forearms. Sweat stains soiled his uniform shirt.

"Karim!" he exclaimed. "You're alive. Thank God! I thought we had lost you last night."

"Get these handcuffs off me quickly, please. Where is your suspect in the bombing?"

Before Saxena could answer, Karim heard a hoarse cry from within the jail. "Sahib, it is Harbans Singh! Tell them who I am! Help me, sahib!" Karim rushed into the building and came upon what he had hoped he would not see. Harbans Singh's wrists, manacled together behind his back, were painfully stretched upward by a rope attached to a roof beam. His pants and underwear were dropped to his ankles, and his bare backside was reddened with blood oozing from half a dozen welts. Head Constable Misra stood by, holding a cane.

"Cut that man down at once!" Karim ordered, his voice quaking with anger. Saxena, who had followed him into the jail, gestured to Misra to obey the order.

"Hafiz-ur-Rehman, take the handcuffs off the superintendent," Saxena said. "I'm terribly sorry you've been treated like a common criminal, Superintendent Sahib." Saxena's words were contrite but his manner was defensive. "We honestly assumed that you had died in the fire. When you came to the railway station my men thought you were the murderer, that you had stolen the pistol and papers and then set the bogie on fire."

Karim paid no attention to Saxena. He knelt down beside the Sikh, who was lying on his stomach on the floor. "I'm sorry for what you suffered, sardarji," he said softly. He stood up, tears welling into his eyes. "Hafiz-ur-Rehman, bring two men and a stretcher. I want this man taken to the District Hospital. I want you to convey to the chief medical doctor my urgent request that this man be given the best possible treatment for his injuries. This man is no longer a suspect in the bombing case, and I want him treated with respect. Understood?"

"But Superintendent Sahib," Saxena argued, "this man is the bomber. He was seen leaving the fire this morning with another person. His hair and beard are singed. His clothing smells of smoke. He had access to flammable materials. The evidence is there. We cannot set him free until he has told us of his collaborator."

Karim thought fast. To berate or embarrass Saxena in front of Misra or Hafiz-ur-Rehman would be dangerous to good discipline.

"I was the man seen with Harbans Singh this morning, Saxena," Karim answered. Then he quickly related what had happened to him and to the bogie. "If it had not been for this man's hospitality, I would truly have been roasted alive this morning."

Hafiz-ur-Rehman and the stretcher bearers carefully helped Harbans Singh onto the stretcher. The end of his loosened turban cloth trailed on the ground as he was carried away.

"Saxena, we have some paper work to take care of," Karim said. "Then I want to talk to you about your interrogation techniques."

"Well, Saxena, where are my quarters? I need a bath and a good night's sleep." Karim lighted a Sepoy, crushed the empty packet, and threw it into a nearby wastebasket. Saxena looked up from his paper-strewn desk.

"Superintendent Sahib, you're in luck. Your bungalow is in the cantonment. It was built for the British, and after the war they installed electricity and running water and a flush system. It has a full staff. You should be very comfortable." Saxena looked wistful. "It's one of the very few compensations for being posted to this godforsaken place."

"Then I take it you would be interested in a transfer."

"I would be very pleased to have an appointment in Lucknow or another large city."

"Too many politicians for my taste," Karim said. What sin had he committed, what crime had he perpetrated, to deserve in one day an assassination attempt, a mistaken arrest by his own police, and now a brutal deputy who was unhappy in his job? "How long have you been in Ramgarh, Saxena?"

"Only four months, sir. Until this morning it has been very boring."

"Well, the least you can stay here is a year, so I expect we'll have to get along with each other. By the way, I'm leaving you in direct charge of the bombing investigation, since it took place before I officially arrived. But keep me informed. Tell me," he added, "have we an officer who knows Ramgarh well? I want to be taken around the city. I want to order some new uniforms also."

"Hafiz-ur-Rehman belongs to Ramgarh. He knows the city as well as anyone. I'm sure he knows the good tailors too. I'll have him collect you tomorrow morning with a pair of bicycles. You can do better with them in the old city than with a jeep."

"Have him come at nine. Meanwhile, I need a jeep to go to my quarters."

"Yes, Superintendent Sahib."

Karim gripped the windscreen frame tightly as his driver swerved the jeep out of the police headquarters gate. They stopped at a small cluster of shops for soap, a razor, and other necessities and then headed down the Grand Trunk Road. They crossed the railway line and entered the cantonment.

After turning onto Tilak Road at a statue of Queen Victoria, they drove past the English cemetery and turned into a compound surrounded by a brick wall topped with broken glass. A dozing policeman jumped up into a startled salute.

The jeep pulled up under the portico of a standard Public

Works Department-style bungalow painted the standard P.W.D. tan. A veranda, shaded by an overhanging thatched roof, stretched along the front of the house. Karim stepped onto the veranda and knocked on the heavy wooden front door, which needed paint and was secured by a huge brass lock. He peered through the dusty windows on either side of the door, praying that his predecessor had left the bungalow in decent condition.

Karim's prayer was interrupted by his driver, who appeared from around the side of the house leading a wizened, spindle-legged old man clad in a khaki shirt and shorts and with his turban slightly askew as if he had been roughly awakened and ordered to present himself *ek dum*. Was this apparition to be his cook–bearer?

The old man approached, his bare feet with their splayed toes padding silently across the broken tiles of the veranda. "*Salaam*, sahib," he rasped, touching his right fingertips to his forehead. Karim recognized his type—an ancient retainer who had served foreign masters since his boyhood, only to be abandoned without a pension when the British Raj departed.

"What is your name, uncle?" Karim asked.

"I am Faiz Khan, sahib. At your service, *huzoor*." Karim breathed a low sigh of relief. Having a Muslim cook–bearer meant that he would be able to have nonvegetarian meals, although pork was forbidden and beef, he knew, was rarely available in this heavily Hindu district.

"How long have you worked here, Faiz Khan?"

"Since the war, sahib. I came here from Muzafferpur with Superintendent Blackwell. He went back to England in '48. I have quarters in the back of the compound, sahib, across from the sweeper."

"So there is a sweeper here also?"

"Yes, *huzoor*. He cleans the floors and toilets and brings coal and wood for cooking. There is not much to do since the flush was installed, so he also helps the *mali*."

"You mean I have a gardener living here as well?"

"No, sahib. The *mali* lives behind the Collector's bungalow next door. He takes care of three bungalows—this one, the Collector's, and the District Medical Officer's."

Karim became aware of movement at the end of the veranda. Turning, he saw five children standing in line, staring at him with calm, open curiosity.

"So how many people are living in this compound?" Karim asked. He feared the answer to his own question.

"Well, sahib," Faiz Khan began counting on his brown fingers, "me, my wife, my nephew and his wife and five children, the sweeper and his wife, the policeman Ram Gopal, who guards the gate, his wife and his two children. That makes fourteen, I think."

Oh no! His life would be complicated enough without his having to settle the arguments of two Muslims, a Hindu, an Untouchable sweeper, and their bickering wives; listen to their noisy children; and breathe the smoke from their three cooking fires. If he had a wife she could at least take that burden from his shoulders. Good God! What had he let himself in for?

"Well, Faiz Khan," Karim said, "I'll have to wait until tomorrow to meet all these people. Meanwhile, heat a bucket of water for my bath. Then get me some supper. You have *chapatis* and *dal*? *Achcha*. Can you make tea and toast and an omelet for breakfast? Good. Eight o'clock. Here are twenty rupees. Go to the market with my driver and buy what you need for the next few days. Do you have a bazaar book?"

"Yes, sahib. Blackwell Sahib left me one."

"Good. Keep a good record of what you spend and show it to me when you need more money." He hoped the old man could count money more accurately than he had counted the residents of the compound.

"Yes, sahib. Sahib?"

"Yes?"

"Your good name, sahib?"

"I am Mohammed Abdul Karim Khan." The old man smiled. "Please open the front door, Faiz Khan, before you go." Faiz Khan pulled a ring of keys from his pocket, selected one with great care, twisted open the lock, and, with much noisy rattling and turning, threw the bolt and pushed open the door. Karim muttered "*Bismillah*" and entered the bungalow.

At first glance the place seemed decent enough. But what a gloomy place it was. A dark living room extended the full width of the house. Those curtains would have to be opened. Ah, now he could see a little better. A cluster of chairs and a sofa stood on his right; on his left, a dining table and six chairs. There were the switches for the lights and the fans. Everything worked.

A door in the center of the back wall led to a corridor. What was back there? He stepped along the corridor. Another door leading to a rear veranda with a storeroom on each side. He looked out. Across a scrubby patch of lawn he saw a row of one-roomed servants' dwellings built against the back wall of the compound. To the right was a small brick building with a blackened opening near the roof—the kitchen.

Turning back into the house, Karim found doors opening off each side of the corridor into bedrooms, each with its own attached dressing room and bath. A door in each bathroom gave access to the outside, a relic of the preflush days when the sweeper came several times a day to empty the soil pots.

Well, it was not so bad after all. Now to choose a bedroom. The one on the right seemed to be a bit cleaner. He hung his clothes in the wardrobe, pulled aside the mosquito net, and lay down on the bed. For a few minutes he watched a gecko waiting on the wall for an insect to come within reach. At the sound of his bathroom's outer door opening and a bucket scraping on the terrazzo floor, he rose, removed his underwear, found a dipper in the bathroom, and began to pour the warm water over his body.

9

"Advantage, Mrs. Siddiqi!"

The umpire, a gray-haired man wearing a blue blazer with regimental badge, turned and nodded to the slim blonde woman. She was about thirty years old and dressed in a simple white tennis outfit. She smiled at him as she accepted a tennis ball from the ball boy, who had darted across the court when her opponent's ball had gone out of bounds.

Ellen Siddiqi brushed a strand of hair from her face and took her position for what could be the final serve of the match. The winner would be the Ramgarh University Staff Club Ladies Tennis Champion for the year. Ellen glanced at her opponent, a tall, rather large black-haired woman wearing a blue *kameez,* or tunic, and white *shalvar* pants, who bent over her racket, shifting her weight from side to side. Mrs. Abda Shamir was the wife of Professor Mohammed Shamir, the chairman of the history department, dean of the Faculty of Arts, and president of the Staff Club Association. She was also head of the Faculty Wives Association and was accustomed to having her way. Abda had held the championship for four years, and she wasn't going to let anyone take it away from her. But the score was 7–5, 5–7, and Ellen was leading in the final set eight games to seven.

Ellen was conscious of the intense interest of the dozen or so spectators sitting behind her on the club veranda. The watchers included certain young male faculty members whose interest in tennis was secondary to the pleasure they took in observing Ellen moving about the court in her tennis outfit, especially when the skirt flew up from time to time. These young men had met only their own sisters and cousins or perhaps a few wives of professors—some of them even more forbidding than Abda Shamir. For them, the female body was something to dream about, or to glance at surreptitiously on the walls of Hindu temples, or to study in movie magazines. When the time came for them to marry, their parents would select the bride and make the arrangements.

Ellen's costume, and the speculative thoughts and discussion it had aroused among these faculty members, were the cause of a certain coolness that had been noticed recently between Ellen and Iqbal Siddiqi. At least, that was what the staff club gossips were whispering as they lazed in the warm afternoon sunshine, sipping their chilled lime and water *nimbu-panies*.

When Iqbal Siddiqi had come back to Ramgarh in 1950 with his brand new Ph.D. in chemistry from the University of Minnesota, he had brought with him his new American wife. Ellen Anderson was the divorced daughter of the chemistry department chairman. She had met Iqbal soon after his arrival in Minneapolis at her father's annual dinner for the graduate students. Iqbal was slightly shorter than she, with light tan skin, wavy black hair, and sparkling brown eyes behind horn-rimmed glasses. His English was excellent, although he used British idioms rather than American.

Ellen was charmed by Iqbal's warmth, good humor, and quick mind. He would sit across from her at a table amid the hubbub and clatter of the student cafeteria and discourse earnestly about Gandhi, Nehru, and Jinnah, about Jane Austen and William Shakespeare. She remembered her ex-husband Paul Anderson's dinner table conversation. When he was not sulking in silence or arguing with another student, it was chemistry, chemistry, and more chemistry. It was a mystery to her that she had not immediately recognized that the young chemical warfare lieutenant who had trained under her father at Edgewood Arsenal, who had told her how he was going to get his Ph.D. and win the Nobel Prize, who had married her at the post chapel in 1943 a week before he would sail for England, was an angry, hostile man.

And Iqbal was quite taken with his professor's daughter. Her blonde hair framed a round face with deep blue eyes, a wide mouth that smiled easily, and a short, straight nose—almost the Hollywood model of the wholesome American girl. She was totally unlike any of the woman in his joint family, the only ones of his own social class that he had ever spoken to. His *purdah*-bound sisters and cousins were trained to be deferential to male family members. They cast down their eyes when spoken to. They had little education, and they were preoccupied with playing with babies, cooking, grinding spices, and picking stones out of the rice.

Iqbal was initially embarrassed by Ellen's frank, bantering manner. He didn't know how to talk to a woman as an equal. But after he had settled into his routine of classes, laboratory research, and library reading, he summoned up his courage and invited her to an Indian dance recital sponsored by the International Students Association.

Ellen accepted, and for the first time she beheld the dramatic movements of the Bharata Natyam dance language and the red, green, and gold of the dancers' costumes and heard the rhythmic chanting and drumming of the accompanying musicians. And here also Iqbal, sitting close to Ellen on the floor, savored her perfume and relished her blonde hair, fair skin, and physical grace. Later that night, in the vestibule of her father's house, Ellen kissed Iqbal. Stammering an embarrassed goodnight, he fled to his furnished room.

Ellen fell in love with India. She spent hours in the library and the museum, reading about Indian history and culture and learning about Moghul miniature paintings and South Indian bronzes. She spent more time with Iqbal, who overcame his shyness and talked to her about life in India and about the career he hoped to make there. Iqbal sent to his village for *saris* and for *kameez*, *shalvar*, and *dupatta*, the graceful tunic, pants, and shawl that Muslim women wear. Ellen delighted in dressing up in Indian costume for graduate student parties and International House affairs. So when Iqbal proposed marriage, once he had successfully defended his doctoral dissertation, Ellen accepted joyfully.

Ellen's arrival at Ramgarh Muslim University had caused a stir. Her friendliness and freedom from social restrictions attracted a following of faculty members—not all of them unmarried—who enjoyed being with her. In a few months a sort of salon had formed in which Ellen's intelligence and cheerfulness kept the men relaxed and amused.

Most of the faculty wives were in *purdah* and never left their homes without wearing the black *burqa*, a voluminous garment that covered them from head to toe with merely two slits of cotton mesh for the eyes. But the wives were not isolated. They were well aware of Ellen's presence and of her effect on the men.

Two of the spectators took more than usual interest in this tennis match. Wahid Sherif, senior lecturer in history, was a candidate for promotion to reader, one step below professor. A jowly, clean-shaven man, he had taken his Ph.D. at Ramgarh under Professor Shamir, Abda's husband, with a dissertation on Shamir's favorite subject, the armies of the Moghul Empire. Then he had joined the faculty as a lecturer. He had diligently served in any capacity that Shamir had demanded: pounding names and dates into the skulls of undergraduates, running errands of all kinds for Shamir and his equally demanding wife, and keeping the Shamirs informed of the currents of gossip that swirled around the university. In the staff club he was known as "Shamir's Shamir."

Wahid's activities on behalf of the Shamirs, however, had taken time, time that should have been spent on the scholarly research that a promotion normally required. There was another senior lecturer in the department whose published work was far more impressive than his. So Wahid was counting on Abda Shamir's good will and influence with her husband. He was rooting—even praying—for her to win.

Ellen Siddiqi wiped some damp strands of hair from her face, raised her racket, and served hard and fast. Wahid Sherif noted the swell of her breasts as she raised her arm and thought fleetingly of an Urdu couplet he had read as a youth. It had celebrated the beauty of Nur Jahan, one of Emperor Jahangir's favorites:

Thy breasts make the clouds feel downcast;
Thy arms bring the solace of the rain.

The serve went into the net. Ellen's second serve, slower than the first, was stroked powerfully by Mrs. Shamir, and Ellen could not reach it. "Deuce!" Wahid Sherif's hands clenched the arms of his chair.

Sitting next to Wahid Sherif was Anwar Hussain, a

bearded young man in his mid-twenties, whose friendship Ellen found a little disturbing. He had visited the Siddiqis at least once a week since Ellen's arrival in Ramgarh. He usually called at teatime, but lately he had been coming by when Iqbal was at work. Ellen enjoyed joking with Anwar about staff club gossip, but she had noticed that Iqbal became irritable whenever Anwar paid a visit.

Anwar was a member of the university community but not because of his academic qualifications. His membership was based on inheritance; Anwar was a direct descendent of the founder of the university. His uncle had been vice chancellor until 1947, when he had migrated to Pakistan and become minister of education.

Anwar had the lean, aquiline look of a Muslim aristocrat and the intense eyes of a fanatic. As an undergraduate, he had been active in the pro-Pakistan, anti-Hindu Muslim Students Association, the young people's affiliate of Mohammed Ali Jinnah's Muslim League. But now Pakistan was a reality, and Indian Muslims voted for the Congress Party and hoped that Nehru would protect them. Anwar was contemptuous of these "Congress Muslims," from the president of India on down. He also was bitter and angry toward the government, because the ancestral estate that he had counted on to provide him a substantial income and an easy life had been sequestered and declared "Evacuee Property." It was being held to compensate Hindu refugees from Pakistan for their losses.

Ellen crossed the court and took her position for the next service. Abda waited, shifting her weight from one leg to the other. Ellen raised her arm and served. The service was perfect, but so was Abda's return. Ellen countered with a high backhand lob. Abda ran to the back of her court and barely returned the ball to the net. Ellen smashed it into the opposite side.

"Advantage, Mrs. Siddiqi!"

"*Shabbash*! Bravo!" Anwar Hussain called out. Abda frowned at the spectators. Wahid Sherif cringed in his chair. Ellen smiled and took her service position. Anwar had said the right thing at the wrong time, as usual.

Ellen served. The service was good and Abda deftly stroked it to Ellen's backhand. Ellen responded with a backspin slice. Abda tried to return the ball but misjudged the backspin, and the ball went into the net. The match was over.

Ellen ran up to the net and held out her hand to Mrs. Shamir, but there was no response. Abda stood silently in her back court, scowling at the spectators. After a moment she marched off the court, snatched her sweater from a chair, and stalked out of the club without a word.

10

The morning haze—a mixture of fog and the smoke of cooking fires—lingered near the ground as Karim and Inspector Hafiz-ur-Rehman slowly pedaled their bicycles toward the old city. Karim was enjoying the unaccustomed physical activity, a change from bounding down the road in a jeep. As he maneuvered the heavy bicycle around the animal excrement that littered the road, he recalled the lighthearted competition he used to have with fellow officers—identifying the animals that had gone before them by the slight variations in the "splat" sound as the jeep's tires rolled over different varieties of manure. He had easily distinguished among cows, water buffaloes, and horses, but separating sheep and goats had been a problem.

"Where shall we go first, Hafiz?"

"Civil and Military Tailors, sir. On Mahatma Gandhi Road. You can be measured this morning. We should get that taken care of before we visit the city police *chaukis*."

The two men joined the queue of cyclists and rickshaw pullers walking their vehicles up the steep ramp leading to the road bridge over the railway. On the far side they turned north, joined the Grand Trunk Road, and, opposite the railway station a few hundred yards farther on, came to the junction with Mahatma Gandhi Road. Karim looked up Mahatma Gandhi Road as it rose to the hill from which the great Friday mosque—the *Jama Masjid*—commanded the crowded, narrow streets of the city and the flat reaches of the Ganges Plain.

"Mahatma Gandhi Road looks very straight and wide, Hafiz Sahib. It doesn't seem to fit in with the rest of the old city."

"Quite right, sir. It's a new road. The British cut it through to connect the station with the *tahsil* headquarters at the top of the hill."

"How many *tahsils* make up Ramgarh District, Hafiz?"

"Six, sir. Ramgarh *Tahsil* is the largest. The city, the cantonment, and about four hundred square miles of land. About 350,000 people."

"I can see corrupting modern influences at work in the shops in this road, Hafiz. Motor spare parts, furniture, insurance, electrical goods—even glass-fronted shop windows. Who knows what else? Just like Connaught Place in New Delhi." Karim smiled. "What would Gandhiji say? Giving his name to a road with such Westernized shops? For shame, Hafiz. For shame!"

"Quite right, sir. Here we are. Civil and Military Tailors." Oh well. Karim had made his little joke. But it had gone over Hafiz's head.

In the next hour, as the smiling proprietors swathed him in measuring tape and spread out bolt after bolt of British worsted, Indian wool, serges, drills, and tweeds, Karim got himself fitted for a full set of winter and summer uniforms, insignia, belts, and civilian clothing. "Nine hundred rupees and twelve annas, eh," he said when he was given the final bill. "Well, Hafiz, how long do you think it will take me to be indemnified by the government for my loss?"

"Start on the necessary documents tomorrow, Superintendent Sahib, and you should easily receive full compensation in . . . uh . . . let us say fifteen years. Twenty at the most."

"So you too have had problems with Lucknow, eh. *Achcha!* Let's get on with our tour. Did you bring along your city map?"

"Yes, sir." Hafiz unfolded a sheet of drafting paper. "This is the general layout of Ramgarh. The railway line and the Grand Trunk Road cross the city from the northwest to the southeast. Here, on the south side, is the cantonment. The university is in this outer part of the cantonment, sir. Here's the old city, north of the railway." Hafiz's hand moved over the paper as a breeze wrapped it around his arm. "Superintendent Sahib, could you please hold down these two corners of the map?"

"Of course. Better yet, let's go into this tea shop and you can spread it out on a table while we have a cup of tea." Karim lighted a Sepoy. "Tell me," he said as they sat down, "where are the *chaukis* located?"

"City Police H.Q., under Subinspector Pathak, is here in the *tahsil* office at the top of the hill. There's a *chauki* with a head constable in charge for each of the four quadrants of the old city." Hafiz-ur-Rehman's finger pointed out four locations on the edge of the built-up area. Karim sipped his tea, holding the cup and saucer off the table to avoid spilling on the map. "We also have a *chauki* here across from the railway station. The last one is over in the cantonment across from the university."

"*Achcha*, Hafiz Sahib," Karim said, rising from his seat and throwing some coins on the table, "where shall we begin? Are the head constables expecting me?"

"They've probably been notified by now that you're in

the area, but they're not expecting a formal inspection. Pathak has been told to get his records ready for you to look over if you wish."

"Well, since I'm not in uniform, I'll first pay an informal call on Pathak and then ride around to the others so they can see what I look like. Ah! It's good to be back at work again, Hafiz Sahib. Let's go."

The shopkeepers on Mahatma Gandhi Road were closing their shutters for the midday rest period when Karim and Hafiz finally finished their tour with the *chauki* opposite the railway station. Karim was feeling pleasantly fatigued after cycling through the narrow lanes of the old city. He had met all the head constables, shared a few anecdotes with Pathak, and gracefully refused the cup of tea that had been proffered at each police station.

Karim had been impressed by Hafiz's knowledge of the city. Not only of its geography but also of other things a policeman should know. Where the young *goondas* and *budmashes* gathered in the evening to plan their escapades. Who were the merchants suspected of black marketeering and dealing in stolen goods. Which *mohallas* were likely places for a communal riot between Hindus and Muslims.

"How about a bit of lunch, Hafiz? Is there a decent restaurant in the railway station?"

"No, sahib. But if you're willing to take a chance on an omelet, you might use the occasion to meet the stationmaster."

"Good idea. When I was there yesterday morning the conditions were not exactly right for a courtesy call."

The two men locked their bicycles and walked through the barrier. Karim paused as they entered the gloomy platform area. Everything looked normal, as if nothing had happened the day before. Coolies were squatting near the wall, puffing *bidis.* Food vendors were preparing their wares for the next train's arrival. A few listless passengers were squatting in small family groups, surrounded by their bedding, steel trunks, and containers of food. The men were softly gossiping and the women were nattering in high nasal voices. Among them were young mothers—too young, Karim felt, too often mothers—each sitting cross-legged with a baby in the lap. The babies' eyes were rimmed with black kohl and they played with their fingers as their mothers jiggled them with one leg. As Karim walked by, one young mother lifted her blouse, exposed a breast, and began to nurse her child.

Had it been only a bad dream? Had he really been nearly assassinated less than thirty-six hours ago? He breathed a silent prayer of thanks, straightened his shoulders, and followed Hafiz-ur-Rehman into the stationmaster's office.

Karim's stomach grumbled as he and Hafiz walked their bicycles over the road bridge after their lunch with Stationmaster Campbell. That lunch! Oh God! That lunch! A greasy omelet sprinkled with bits of green chili that made it look as if it had some rare skin disease, hard black toast, and tea served in a cup that reminded him of the cracked tiles on his veranda. Only the waiter's uniform was filthier than the tablecloth.

They joined the busy stream of traffic on University Road. The road was about sixty feet wide, but only the middle was paved—an asphalt strip with two narrow lanes. As usual, they had to contend with a hodgepodge of traffic moving at different speeds: cattle, buffaloes, bicycle rickshaws, horse-drawn *tongas*, bicycles, and every now and then a lorry or a bus, racing along the narrow pavement, its driver frantically squeezing the rubber bulb of its horn.

As they made their way up the road, Hafiz pointed out the District Court, the Sessions Court, the collector's office, and the English church.

"What's that bungalow over there, Hafiz?" Karim asked. He pointed to an impressive mansion set in a large compound. When they came closer, he saw that parts of the thatched roof had fallen in and large pieces of plaster had fallen off the walls. The lawn had become a scrubby pasture, with cows and buffaloes picking at tufts of spiny vegetation. The verandas had been subdivided into cubicles by curtains of old burlap sacking. Women could be seen playing with children and preparing food. A sign on the open gate said "Aman Manzil," House of Peace.

"That's the Hussain bungalow, sir. It's evacuee property now. Those are Hindu refugees from Pakistan living on the veranda."

"Which Hussain is that?"

"Liaquat Hussain Khan, the former vice chancellor of the university. He went to Pakistan in '47, and his house and lands were declared evacuee property."

The two men walked their bicycles through the gate to the bungalow. As soon as the women noticed them they stopped making *chapatis* and retreated with their children behind the sacking. Four men, apparently the family heads, came out to the front and stood, staring suspiciously at Hafiz-ur-Rehman's uniform. Something about their appearance was wrong. They bore no resemblance to the dark-skinned Doms, the gypsies that the police so often had to evict from abandoned buildings and send on their way.

"*Namaste*," Karim said, joining his palms in the Hindu greeting.

"*Namaste*, sahib," the men responded warily.

"I am the district superintendent of police." Karim's announcement triggered a shriek from behind the nearest curtain. The four men suddenly adopted a pleading, whining attitude, touching Karim's shoes and grasping at his trouser cuffs.

"Oh, sahib, help us! We are poor refugees. We have lost our land and houses in the Punjab riots. Please let us stay here. We have no other place to go!"

"Get up, all of you!" Karim ordered, repelled by their begging. "I'm not going to evict you. Just tell me who you are and where you come from. Inspector Hafiz, take their names."

The tale the refugees told was familiar. They were all members of a joint family that had fled from Lyallpur, in the irrigated area of southern Punjab. One brother had had a flourishing law practice, two had been grain merchants, and the fourth man, a cousin, had been the local distributor of agricultural equipment and fertilizers. All of them had owned land and houses.

"We escaped with only our lives, Superintendent Sahib," the oldest man said, "and not even that. My father and mother were killed in the train, my brother's daughter was kidnapped, and his wife was raped. Oh, sahib," the man's shoulders shook with anguish, "help us. We are your children."

Karim stepped back involuntarily. Poor, sad people. And similar awful atrocities had been committed on Muslims fleeing from India to Pakistan. "How long have you lived here like this?" he asked gently.

"Nearly a year, sahib, since we left the refugee camp outside Delhi."

"Well, won't you be able to settle down once the Evacuee Property Exchange Treaty is signed?"

"But sahib, we are not farmers or manual workers. We

are professional men and businessmen. How are we to be compensated by what Muslim peasants and workers left behind?"

"What about my daughter, sahib? How will I be compensated for her?"

Oh Lord, all he could do was offer them meaningless reassurance. And get away as quickly as possible. "*Achcha*," he said to the squatters, "if you stay here, you must not damage the property. It is still under the control of the government."

Karim and Hafiz continued their ride up University Road. Just before they reached Netaji Park there was a gap in the flow of traffic. A crowd of men and boys was blocking the road ahead.

"What have we here?" Karim asked.

"Looks like a road accident, sahib."

They dismounted and walked their bicycles into the crowd, with Hafiz-ur-Rehman shouting, "Police! Make way!" When they reached the center of the crowd a hush fell. The eyes of the watchers turned toward the two officers. Look at this, Karim felt they were saying. What are you going to do about this?

There was an overturned *tonga* lying on its side. The horse, still in the traces between the shafts, was lying with a grotesquely twisted right front leg. Karim stared at it. The animal was silent, but—oh God, its eye—in its eye were pain and shock and fear. The *tongawallah* was squatting beside the horse, his whip across his lap, a picture of passive dejection.

But what drew his eye was a blonde European woman, dressed in flowered *kameez* and white *shalvar*. Her shoulders were shaking as she held on to the overturned *tonga* with both hands.

"Madam," Karim said in English, "I am the district superintendent of police. Are you injured? Can I assist you?"

The woman turned and looked at Karim. Her face was streaked with tears, her *kameez* was torn at the shoulder. Karim felt an unexpected surge of fatherly tenderness for the young woman. He wanted to rest her head on his shoulder and murmur soothing words to her.

The woman sucked air in, blew it out, and wiped her sleeve across her mask of tears and dust. She continued to clutch the *tonga* with her free hand like a sailor in a storm-tossed boat.

"Please. Can I help you, madam?" Karim asked. Her tear-filled blue eyes swept across Karim's face and down over his worn civilian jacket and pants. She swallowed.

"Who are you?" she whispered.

"The police, madam. Can we help you?"

"Help this man. He's ruined. He hires the horse and *tonga* and he'll be in debt for years." She was still breathing hard but her voice was getting stronger.

"Try to be calm, madam," Karim said gently. Good. She seemed to be getting control of herself. "Tell me what happened."

"A big truck. It sideswiped our wheel and knocked us off the road. The *tonga* tipped over and I fell out."

"Hafiz. Write this down," Karim said. She seemed much stronger and calmer now.

"The horse was thrown down when the *tonga* fell over."

"Are you injured?"

"I don't think so. Just a few bruises. My shirt is torn. But this horse will never walk again and the driver will have to pay." She looked around at the men and boys who were pressing close and staring at her. "Who are all these people?"

"Get back, all of you!" Hafiz-ur-Rehman shouted. The nearest men moved back slightly.

"Could you identify the lorry, madam?" Karim asked.

"It was big, with four wheels in the back." The woman knitted her brow. "It was green, I think. Yes. Green paint with some gold flower designs. And it was carrying something in burlap bags." She took another deep breath and wiped her face once again. "I don't think the driver even knew he hit us, he was going so fast."

"Which direction was he going?"

"Toward the city, I think." She took her hand away from the *tonga* and fluffed up her hair. A brightly painted bus ground by, packed with passengers who stared silently at the *tonga* and the horse and the European woman.

"Hafiz Sahib, take the name and address of the *tonga-wallah*. Also any witnesses. Then go back and tell Saxena what has happened. I want a search organized for the lorry. *Achcha?* It probably will be near one of the wholesale grain markets. Notify all the octroi posts to hold it if it tries to leave the city. Where do you think it entered the city?"

"It probably was checked in at the end of University Road, sir."

"Send a man to copy the records of incoming lorries since noon today. And question the octroi clerk. Green with gold flowers. It shouldn't be too difficult to find. *Thik hai?* I'll get a cycle rickshaw and take her home."

"Yes, Superintendent Sahib."

"Madam," Karim said, turning to the woman, "We shall find the lorry. Your *tonga* driver will not have to pay for the accident."

"Superintendent Sahib," Hafiz said in English, "I will need the lady's name and address for this statement."

"My name is Ellen Siddiqi. I'm the wife of Doctor Iqbal Siddiqi, reader in chemistry at the Muslim University. I live at Number 2B Fazlullah Road." Ellen gave the details slowly in a calm voice. Karim lighted a Sepoy cigarette.

"Let me take you to your home, madam. This unfortunate accident has upset you. But you are lucky not to be seriously injured."

"You're very kind, Superintendent." Ellen brushed some of the dust off her clothes. "Please excuse me but I didn't catch your name." She smiled when Karim told her his name. Was it because it was a Muslim name? "Thanks, I can get into the rickshaw myself."

Karim followed the rickshaw on his bicycle for the few minutes it took to reach the Siddiqi's small faculty house. It was a duplex; each half had its own walled garden front and back. Karim dismounted and opened the gate.

"Good afternoon then, madam. I hope you will not suffer any ill effects from your accident. A police officer might be calling on you for identification when the suspected lorry is found." Karim paid off the rickshaw driver and prepared to mount his bicycle.

"Please don't go away so fast, Superintendent." Ellen smiled. "I can't let you leave without a cup of tea. You've been so kind."

Karim hesitated. He gripped the handlebars tightly and looked up and down the secluded street. The rickshaw man was turning into the main road. Then he turned back to Ellen, who was resting her hand on the saddle of his bicycle. "Madam," he said, "I'm not sure I should accept your kind offer."

"Oh, don't worry," Ellen said. "My husband won't mind. Anyway, he'll be home in a little while and you can meet him." She smiled again. "Do come in. I'd like to get to know you better. You sit in the living room while I change my clothes and have the tea made." Ellen entered the compound and Karim followed with his bicycle.

They were led into a small sitting room by a woman

servant and a dachshund. The dog yelped and wagged a warm welcome for Ellen and, after sniffing at Karim's trousers, decided that he could be tolerated.

What a pleasant room it was—smaller than his own sitting room, but the printed curtains and matching seat cushions made it look like a home. Not like his own official quarters.

"Schnitzel's a friendly dog," Ellen said. "Almost too friendly. He'll bark at strangers, but he'll make them welcome once they get into the house. Do you know Doctor Shamir's Alsatian bitch, Hilda? That dog is dangerous! She almost tore my dress off when I visited there a year ago." Bending down to rub Schnitzel's stomach as the dog lay on its back, Ellen cooed, "You're not that kind of dog, are you, Schnitzel. You be nice to the superintendent, now!

"Sit down, Mr. Karim. Alice," Ellen said to the servant, "make a pot of tea, please, and bring some biscuits." Turning back to Karim, she said, "Will you excuse me for a moment? I'll just wash up and change." She left the room through a curtained doorway. Schnitzel followed, his claws clicking on the tile floor.

Karim remained standing, plucking nervously at the threadbare sleeves of his jacket. He pulled out his pack of cigarettes, hesitated, and replaced them in his pocket. He looked around the room and saw some photographs and a silver bowl on a sideboard. He read the inscription on the bowl. So she had won a tennis prize, eh? He smiled. Good for her.

He looked at the pictures. There she was with her parents in a family portrait. The Indian in the other picture was probably her husband. An ordinary face. But the horn-rimmed glasses made him look sort of distinguished.

That bookcase over there. They wouldn't mind if he took

a look at the titles. Novels. Hadn't seen them before. Must have been brought from America. The *Oxford Dictionary*. He had used it as a student. What were these, down on the bottom shelf? Nehru's *Discovery of India*. A good one. *A Passage to India*. E. M. Forster. What could that one be about?

"Well, Anwar. So you're here again." The soft male voice, its tone verging on the menacing, came from the direction of the door. Karim stiffened, rose to his feet, turned around, and saw the man from the photograph on the chest.

"Who the devil are you?" Iqbal Siddiqi's voice rose, his head jutting foward toward Karim.

"Please forgive me for intruding, Doctor Sahib." Karim said. "I am Mohammed Abdul Karim Khan, the new superintendent of police. Your wife has invited me for tea." Siddiqi glared at him from behind his glasses. He opened his mouth and was about to speak when Ellen stepped into the room carrying a tray of biscuits.

"Well," she said brightly, "have you two gotten acquainted? Iqbal, this is Mr. Karim, the police superintendent for Ramgarh. He brought me home this afternoon after my *tonga* was tipped over by a truck and I fell out onto the pavement. Don't worry. I'm not hurt. But Mr. Karim is going to catch the truck driver and make him pay for the *tonga* and the pony." The two men bowed and greeted each other warily with the Muslim *salaam*.

"I feel a lot more presentable now that I've changed," Ellen said. And she looked more presentable too. The printed cotton dress, the sandals, and the sweater over her shoulders also made her look more normal. Why did European women wear Indian dress? Didn't they know that they looked incongruous, with their light hair and their pink skin and their pink feet sticking out from under the folds of a *sari*. Let them wear their own clothes; that was more fitting.

"Please take your seat, Superintendent," Iqbal said without enthusiasm. "Thank you for helping my wife."

"Oh, come on, Iqbal!" Ellen protested. "Relax. Mr. Karim is just having a cup of tea. He's not staying the night. Good, here's Alice. Just put it on the coffee table, Alice, will you please. I'll pour. Mr. Karim?" She held out a cup of tea and the sugar bowl.

"Thank you, madam. I'll just drink my tea and be off. My deputy will be wondering what happened to me." Schnitzel scrambled onto Ellen's chair and settled down next to her, keeping an eye on the biscuits.

"When did you come to Ramgarh, Superintendent Sahib?" Iqbal's innocent question sounded only slightly less hostile than before.

"I came only yesterday morning, Doctor Siddiqi. I was transferred from Raipur District." He knew he should not have come into the house.

"Raipur, eh? Were you on the Raipur train the other night? The one that burned up?" Iqbal removed his glasses, wiped them on his handkerchief, and leaned toward Karim. A hint of a smile showed on his face and as quickly disappeared.

"Yes I was, Doctor Sahib. I escaped with my life and these civilian clothes that I'm wearing."

"Mr. Karim!" Ellen cried out. "That's terrible!" She leaned over and put her hand on his arm. "You poor man. What a way to arrive. Whatever caused the fire?" Iqbal's fingers tightened around his teacup. Karim moved slightly and Ellen withdrew her arm.

"It was a fire of mysterious origin, madam. Deputy Superintendent Saxena and his men are investigating."

"Saxena? That brute Saxena?" Iqbal's face contorted. "I wouldn't put it past that man to burn it himself to do you in."

"That is a very serious accusation, Doctor Siddiqi."

"You may not be aware of it, but since Saxena has been in Ramgarh the feelings of the Muslim community have been treated with contempt by the police. Muslims, especially our students, have been arrested without cause and mistreated by this man Saxena. I hope you will put a stop to this."

Karim stood up. "There will be no arrests without cause while I am superintendent, Doctor Siddiqi. And all persons will be treated equally, regardless of their community. If you have evidence of false arrest, please submit a formal complaint to me and there will be an investigation."

"Oh yes. Yes. A formal complaint." Iqbal turned away.

"Now then," Karim said, "I must make a move. Mrs. Siddiqi, Doctor Siddiqi, I am happy to have met you. Thanks for the tea and biscuits. Mrs. Siddiqi will be contacted in connection with the road accident."

"Goodbye, Mr. Karim. Thank you so much for helping me get home. I'll see you to the door." Ellen led Karim to the front door, opened it, and stood aside to let him out. As he passed, she held out her hand. Karim hesitated. He hadn't touched a woman since his wife had died. Ellen smiled and took his hand in hers.

"Goodbye, Mrs. Siddiqi." He felt Ellen slowly release his hand. Finally only their fingertips touched. Ellen looked into his eyes.

"Thank you again, Mr. Karim."

The bungalow door closed behind him. Karim pushed his bicycle through the gate in the compound wall. He mounted the bicycle and started to pedal back to his office. It was then that he heard Iqbal Siddiqi shouting angrily at his wife.

11

"*Arrey*, Shri Gupta! Where are you bound in your fancy *achkan* this fine evening?"

Irritated, Surendra Gupta turned in his rickshaw seat to see who had asked such an impertinent question. He was wearing an *achkan* of fine tan silk with silver buttons. It was his best coat and with it he wore a *dhoti* and a turban of pure white cotton.

"Well, well, Subinspector Pathak, my friend from the *tahsil chauki*. Good evening, Subinspector." Gupta warily shook the police officer's hand as Pathak steered his bicycle alongside Gupta's rickshaw in the congested traffic of Mahatma Gandhi Road. "You're going home late this evening, isn't it?"

Pathak dismounted from his bicycle as Gupta's rickshaw driver pulled over to the side of the road. "I haven't worn a coat like that since my wedding, Guptaji!" He laughed and winked one eye.

"I've no time to joke with you now, Pathakji. I have an engagement for the evening."

"Does your wife know about this important engagement you've gotten all dressed up for, Guptaji?" Pathak held up his hand and rubbed his forefinger over his thumb in an obscene gesture.

Gupta winced. "Please, Pathakji! You know me well enough to answer the question yourself." Pathak winked again. "If you have nothing serious to say to me, please let me take my leave."

"I'm not sure how serious it is to you, but our new superintendent has arrived. He's a Muslim. He came around to all the city *chaukis* yesterday on an inspection tour."

Gupta stiffened. He turned away from Pathak and looked across the crowded road. He squeezed his eyes shut, wiped his face with his hand, and turned back to look at Pathak. "What is this new superintendent's name, Pathakji?" he asked, trying to keep his voice calm.

Pathak described Karim and the circumstances of his arrival in Ramgarh. Gupta listened closely. When Pathak had finished he said, choosing his words carefully, "It's a miracle that the superintendent survived, Pathakji. I hope the police will quickly track down the culprit and bring him to justice. Now, please excuse me, I really must make a move."

"But Guptaji, don't you want to . . . ?" Pathak's voice trailed off plaintively as Gupta ordered his driver to pedal on toward his destination.

A convulsive shudder broke Gupta's self-control as the rickshaw rolled down Mahatma Gandhi Road. Tears welled up in his eyes. So it was true, after all. That Muslim pig had escaped. Bahadur Singh had . . . No, it must have been a mistake. It must have been the wrong bogie. "My God! What will happen now?" Gupta said aloud.

"Sahib said something to me?" the rickshaw driver asked.

"What? No. Nothing. Talking to myself." Gupta wiped his eyes and blew his nose. He took a few deep breaths and felt better. Time enough later on to worry about this Muslim superintendent. Just now he had to concentrate on the evening ahead.

Gupta's rickshaw dropped him off in front of the heavy

wooden gate in the Shiva Prasad compound wall near the Vishnu temple. A small enameled sign told him that the residence was called "Security House." Old Shiva Prasad. He had made so much money that he could have built his house in the cantonment near the other newly rich. He could have bought an acre or more of ground and put up a large mansion. But the shrewd old tyrant had never wanted to be very far from his business, so he had bought a piece of land on the edge of the old city, kicked out the tribal people squatting on it, put up a high brick wall topped with broken glass, and proceeded to build himself a home.

Gupta pressed a button next to the door and a moment later it was opened by a bearer in a white uniform with sash and turban. Just like the bearers in European-style hotels! The man bowed and extended his arm in the direction of the house.

Gupta was surprised by the house. It wasn't a flamboyant mansion in the style the wags in the tea shops sardonically called Black Market Modern. It was only an ordinary flat-roofed bungalow with verandas in front and back, similar to dozens of bungalows in the cantonment. He understood. What old Shiva Prasad had wanted was a cantonment bungalow just like the English but here in the old city, near his business and among his own people. The best of both worlds.

Ram Lal Prasad was waiting on the veranda. "*Namaste*, Guptaji," he said, joining his palms. "What a handsome coat you're wearing."

Gupta suddenly felt overdressed, out of place. Prasad was wearing clean white pyjamas and a *kurta* shirt with a white wool waistcoat. Simple, everyday clothing. Gupta coughed, cleared his throat, and wiped his mouth nervously with his handkerchief.

"Have you caught cold, Guptaji?"

"Ah, Prasadji, I've heard so much about your late father's cultural evenings. I'm so happy to be here that my throat suddenly tightened."

"Really?" Prasad looked at him skeptically. "Feel better now? Good. Come in and meet my friends. We're just about to have a meal."

Prasad led the way into a large room, brilliantly illuminated by an ornate crystal chandelier. Five middle-aged men, all of them dressed in clean white homespun, were sitting cross-legged or leaning against white bolsters on a thick Persian rug. Gupta recognized them as merchants, members of the Municipal Committee, and leaders of the Hindu Mahasabha. They struggled painfully to their feet to greet him. How fat and flabby they were, these wealthy merchants, men who spent their days sitting in their shops or offices with their cash boxes close by.

But these were the most powerful men in Ramgarh. These were the men whose word could cause an electrical connection to be installed in a month instead of the usual two years, or a plot of land to be allotted to an ineligible applicant to build a house or a factory. These were the men he hoped would befriend him and take him into their confidence.

Ram Lal clapped his hands. The bearer appeared at a curtained doorway across the room. "Bring the food," Prasad ordered. When the men had seated themselves, the bearer returned with a silver ewer, a large basin, and a white towel folded over his arm. Beginning with the senior guest, he poured warm perfumed water over their outstretched hands and waited while they dried them on the towel.

Then a Brahmin cook entered the room, bearing a silver tray of food in each hand. He set one tray on the carpet in front of each of the two senior guests, left the room, and reappeared with more trays. When all had been served he brought in silver cups of water.

The meal was simple—a mound of saffron rice and *chapaties* in the center of the tray and around it small silver cups with vegetable curries, yogurt, and *dal*, a thick lentil gravy. The men ate quickly, with little conversation. They expressed their appreciation by belching and noisily sucking their fingers. Gupta was asked about his health, his wife's health, and his law practice. When would they get around to talking about something serious?

When the meal was finished and no one wanted to have more, Prasad clapped his hands. The bearer came and removed the trays, and the cook reappeared with plates of the *halva* and other sweets that Ram Lal had so appreciated at Gupta's office. Murmurs of approval and delight rose as the guests gorged themselves on the sweets. Finally, after the last bit of *gulab jamun* had been finished, the bearer returned with warm water and the towel. This time each guest noisily washed his mouth as well as his hands.

Feeling full and a bit sleepy, Gupta sat quietly, waiting to see what was next on the program. It was clear that business was the last thing his fellow guests wanted to talk about. Could it be that they were waiting until after the music?

There was a commotion at the door. Voices raised in protest. Prasad rose quickly and threw open the door. The turbaned bearer, staggering under the weight of two large instrument cases, lurched into the room, nearly fell on the carpet, and panted, "The musicians, sahib." Gupta got up and relieved the bearer of the largest case, only to have it snatched away from him by a teenage boy who had entered the room with the two musicians. While the musicians were setting up their instruments at the end of the room, Prasad addressed his guests.

"As you know," Prasad announced, "ever since my father died, I have hoped to take up his custom of having cultural evenings. They gave him so much pleasure. They gave his friends so much pleasure. So this first cultural evening means much to me." A smile illuminated his smooth, youthful face. Gupta watched the fat merchants making themselves comfortable on the carpet, arranging the bolsters, ignoring Ram Lal's remarks. Had they been so inattentive when his father had spoken?

"This is *Ustad* Bashiruddin Khan," Ram Lal continued, "the master of the sitar." The older of the two musicians bowed low and raised his right hand to his forehead in the exaggerated courtly style of the old-fashioned Muslims of Lucknow. A Muslim musician hired to play in a Hindu home, a Muslim playing classical Hindu melodies on an ancient Hindu instrument. Almost all of the great musicians in North India were Muslim, since the Moghul emperors had developed families of court musicians for themselves and their nobles. Hindu musicians had been relegated to wedding processions and folk music.

"This is Chandra Bhal, the *tabla* master." The younger man bowed and pressed his palms together in the Hindu greeting. Gupta felt proud.

The musicians busied themselves arranging their instruments, tuning them, and finding comfortable seated positions on the carpet. The *tabla* player tapped the leather bindings on the edges of his two drums with a small mallet and tested the skins with his fingertips. The sitar player adjusted the movable frets and twisted the pegs that tightened the six steel playing strings and twelve sympathetic strings of his ornate wood and ivory instrument.

"The first *raga* we will play is *Raga Ahir Bhairav*, a morning *raga*," *Ustad* Bashiruddin Khan announced when all was ready.

The tinkling descending arpeggio that begins every sitar movement brought Gupta to attention. He shifted his body around to get comfortable and glanced at the other men. Their faces were raptly expectant as they waited for the *ustad* to begin the *alap*, the slow improvisational invocation and exploration of the *raga's* melody.

The sitarist slowly moved his left hand up and down the length of the sitar, his fingers pressing and stretching the steel wires as his right index finger plucked the tones and his right thumb picked out a drone note. The audience sat with their heads swaying gently, captivated by the *ustad*'s sensitive evocation of the *raga*'s devotional mood.

Gradually Bashiruddin began to introduce rhythmic variations on the melody as he entered the *jor* phase of the performance. His speed increased; his variations became more complex. The sympathetic strings were sounding in response to the playing strings. The left hand moved swiftly up and down over the frets and the right index finger moved so fast that it blurred as he moved into the *jhala*, the lightning virtuoso display that concludes the first half of the piece. The listeners sat with their fingers tapping against their thighs, smiling at each other after a particularly inventive improvisation. The *jhala* ended with another tinkling arpeggio. "*Wah! Wah!*" the guests cried out. *Ustad* Bashiruddin Khan smiled and touched his forehead with his hand.

Now the *gat* began. Chandra Bhal struck the first beats of the *rupaktala* rhythm cycle: three beats, two beats, three beats. His fingers struck the skins of his small right-hand drum and his large left-hand drum with clarity and precision. Then the sitar picked up the lead. *Tabla* and sitar joined in a rhythmic and melodic display, slow at first, then faster and faster. Bashiruddin improvised a variation on the sitar; Chandra Bhal followed with the same variation on the *tabla* and then contributed one of his own, to which the sitar responded. The two musicians grinned, challenging each other to come up with a more difficult improvisation.

The audience loved it. Their fingers beat an accompaniment, their heads swayed with pleasure. Gupta, caught up in the shared ecstasy of the experience, closed his eyes and tried to feel the music with his entire body. Suddenly, after a lightning-fast sequence in unison, the music abruptly stopped; a final arpeggio brought the *raga* to a close. Gupta opened his eyes as Prasad and the others broke out into shouts of delight and approval. What a difference it made when you were close to the musicians.

Prasad clapped his hands and the Brahmin cook appeared with a tray of fruit juices. The men sipped and talked quietly, waiting for the next *raga* to begin.

It was well past midnight when the musicians concluded their final *raga*. Gupta felt emotionally drained. Not so the other guests, who rose and chatted with each other and the musicians.

"Well, Guptaji, did you enjoy the concert?" Prasad inquired.

"I could not have enjoyed it more, Prasadji. I've never been so close to the musicians where I could see every movement of their fingers." Gupta noticed the other guests still talking among themselves. Was Prasad trying to tell him something? Was he trying to get rid of him? "But it's very late and you must be tired after making all these arrangements. Shall we make a move and let you get your rest?"

"*Achcha*, Guptaji. I'll send my bearer to get you a rickshaw."

Five minutes later Gupta found himself sitting in a rickshaw, riding away from Prasad and his wealthy guests. At this hour it was impossible to find a rickshaw so quickly. The fellow must have been waiting at the gate by arrangement. He'd been gotten rid of! He'd been sent away so they could make their deals without him!

So that's the way it was, he thought. The poor lawyer was excluded from the plans of the great men of the Hindu Mahasabha. Well, who needed them? The R.S.S. would go it alone. They would sing a different tune when the great day of *Hindu Raj* came!

The road was dark, so dark that the rickshaw man could not see Gupta silently sobbing as he took him back to the narrow alley in *Mohalla* Kanungoyan.

12

"Well, Saxenaji, anything to report on the railway bogie fire?" Mohammed Abdul Karim was sitting behind his desk at police headquarters, wearing his new winter uniform. How comfortable he felt in the brown worsted jacket with its brass buttons and insignia. Wearing a uniform again gave him the feeling that he had defeated his unknown assailant, at least for the time being.

Karim lighted a cigarette, inhaled deeply, and blew the smoke upward toward the ceiling fan that hung motionless in the cool winter air. He glanced at his three assistants, sitting facing his desk like schoolboys called to the headmaster's office. And, like schoolboys, they needed supervision, discipline, encouragement. Especially Saxena. A violent man. Om Prakash? Young, still enthusiastic. Hafiz-ur-Rehman, a Muslim. Pleasant fellow. But Saxena. Could be trouble.

All right, so the routine business was finished. The lorry driver who had knocked over Mrs. Siddiqi's *tonga* had been identified and was being charged. Then there was that case of pistol cartridges, missing for over two months. It had been reported to Lucknow. Next week Karim would start visiting the police *chaukis* out in the district. The annual reports were being worked on. Now it was time to deal with the fire bombing.

"Superintendent Sahib, I've had five men working on it." Saxena read in his harsh voice from a file folder. "We've followed up your suggestions. Not one of the coolies can read English. None of them had the smell of petrol or burned material about their persons. No sign of singed hair or burned skin. Every coolie was able to account for his movements from midnight until the time of the fire." Saxena closed the file and looked up, his eye pouches jiggling as he moved his head. "It is true, though, that most of the coolies were only backed up by other coolies."

"Hmm. What does that mean?" Karim pulled at his mustache. "Can we assume that someone's lying? Because it's not easy to prove that someone does not know something. So there could be a coolie who does know English but denied it when you questioned him."

"Yes, sir, but we . . ."

"No, no, Saxenaji. I'm not saying that you didn't do the right thing." Karim took a final puff of his cigarette and tamped it out in the ashtray. "I'm . . . I'm sort of . . . uh . . . thinking out loud. You know? Letting the mind play with the evidence. It helps sometimes."

"Yes, sir." Saxena shrugged and seemed to relax.

"Superintendent Sahib?" Hafiz-ur-Rehman raised his hand to speak.

"Yes, Hafiz?"

"We could find out. We could send men into the *mohallas* and question their neighbors and relatives." Hafiz spread his hands in a gesture of futility. "But it would take a long time."

"Exactly," Karim said. "So what's the alternative? Now. Let me see. I was in the bogie looking out under a window that was raised about two inches. I saw a coolie with a lantern come up and read the reservation paper pasted on the door. The reservation paper was in English. So where are we?"

No one spoke. The sound of a lorry horn came in through the window, followed by the chuck-chuck-chuck of a flour mill as it began grinding grain for its morning customers.

"I think we need some stimulation, gentlemen. Misra!" Karim called to his head constable through the open door of the office. "Bring some tea, please. *Achcha*. What next? Have you found any physical evidence, Saxena?"

"Sir, Om Prakash has searched the railway yard and the remains of the bogie with great care. May he report on his findings?"

"Superintendent Sahib," Om Prakash began as Karim nodded to him, "my men have found this burned petrol tin under the bogie and this brass lock on the outside of the compartment door." He put the two pieces of physical evidence on the desk. Karim's heart began to pound as he smelled the acrid odor coming from the charred metal and saw again the inferno in which he had almost been incinerated.

"The petrol tin has no identifying marks," Om Prakash said. "The lock is marked SPL. This means that it was made here in Ramgarh by Shiva Prasad and Son. But these locks are available anywhere." He cleared his throat. "It's not an overly strong lock, but it could easily have prevented anyone trapped in the bogie fire from getting out." He paused, coughed and cleared his throat again. Where was that tea, Karim wondered.

Om Prakash continued. How soft his accent was. Not like the hard, clear Hindi these Ramgarh people spoke. "There's a small opening in the barbed wire at the closest point to the Grand Trunk Road, but from the rust I would judge that it's not a new break. It's probably been used regularly by ticketless travelers." Karim smiled inwardly. Well done, Om Prakash. You've got a good head on your shoulders.

"That's the opening Harbans Singh and I used when we left the bogie. The coolie didn't seem to come from that direction." Karim started doodling on a sheet of paper. "After the explosion there were those witnesses you found who saw the two of us, but did anyone report seeing a lone man passing through that break in the fence?"

"No, sir, no one did," Saxena answered.

"I don't want to completely eliminate that possibility, but I'm inclined to think the man came from the direction of the station. Was anything else found in the yard? A sandal, a box of matches, anything the bomber might have left?"

"We haven't found anything like that, sir."

"Well then. So we're at a dead end?" Karim asked.

"Sir," Saxena began, "Inspector Hafiz-ur-Rehman has been making inquiries in the city. We have our sources, you know."

Karim turned to Hafiz-ur-Rehman. "Sorry, sir," the inspector said with a wry smile. "Nothing to report. None of our local *budmashes* did this job. It just doesn't fit their pattern. No money in it." He crossed his legs and sat back in his chair. "Could it be political, sir?"

"That's the obvious question, Hafiz. Whenever a government officer is attacked, you suspect a political motive." Karim wrinkled his nose in distaste. "I hope not. That would mean big trouble." He paused. "But . . . I've been thinking. Maybe I was wrong about the man with the flashlight. Maybe I thought he was a coolie because he was dressed as a coolie. Maybe he wasn't really a coolie at all. What do you think?"

"That's it, sir!" Om Prakash nearly leaped out of his chair.

"Everything fits if he was only dressed up as a coolie. It fits!"

"Not so fast, Om Prakash," Karim cautioned. "Did any of the coolies or the railway personnel notice any stranger lurking about in the railway yard or in the station during the night? Someone who might not have acted like a legitimate railway passenger?"

"Superintendent Sahib," Saxena asked with more than a trace of a sneer, "how would anyone know who is a legitimate passenger and who is not?"

"Think about it for a moment, Saxenaji," Karim replied gently. Damn that man! If only he knew when to keep quiet. "Let me see, now. The legitimate railway passenger usually has some baggage, maybe a bedding roll and a steel trunk or a suitcase of some sort. He hires a coolie to carry his baggage. He goes to a ticket window and purchases a ticket to some destination. It's printed on the ticket, isn't it? Right! What then?"

Karim leaned forward, looking from one face to another, commanding their attention. "The passenger shows his ticket to the guard at the barrier, enters the platform, and waits until the proper train arrives. When it does, he finds a seat, has the coolie put his baggage on the rack, pays the coolie, and leaves on the train. Do you agree, Saxenaji?

"Now," Karim continued, "when the passenger reaches his destination he hires another coolie to take his baggage out of the station. He surrenders his ticket to the guard at the barrier, who checks to see that it is correct. Then he looks for a *tonga* or a rickshaw outside of the station to take him to where he is going." Karim leaned back in his chair and lighted a cigarette. "The normal pattern. Right?" Saxena was silent.

"I think I see what you're driving at, Superintendent

Sahib," Hafiz-ur-Rehman said slowly, nodding his head and smiling. "It would not be normal for a passenger with baggage to purchase a platform ticket. No. That wouldn't permit him to travel, unless he intended to jump off the train before he reached his destination. Also, a traveling ticket inspector might catch him anad make him pay a fine."

"That's true, Hafiz Sahib, but isn't it perfectly normal for a person to purchse a platform ticket if he's . . . uh . . . seeing someone off or maybe meeting an arriving passenger?"

"Yes, sir," answered Hafiz-ur-Rehman. "But sir, we're looking for a man who's probably carrying a tin of petrol. He can't carry the tin onto the platform. He has to have it hidden somewhere in the railway yard so he can get it when he needs it . . ." Hafiz-ur-Rehman's voice trailed off as his thoughts failed to come together.

"Good!" Karim said. "Here's Misra with the tea. Just what we need at this moment, isn't it? Get's the brain going again."

Each man took his tea from Misra's serving tray. Saxena tipped a small amount into his saucer, slurped it, and smacked his lips.

"Hafiz Sahib," Om Prakash said, "how would your bomber get the petrol tin into the railway yard without someone noticing it?" He looked to Karim for confirmation. Karim nodded and looked to Hafiz for an answer.

"Wait, I think I have it." Hafiz stood up, put down his teacup, and began to pace back and forth in front of the desk, counting off his points on his fingers. "First, the man is dressed in ordinary clothes. Second, he's carrying a suitcase. Third, in the suitcase is a tin of petrol and . . . wait, wait . . . yes! A red smock and a turban, just like the platform coolies wear!"

"*Achcha, achcha,* Hafiz Sahib! Go on!" Karim leaned over his desk.

"He buys a platform ticket," Hafiz continued, "enters the platform, goes to the end of it, and finds some dark corner behind one of the sheds in the yard. There he takes the petrol tin out of the suitcase and puts on the red smock and turban. In the dark no one will notice he's not wearing a badge. Right? Then he finds the bogie, spills a bit of petrol under it, leaves the tin lying open, throws a match, and runs back to where he's hidden the suitcase. Wait. No! *Before* he throws the match he puts the lock on the outside of the compartment door. *Achcha*! When he gets back to the suitcase, he takes off the smock and the turban, returns them to the suitcase, and walks back to the platform. He gives his platform ticket to the guard and leaves the station. Meanwhile, everyone else is running to the fire." Hafiz sat down, exhausted but smiling.

Saxena's puffy eyelids had narrowed while Hafiz had been thinking out loud. Beads of sweat had appeared on his forehead.

"But what has happened to this imaginary suitcase?" Saxena demanded. "Wouldn't he be likely to attract attention if he's carrying a suitcase when he shows a platform ticket to the guard? Did he leave it in the yard after he changed his clothes?" A plaintive note had crept into Saxena's voice.

"Om Prakash and his men didn't find any suitcase in the railway yard, did they?" Karim asked.

"No, sir, we did not. But we weren't looking for a suitcase. I think it would be a good idea to make another search of the whole railway area. The suitcase might even be in the left luggage office waiting for someone to pick it up."

"Right! Om Prakash, take extra men and go through the

station and the yard. The suitcase may be hidden away somewhere. If you find it, don't touch it. We might get some fingerprints from it."

"Yes, sir!"

"And what about that lock?"

"Sir?"

"Would it be worthwhile to send a man around with it? I'm just wondering. It might be a waste of time." Karim paused. "*Achcha*! When you've finished your search, take the lock over to the Prasad factory and get a list of all the local dealers who bought that kind of lock during the past . . . let me see . . . six months. No! The past year."

"Yes, Superintendent Sahib. Then I'll visit those dealers and see if anyone remembers who bought it."

"Don't visit the dealers yourself. Send a plainclothes man. But you go to see Prasad personally. What's his name?"

"Ram Lal, sir."

"You visit Ram Lal Prasad. But don't tell him where the lock was found." Karim paused. "Saxenaji, you need to interview the platform guards and other station personnel who were on duty that night. Find out if they noticed anyone who purchased a platform ticket but was carrying some kind of baggage. You and Hafiz take care of it. What next?" Karim made circles with his forefinger on the scarred surface of the desk. "Right! Saxenaji, put a good plainclothes man on duty in the left luggage office. Have him sniff every suitcase for the smell of petrol. The suitcase should not be very heavy. There may also be marks from the cinders and soot in the railway yard."

"And if he finds the suitcase?" Saxena asked.

"What should he do? What should he do? Well . . . uh . . . if it *is* the suitcase, he should not touch it any more than necessary. We can dust it for prints when the office is closed. In any case, get the locks picked open on any suspicious luggage."

"I'd better put two men on it, sir. If we find the suitcase, we can wait until it's claimed. Then our second man can follow the bomber and see where he goes. He'll be waiting outside the office for a signal from the man inside."

"Good idea, Saxenaji. If the suitcase is found, let me know immediately."

"Yes, Superintendent Sahib." The officers stood, saluted, and left the room.

Karim leaned back in his chair and pensively stroked his mustache. Not much chance of finding the bomber. The man probably wouldn't come back for the suitcase, if there was a suitcase. Hafiz-ur-Rehman. There was a man with a good mind. The way he had picked up his idea and made it something workable.

The political angle. It was risky. It could be quicksand. Who could have known he was arriving on that bogie? Saxena and the officers, of course. But who else? And why would they want to kill him? Was it someone who hated him personally? Someone who hated the police, the Muslims, the government, or what?

He looked at the safe in the corner where the political files of the C.I.D. were kept. Did they contain the names of informers who could find out who or what was behind the bombing? Was Harbans Singh recovered enough to help? He lighted a Sepoy, leaned back in his chair, and inhaled the comforting smoke. The polished brass buttons of his new uniform jacket glinted in a shaft of morning sunlight.

13

Ellen Siddiqi woke up in the middle of the night when a dog barked in the distance. It was very cold so she moved onto Iqbal's half of the bed, fitting her legs close behind his, and slipped her arm around his chest. Iqbal groaned and woke up. "Damn!" he muttered, got out of bed, and went to the bathroom. Ellen heard the splashing in the toilet, specially installed by the university when they had arrived, and the clanking as Iqbal pulled on the chain five times before the flushing water siphoned out of the tank high on the wall and rushed into the toilet.

"We should have brought an American toilet back with us," Iqbal grumbled when he came back and lay down on his side, pulling the quilt over his shoulders. Ellen resumed her position, fitting her body tightly against his and holding his chest in her arm. Iqbal stirred slightly, took her arm, and held it close under his own.

"What did your mother say in the letter? The one that came today," Ellen murmured sleepily. Iqbal's mother dictated her letters in Urdu to the village scribe. Ellen had seen the letter in the morning post, but Iqbal had not mentioned it at supper or during the evening while they listened to the "Voice of America."

"The usual. When are you coming to visit me? When are you doing to have a baby?" Iqbal's voice was muffled by the quilt.

"Oh Iqbal!" Ellen cried out. "When are you going to tell her?" She turned around and faced away from Iqbal, tears wetting her face and pillow.

Ellen's memory of her first meeting with Iqbal's mother in his ancestral home in Sitapur District was so vivid she could repeat almost word for word what had been said. Iqbal's father had died while they were en route from America. When Iqbal had crossed the threshold of the fortresslike landowner's home after three years' absence, the family had gone into a state of shock. The grief that his mother and sister had felt when his father died had to be revived and shared with Iqbal. His mother had sequestered herself in her room, allowing Iqbal to see her only on the day after his return as if to punish him for not being there when she had needed his comfort and support. Iqbal had spent most of the next two days talking with his mother in her room or praying at his father's grave in the Muslim cemetery at the edge of the village.

"She will like you, Ellen. I promise," Iqbal had told her as they lay under mosquito nets on wood and rope *charpoy* beds in the open courtyard, hoping to get some sleep after the heat and emotional turmoil of the day. Ellen had not responded. The diarrhea and cramps she had developed in Bombay had lasted for a week, and she was utterly without strength. Her sister-in-law had given her cups of hot tea and small clay bowls of yogurt mixed with sugar. Iqbal had given her Entero-Vioform, but she had exceeded the dosage and he was afraid to give her any more. There was no doctor in the village, and Iqbal didn't trust those in the nearby town. He had wanted to wait until he could get her to Dr. Abbas in Ramgarh.

"Ellen. We are man and wife. You are her daughter-in-law. She will love you." Iqbal had reached under the mosquito nets to caress her breast. Ellen had clutched his hand to her mouth and used it to stifle her sobs.

On the fifth day Ellen had been taken in to meet her mother-in-law. She had held Iqbal's hand tightly as she had entered the dark, curtained bedroom. When her eyes had adjusted, she had seen Siddiqi Begum sitting on a *charpoy* with one leg drawn up, fanning her face with a woven reed fan. How closely she resembled Iqbal! Put a pair of horn-rimmed glasses on her and you couldn't tell them apart.

Iqbal had brought Ellen close to the bed and said something in Urdu. His mother had smiled, exposing teeth reddened by *paan*, and had gestured for Ellen to sit next to her on the bed. "She wants you to sit next to her, Ellen. Sit down. She likes you," Iqbal had said. Ellen had complied, careful not to sit on the embroidered silk garments that she was sure the woman had worn for the occasion. She had held out both her hands and Siddiqi Begum had put down the fan, taken them in her own brown hands, and looked down at them and up at her face. "She is saying how fair your skin is. Indian women with fair skin are highly prized." Her blonde hair delighted his mother, who touched it as if she were arranging flowers in a bouquet. "Just like the English district magistrate's children!" Iqbal had translated.

"Iqbal! What is she doing?" Ellen had cried out, startled as her mother-in-law, laughing lustily, had run her hand down over Ellen's belly and rubbed it. Her voice had become gleeful as she rubbed.

"She says she thinks you will be a good bearer of children. She wants to have grandsons to carry on the family. When my sister has sons they'll belong to her husband's family. She wants you to have a son right away."

"Oh Iqbal! Tell her I love her very much!" Ellen had taken her mother-in-law's hands in hers and kissed them. Iqbal had pulled up a chair and the three of them had spent the day talking and laughing as Ellen had told Siddiqi Begum about her family and the home she had left to come to India.

"It might not be my fault, Ellen." Iqbal's answer came after a pause, and his voice sounded as if he was trying hard to control his feelings. He turned to Ellen, leaning on his elbow and bringing his face close to her shoulder. "There were other chaps working next to me in the lab. No one has written to me that they have any problems having kids."

"But Iqbal, we've been trying for so long. I don't know what's happening sometimes."

"I'm not sure it's my fault, Ellen." He turned away.

"Oh Iqbal, I'm so sorry!" Ellen moved closer and leaned over Iqbal to kiss him on the lips. Then she snuggled against him, one hand holding his penis. Her tongue explored the inside of his ear. Iqbal took a deep breath and expelled the air. Ellen lay there without moving, waiting for a response. Then, resignedly, she turned over and moved to her side of the bed. She finally fell asleep as dawn was breaking and the *muezzins* were calling the faithful to prayer.

14

"Fifty million Muslims, Prime Minister! Fifty million Muslims!" Mohammed Ahmed Salim's jaw was quivering. His horn-rimmed glasses had slipped from the bridge of his nose. "What are we to say to the fifty million Muslims of India, Panditji?" He leaned back and looked at the other men around the conference table. "After all, I *am* the communications minister," he said.

Jawaharlal Nehru spread his fingers on the polished rosewood table in the Cabinet Room. Yes, it was a good question. What were his old Muslim colleagues Salim and the education minister, Maulana Mohammed Ashraf, going to say to the Indian Muslims. And, for that matter, what was Victor Russell, the magazine editor, going to say to the Anglo-Indians?

Damn that Uttar Pradesh government! Just when Hindu-Muslim violence was quieting down, those fools talked of making Hindi the only language for state business. Instead of waiting a few years. Now the Muslims and Anglo-Indians were frightened and angry. Who could blame them?

"Prime Minister," Victor Russell said, "the Anglo-Indian community also is concerned about the developments in Uttar Pradesh." He could pass for an Englishman, that

Russell. Fair skin, light eyes, English suit, and that ridiculous pith helmet on the table in front of him. Prasad and Rao had smirked when they sat down at the table. Missionaries and Anglo-Indians. You could tell them by their pith helmets. "The Anglo-Indians feel that . . ."

"All right, Russell," interrupted Maulana Ashraf. "We already know what the Anglo-Indians feel. We've heard it many times. You have your own Anglo-Indian schools and no one will stop you from using English. But Panditji," he turned to Nehru, who had picked up a pencil and was doodling circles on his note pad, "Salim Sahib has asked the critical question. What are we to say to the fifty million Urdu-speaking Muslims still in India?"

"Maulana Sahib," Nehru said gently, twirling his pencil, "let me rephrase the question. Let me make it a little more complicated. Let me make the question reflect the real concerns of the Indian Muslims." The prime minister smiled, aware that he was playing the role of barrister trying to put a nervous witness at ease. Ah, to leave this office and go back to his law practice. How pleasant it would be. "The real question, Maulana Sahib—and you too, Salim Sahib—is this. How can you, the leaders of the Muslim community, stop Uttar Pradesh from replacing English with Hindi in government business, the courts, and the schools. And if you can't, what will happen to Urdu, to Muslim culture, and to the economic position of the Muslims. And to the position of the Anglo-Indians too, Victor. Have I clarified the issue just a little bit, gentlemen?" Salim and Ashraf nodded. Victor Russell flushed slightly and straightened his necktie. Mahavir Prasad, the law minister, and A. V. P. Rao, the home minister, sat back in their chairs as if withdrawn from the discussion.

"Let me continue, then," Nehru said. He turned his pencil over and began to erase the circles on his note pad.

"To complicate the issue a little more. The Anglo-Indians—how many are you, Victor? One hundred thousand? One hundred fifty? A drop in the ocean. India has—let me see—360 million. Not even a drop in the ocean, Victor. To be sure, the British acknowledged your blood relationship to them, but they did not accept you as equals. Now that they're no longer here to protect you and guarantee you jobs, you're worried about your future. Am I correct, Victor?"

"Yes, Prime Minister."

"Yes, Victor, you are worried and fearful." Nehru looked around at the others. "And we should all be worried and fearful about the Anglo-Indians, gentlemen. All of us. Where would our railways be without the Anglo-Indians? Our police? Our army?" He turned back to Russell. "You are our cousins, Victor. You have no political influence, no economic power, but you are Indians, Victor."

Nehru stood up and went to a window that overlooked the gardens surrounding the parliament building. "It saddens me, Victor," he said, rubbing his cheek as he looked out of the window, "whenever I read about Anglo-Indians emigrating to England, to Canada, to America. What are they running away from? They have good jobs here, they have their Anglo-Indian schools. How much better could it be elsewhere? Especially for the darker-skinned Anglo-Indians, Victor."

"Your point is well taken, Prime Minister."

"You people have English as your mother tongue, Victor. You speak it better than any group in India. We will always need good English speakers in India. You need have no fear of that, Victor. We will always need the Anglo-Indians here in India."

"May I quote you on that in my magazine, Prime Minister?"

"Of course."

"I wish the Urdu question could be settled so easily, Panditji," Salim said. He had removed his white Congress cap and was fanning himself with it.

"Who said anything about an easy settlement, Salim Sahib?" Mahavir Prasad peered at Salim through his thick glasses. "You know what the Constitution provides for the Anglo-Indians. Ten years. That's all the time they have. After that there will be no more reservation of posts or special grants to their schools. These people are going to have to stand on their own feet like the rest of us." He turned to Victor Russell. "You are aware of that, Victor, are you not?"

Russell's face reddened. "*Every* Anglo-Indian is fully aware of Articles 336 and 337, Minister Prasad, I assure you." He wiped his forehead and cleared his throat. "We want to stand on our own feet, gentlemen. But we're a poor community, and it will take more than ten years. It will take a generation. And when we read what these Hindi fanatics are saying, we wonder about our future." He turned to Nehru. "I'm grateful to you, Prime Minister, for your confidence."

A. V. P. Rao, the home minister, leaned toward Russell and smiled. "With sincere apologies, Victor, it is time to turn to the more important question of Urdu. We've got an amendment to the Criminal Procedure Code coming up for debate, and I have to be on the floor of the House.

"Prime Minister," he continued to Nehru, "I am in agreement with my Muslim colleagues. The Urdu question is a political mine field, especially in North India and in my state of Hyderabad. We need the Muslim votes. Who knows what will happen if the Muslims begin to feel that Congress no longer looks after their interests?"

Nehru turned again to look at the gardens. How beautiful the roses were in the sparkling winter sun. He watched a *mali* watering the cannas from a goatskin bag. Finally he said, "Gentlemen, we're dealing with the ultimate moral problem here. You know what I mean, Maulana Sahib? It's not the problem of right and wrong. That would be easy. The Bible, the Koran, the Shastras—every great religion has the answer to right versus wrong. Eh, Maulana Sahib?" Maulana Ashraf nodded his head. "What we have here is the problem of two conflicting *rights*. The Urdu-speaking minority, the Muslims, has the *right* to preserve its language and culture, guaranteed by the Constitution." Nehru returned to his seat at the head of the table. "What are those articles, Prasadji?"

"Twenty-nine and 30, Panditji."

"And the Hindi-speaking majority in Uttar Pradesh has the *right*—not only the right but the *duty*, according to the Constitution—"

"Three fifty-one," Prasad interjected.

"—to promote the development and spread of Hindi. What do you think, Maulana Sahib? And Salim Sahib? If it's a political problem, we look for political solutions. If it's a moral problem, we have to find a moral solution."

"You have not only complicated the question, Panditji," Maulana Ashraf chuckled, "you've turned it into a conundrum. I am perplexed. For the first time in some years, I am perplexed." He removed his fur cap and wiped his forehead with a handkerchief.

Nehru smiled. "Remember those arguments we used to have with Gandhiji? Remember? We'd go to him with a simple question and come away with five questions. Talk about perplexed!" Nehru laughed out loud. After a moment he said, "Ah, Gandhiji. Why did they take you away from us? We need you now more than ever."

Once more the room was silent as each man seemed to

recall the black day in 1948 when Hindu fanatics had put three bullets into the thin brown body of Mahatma Gandhi, the one man in India who might have brought peace to the bloody, refugee-choked roads of the Punjab. "The light has gone out of our lives and there is darkness everywhere," Nehru had said on All-India Radio.

A bell rang somewhere in the building. A. V. P. Rao cleared his throat. "Forgive me, Panditji, but I'm needed in the House. Can I say a few words about the political situation as I see it?" Nehru nodded. Rao looked sharply at Ashraf and Salim. "With suspicion, gentlemen. With suspicion. This is how the Hindus in North India and Hyderabad view the Muslims. Where do their loyalties lie, they are asking? No, wait, Salim Sahib, let me finish. What I have to say must be said." He waggled his index finger. Like an angry schoolteacher, Nehru thought. "The Hindus see the educated Muslim boys running off to Pakistan. Who paid for their education, they are asking? They see ex-Muslim Leaguers like Nurul Hussain get elected to the Indian parliament and then run away to Pakistan. Who are these Muslims, they are asking? Are they Indians? Are they Pakistani spies ? Can they be trusted, they are asking?"

"Nonsense!" Salim's jaw was quivering again. "Utter nonsense, I tell you! You cannot name an Indian Muslim who has spied for Pakistan!"

"I don't have to, Salim Sahib! That's not the point!"

"What is the point, then?"

"The point is that the Hindus *believe* they are spies. The Hindus *believe* they are disloyal. It's only four years since Partition. People don't forget so easily. The Muslims have to demonstrate that they're not disloyal to India."

"Impossible!" Ashraf said. "How can you demonstrate that you're not disloyal? That you're not a spy? It's not possible." He shook his head. "I'm amazed that you, a lawyer, should say such a thing."

"Amazed or not," Rao replied, "that's what you have to do. Now, Prime Minister, you must excuse me. I have to get to the floor of the House." Joining his hands and making *namaste*, Rao hurried out the door.

Salim and Ashraf looked at each other. Ashraf turned to Nehru and then to Prasad and Russell, who looked down at their hands. Nehru opened the collar of his *achkan* jacket and wiped his neck with a handkerchief. He fingered the rose that was fixed in the third buttonhole of his jacket.

"What are you thinking, Maulana Sahib? Salim Sahib?" Nehru asked after a few moments.

"I'm thinking that if Rao is correct," Salim said, "the question of Hindi is the least of our worries." Ashraf nodded in agreement. Salim added, "Our very existence as a community, as Indian Muslims, is under attack."

"Yes," Nehru said, twirling his pencil between his thumb and forefinger, "you might be justified in feeling that way. These are legitimate fears for any minority community when feelings are running high. But tell me this, gentlemen. How will the Indian Muslims—no, let me put it this way. Is India a secular state, with freedom of religion and culture for everyone? Salim Sahib?"

"It's in the Constitution, Panditji."

"*Achcha*. Another question. Can any political solution acceptable to the Hindu majority and the Muslim and Anglo-Indian minorities be found in an atmosphere of hostility and fear? The answer is obvious."

Salim and Ashraf looked at each other with raised eyebrows. Russell and Prasad stared expectantly at Nehru. A puff of wind came in through the window and stirred the papers on the table.

"As I said before, gentlemen, the problem is a moral one. We should be seeking a moral solution." Nehru stood up and fastened his collar. "A moral solution is not like a political solution. It's not a matter of give and take—you give me this privilege and I'll give you that benefit. Not at all. A moral solution demands wisdom and courage. Wisdom comes from the mind, and courage comes from the heart."

Nehru put his hand on the door handle. "I've often asked myself a question in situations like this one. You should do the same. Ask yourselves this. What would Gandhiji have done?" And Nehru opened the door and left the Cabinet Room.

15

"Scotland the Brave" skirled over the flat green cricket ground of Ramgarh Muslim University as the Ramgarh Police Pipe Band—twelve bagpipers, four drummers, and a pipe major—paraded smartly past the reviewing stand, their brown legs oscillating rhythmically inside their starched, oversized khaki shorts. Their turbans, fan-pleated like the napkins at a diplomatic banquet, bobbed up and down with each step. The pipe major, a fiercely mustachioed head constable, twirling his baton, swung it across his chest in salute, and snapped an "eyes right" as he came abreast of Dr. Ibrahim Shamir Khan Gilani, principal of the Delhi Medical College and soon-to-be vice chancellor of Ramgarh Muslim University.

Dr. Gilani raised his hand to return the salute. Then he paused, turned to his right, and looked inquiringly through thick-lensed glasses at Major Mehboob Ali, the commandant of the Ramgarh University Detachment of the National Cadet Corps. The major nodded vigorously. Dr. Gilani drew himself erect and swung his arm up to the salute with such force that he knocked askew his gray karakul cap.

The band marched to the edge of the field, reversed direction, and returned to the center. There it formed up on the cricket pitch, opposite the saluting platform and the grandstand. Behind the band three hundred cadets stood at attention.

"What do I do now?" Dr. Gilani asked.

"Now you will review the cadets, Doctor Sahib," Major Ali replied. He stepped forward four paces. The bagpipes moaned into silence; the drums were mute. Major Ali looked to the left and to the right at the khaki-clad ranks of cadets.

"Paaaaaassssss . . . in review!" The last word of Major Ali's command came out as a high-pitched shriek. The bass drum boomed, the snare drums snapped, and "Scotland the Brave" skirled again. The detachment of cadets, swinging their arms with varying degrees of smartness, paraded past their future vice chancellor and disappeared from view behind the tennis courts.

Two men, dressed in tailored European clothes, were watching the parade from a position near the cricket ground. "There goes the new officer corps of the Pakistan Army," muttered Bharat Chaudhri, the Ramgarh district magistrate and collector. He was standing with his hands in the pockets of his gray flannels. His blue blazer had an ornate crest on the breast pocket.

"As soon as they have graduated they'll be off," said Dr. P. C. Lalchand, the civil surgeon. "The government should make this a secular university." He spat on the ground in disgust.

"Ah, here comes our good friend the superintendent of police," said Chaudhri. "I hope you've committed no major crimes, Doctor Sahib."

"Good afternoon, Collector Sahib," Karim said and saluted.

"Ah, Karim. Replaced your uniform, I see. Well done. Well done! Mustn't let the side down, eh?" Chaudhri chuckled. "Mustn't let the buggers think we're beaten. How goes the investigation?"

"Not much progress, I'm afraid, sir. We think it was an outsider, not one of the licensed coolies. In that connection, might I call on you to discuss the case? There are certain aspects that I need to have your advice about."

"Of course, Karim. Come to my office on Monday morning at eleven."

"Your sardarji friend was discharged from the hospital on Wednesday, Superintendent Sahib," said Dr. Lalchand. "He shouldn't have any difficulty getting back to work."

"Thank you, Doctor Sahib. That's a relief. He seemed in good spirits last week. By the way, what about the cost of his treatment? I want to pay it myself."

"*Achcha.* We'll see that you get the bill. But remember, you can't make a habit of this. You'll go bankrupt. Ha ha!"

"Come on, Doctor Sahib. The parade's over. Introduce me to Doctor Gilani. You were his student, I understand." Chaudhri led Dr. Lalchand by the arm away from Karim.

Looking around, Karim noticed Ellen and Iqbal Siddiqi among the spectators who had crowded into a large striped tent set up near the reviewing stand and were queuing up for tea, fruit juices, sweet biscuits, and *halva.* He adjusted his jacket and cap and joined the tea queue.

"Mr. Karim! Mr. Karim! How are you?" Ellen called out when she caught sight of him in the line. Karim was suddenly aware that nearly everyone in the queue had turned and was looking at him with friendly curiosity. Only Iqbal Siddiqi seemed to frown.

As Ellen carried her tea and biscuits over to Karim, he contemplated her Muslim dress—a blue *kameez* and white *shalvar* with a white *dupatta* shawl over the bosom.

"What a handsome uniform, Mr. Karim. You really look like a superintendent now. By the way, I've been wondering if you've found that truck driver who knocked over my *tonga*."

"Yes, madam, we've found him and he's being charged. We'll be asking you to appear when the trial takes place."

"Appear?"

"In court. To testify." How beautiful she was. She stood out from the Indian crowd like a lotus in a dark pool. But what was he thinking of? No woman had interested him like that since his wife had died.

"Oh, that's great! I can hardly wait." Her pleasure at his news gave her face a radiance that he had not seen before. "Who'll pay? For the *tonga* and the pony, I mean."

"That will be up to the judge, madam. He may order the lorry to be sold to pay the costs and damages. Just like in your country, I think. Yes?"

"When is the trial?"

"That is hard to say, madam. This is India," Karim grinned. "These things move slowly. There are many cases ahead of this one. This lorry owner, I'm told he's a powerful man in the city. He has a lawyer. The lawyer may get postponements. I don't know."

"That's terrible!" Ellen's face was suddenly transformed. "What about the poor *tonga* driver? What will happen to him in the meantime?"

"What's this about a trial?" Iqbal Siddiqi broke in when he had joined them with his tea. His eyes behind their thick glasses looked sharply from Ellen to Karim and back to Ellen.

"That driver. The one who knocked over my *tonga*. Mr. Karim says I'll have to testify against him."

"We'll see about that, Ellen. I'm not sure I want you in any court case like that." Was that a note of warning in Iqbal's soft voice? Was Iqbal reminding him that Ellen was off limits?

"Iqbal, I can't turn my back on that poor *tonga* driver. If my testimony is necessary, I'm going to give it." Ellen turned angrily away from Iqbal. She handed her cup and saucer to a passing servant, put her two hands on Karim's arm, and said, "Mr. Karim, I want you to meet some of the faculty members. I'm sure they'd like to meet you."

"Please don't trouble yourself, madam." What could he say to these sophisticated professors? He had not spoken to a single academic since law college in Lucknow before the war. Of course, it would be nice to go around with this pretty woman. But . . . should he risk making an enemy of her husband?

"Nonsense. No trouble at all. Let's start with Doctor Mirza. He's acting vice chancellor. You'll like him."

Pulling gently at his sleeve, Ellen led Karim over to Dr. Gilani and Dr. Mirza, who were talking. As he caught sight of Ellen, Dr. Mirza ran his hand over his abundant white hair and said, "Doctor Gilani, let me introduce my favorite faculty wife, Mrs. Ellen Siddiqi from America." His voice boomed clearly to the crowd at the tent. "She's married to our reader in chemistry, Doctor Iqbal Siddiqi." Mirza put his arm behind Ellen and gently moved her closer to Gilani. "Mrs. Siddiqi has made an excellent adjustment to life here in Ramgarh. We think very highly of her. She just won the Women's Tennis Cup. Don't you think she wears the *kameez* and *shalvar* well, Doctor Sahib?"

Dr. Gilani declined Ellen's outstretched hand and touched his right hand to his forehead in the Muslim greeting, murmuring "*Salaam*, Siddiqi Begum." He looked inquiringly at Karim and at the badges of rank on his shoulder straps and then turned back to Ellen.

"I just wanted to introduce our new superintendent of police, Doctor Mirza. I didn't know that I would also meet our new vice chancellor." Ellen flashed her most winning smile, but Gilani maintained his wary expression. Was he a conservative Muslim or was he inexperienced in dealing with Western women?

"I am Mohammed Abdul Karim Khan, sir, superintendent of police, Ramgarh District, since January first of this year." Karim saluted both men.

Other spectators had taken a keen interest in Ellen Siddiqi's bold advance to Dr. Gilani.

"Do you see what I've been telling you?" Abda Shamir whispered fiercely to her husband. "You are his relation, yet she is the first one to meet him. You are the dean of the arts faculty, not some smelly chemistry teacher. You should have been the first."

"Calm down, Abda. Don't worry. All in good time, all in good time," Mohammed Shamir said in a comforting tone. He looked wistfully at Gilani. "He's come a long way since we went to England together in '35. I never expected to see him as our V.C."

"That Siddiqi! A reader in less than two years. And don't you know why? It's because of her. She gets the invitations to Mirza's house, she gets paraded out whenever an important visitor comes to the university, and Siddiqi gets the promotions. The poor man slaves away in his laboratory, thinking he's been promoted on merit. It's her, I tell you . . . !" Abda was glaring down at her husband and gripping his arm.

"Abda! You're hurting my arm!" Professor Shamir whispered. "Listen to me, Abda. Stop worrying about Ellen Siddiqi. I'm not bothered if she's introduced before me."

"Don't be a fool! Do you think you'd be dean of the faculty if I hadn't pushed and pushed for you? You'd still be a lecturer with a tiny office in the back of the library. So don't tell me not to worry about that Siddiqi woman!"

"Did you see that Hindu pig spit on our soil? Wahid Sahib, did you see that?" Anwar Hussain's bearded face was no more than two inches from Wahid Sherif's. Hatred flashed from his dark eyes; his hand shook as it clutched the sleeve of Sherif's black *shervani*.

"What are you talking about, Anwar Sahib?" Sherif pulled back from Hussain's intense stare. Lately his friend's hatred of the Hindus and of the government had become rather excessive. Such strong feelings might be all right for a common man but not for a man of culture, a man of honor, a *sherif admi* in the Ramgarh Muslim University tradition.

"That civil surgeon, that Hindu moneylender with an M.B.B.S., he *spat* on our Muslim University!"

"Anwar Sahib, you're hallucinating again. Why don't you keep your eyes on our tennis champion. She's brought along that new police superintendent. You know, the one who nearly got burned up in the railway fire. I wonder what she sees in him. He's one of us, I understand."

"Yes, I heard about him." Anwar looked over to Karim, Dr. Gilani, and Dr. Mirza standing in a circle with Ellen in the center.

"I would prefer to see her in that tennis costume of hers, wouldn't you?" Wahid put his hand on Anwar's shoulder. "Look, Anwar! Look at her with Gilani. Like she's known him all her life. Abda must be fuming."

"That Muslim policeman makes me ill. Dancing to the tune of his Hindu masters."

"She's coming this way, Anwar. Look at the way she

moves. That hair. Ah, Iqbal Sahib, I'm not responsible for my thoughts. You had better make her wear the *burqa* when she leaves your house. No man should see her face."

"I'm leaving. I don't want to meet him." Anwar Hussain turned to leave, but Wahid held on to his arm. "Let me go, Wahid Sahib! What are you doing?" Anwar's voice was soft but it trembled with fury.

"Don't make a spectacle of yourself, Anwar. All those people! Don't let them see you lose control. Anwar!"

Wahid's voice became ingratiating as Ellen and Karim approached. "*Salaam*, Superintendent Sahib. *Salaam*, Mrs. Siddiqi." Wahid bowed with exaggerated courtliness.

"Mr. Karim, this is Doctor Wahid Sherif, senior lecturer in history, and Mr. Anwar Hussain. Anwar, where have you been for the past month? You haven't come to see me." Ellen's voice teased lightly.

Anwar looked away from Ellen toward the tent, where he could see Iqbal Siddiqi watching them.

"I . . . uh . . . I've been very busy, Ellen. Working on my property case. Those Hindu squatters have been running the property down."

"Which property is that, Anwar Sahib?" Karim inquired.

"Aman Manzil, my family's ancestral home. We lost it as evacuee property when my uncle migrated to Pakistan. I've been trying to get the decision reversed, but so far it's been no use. This damned government hates Muslims!"

"Have you been practicing your tennis, Ellen?" Wahid Sherif asked, breaking into the silence that followed Anwar's outburst.

"I've seen the property, Anwar Sahib," Karim interjected, looking sharply at Hussain, "and I've warned the occupants to take care of it."

"Yes, I'm sure you have, Superintendent Sahib," Hussain replied.

"Why did you ask about tennis, Wahid?" Ellen said. "The tennis competition is finished."

"Abda Shamir's out to get that championship away from you. She's out early every morning practicing her serve against the backboard. You'd better watch out, Ellen," Wahid laughed.

"What's that noise, Wahid?" Ellen asked. "Do you hear it?"

"What noise?"

"Listen. There it is again. Sounds like someone screaming."

"Look there!" Karim shouted. "Near the tennis court. My God! It's someone on fire!"

A man—his clothing on fire, his hair ablaze—ran onto the cricket ground, weaving erratically from side to side, screaming, waving his arms, trying to put out the flames. He was pursued by a crowd of shouting students, some carrying blankets. They caught up with him as he ran headlong into the boundary fence and fell to the ground. Quickly they covered his agonized body with blankets, but his screams would not be stilled. The sound hovered over the cricket ground like a pall of anguish.

Dr. Lalchand and Karim were the first to overcome their shock and run to the man. They pushed their way through the stunned crowd and knelt beside the blanket-covered form. The man was shuddering as the civil surgeon carefully pulled back the blanket and exposed his face. The onlookers gasped with horror, a woman screamed, a student vomited. The man's lips, nose, eyes, and ears had been burned away; his face and hairless scalp had been charred black. The screams that had come from his seared mouth had subsided into the squeals of a dying animal.

Dr. Lalchand pulled the blanket further and exposed the body. The fire had charred most of the man's skin. He gently replaced the blanket and looked at Karim. Tears filled his eyes.

"I . . . I've never seen anything so bad. Third degree. Most of his body. I've never . . . He hasn't a chance." Dr. Lalchand rose wearily to his feet. "I'll fetch some morphine from my car and then we can take him to the hospital." The shocked and silent crowd made way for the doctor. He said a few words to Dr. Gilani and walked quickly to his car.

"Don't look, Ellen!" Iqbal Siddiqi begged, holding Ellen tightly to him. "Don't look! Don't look! Don't look!" He pressed her cheek to his chest. "Here. Let me wipe your eyes."

"Oh my God, Iqbal!"

"I'll take you home. Come on. Let's go home." They stopped and hugged one another as a gust of wind blew a dust devil across their path. Then they moved on.

Karim stood up and looked around. He was surrounded by students and faculty. Looking over their heads and seeing the band at the edge of the crowd, he called the pipe major to his side.

"Head Constable!"

"Sahib!"

"None of these students are to leave this area until their statements have been taken. Have your men see that they stay here."

"Yes, Superintendent Sahib!"

"Wait. Send one of your men to headquarters *ek dum* with this note." Karim quickly wrote a message with instructions to the duty officer, gave the note to the head constable, and turned to the students. He raised his arms.

The students stood quietly, waiting for him to take charge.

"Now then," he called out, "Who can tell me what happened?"

A dozen students began to shout their versions of the incident. Karim waved his arms to silence them. He pointed to the nearest man. "You! What is your name? Can you tell me what you saw?"

"I am Enayat Khan, sahib. You must come to the hostel and see for yourself. Come this side." The student extended his arm and gestured Karim toward the opening through which the burning man had come.

"Right! Let's all move to the hostel and have a look." Karim strode quickly across the field, followed by the students, the police musicians and their instruments, Dr. Mirza, and Dr. Gilani.

"Here it is, sahib," Enayat Khan said. "The hostel warden's office. Mr. Rafiq. He's visiting his parents this weekend."

Karim looked carefully at the red brick building. There wasn't much damage, just a few blackened bricks under the barred ground floor window, some sooty panes of glass, and a black stain that spread upward, almost to the cornice at the top of the second floor. He stepped closer and noticed the burned and wilted flowers and bushes under the window and the smell of petrol. What was that, there in the bushes? A burned petrol tin. Just like the one from the railway yard?

"Did anyone actually see what happened? Was anyone here when he caught fire?"

"None of us were here, sahib." Enayat Khan looked at his fellow students for confirmation and continued. "We were all coming back from watching the parade. We saw this man on fire, so we grabbed some blankets and tried to put it out.

But he wouldn't let us touch him." The students nodded and murmured in agreement. Karim looked around and caught Dr. Mirza's eye.

"Vice Chancellor Sahib, would you kindly arrange to have the names of these witnesses recorded and sent to me. There will have to be a judicial inquiry into this event. We will need their testimony."

Karim turned back to the scene of the fire. Who would be so inept as to set himself on fire this way? Was it the same man who had set his bogie on fire less than two weeks ago? Was it one of the men Harbans Singh had heard plotting in a tea shop? Why had he chosen to do it today? How had the man entered the quadrangle? What was his planned escape route after the fire had been set?

Karim rummaged among the burned bushes and picked up the petrol tin. It was burned badly, and yes, it did resemble the one from the railway station. But nearly all petrol tins look alike. Only their labels differ. Could it be traced? It would be difficult but not impossible.

He straightened up and looked around at the two-storied quadrangular building—only two entrances, one leading to the cricket ground and another leading through an archway to a neighboring quadrangle. No, there was another one. Down at the corner of the building. A small postern gate—wood, but painted red to resemble the bricks. Had the man come in by that gate?

Karim quickly walked the thirty or so yards to the gate, followed by the students. He paused. He pushed the wooden door; it didn't move. He covered his hand with his handkerchief, grasped the handle, and pulled. The door squeaked open. Karim stepped through the gate and found himself in a narrow, shady arbor. At the end of it, only a few dozen yards away, was a well. It was the *bhishti's* door, the waterman who brought water to the hostels in his goatskin bag to keep the red clay *chatties* filled.

Karim stepped into the arbor. In a moment he saw it, partly hidden by leaves. A battered suitcase, smudged with soot and coal dust.

16

Arranging the end of her *sari* over her graying hair, Zakia Begum pulled aside the curtain printed with scenes of blue-faced Krishna frolicking with his dairy maids. She looked into her waiting room and beckoned to Ram Lal Prasad. He was her first customer this evening.

"Come, sahib. Aijana Bibi has just finished her bath. She is waiting for you."

Zakia Begum's reputation as the best brothel keeper in *Mohalla* Tavaif was based mainly on the beauty and accomplishments of her girls. But for Ram Lal her high prices were justified also by Zakia's insistence that they bathe before each encounter with a client. He pushed aside Zakia's tray of sweets and wiped his hands and mouth on one of her perfumed towels. Taking a small package from beside him, he rose from his cane chair and, grinning, followed Zakia down the narrow corridor.

Zakia Begum led the way to the last curtained door on the left. She held the curtain aside and unlocked the door. Handing Prasad the key, she whispered an endearment and gently pushed him into the room.

Aijana Bibi—wearing lace-trimmed *shalvar* pyjamas and a flowered silk *kameez*—was sitting on a white padded cushion, the size of a mattress. One leg was drawn up, her chin rested on her knee, and she was leaning against one of several white bolsters that lay along the wall. The window of the small room was closed against the cold. A small electric heater glowed red in one corner.

Prasad stood quietly, gazing at Aijana's smooth face with its regular, almost childlike features. Her eyes were darkened with kohl, her lips were reddened with lipstick, and a small diamond was fitted into the left side of her nose. Her skin was fair, the light brown "wheatish" complexion that his mother preferred when she looked for a bride for him. With her looks Aijana could have made a good marriage, even if her father had been poor and had not been able to give a large dowry. How had she become a prostitute? Had she been kidnapped? Had she been sold by her father to pay off a debt to the village moneylender?

Prasad reached out toward the girl, who rose to her feet and stood facing him, her eyes cast down. He removed her yellow silk *dupatta* scarf, let it drop to the floor, and gathered her into his arms. He grasped her long black hair in both hands, holding it to his face and breathing in its sweet coconut oil scent. He kissed her neck. She fumbled with the knot that fastened his *dhoti*, as if to hurry things along and get to the next client. Prasad held her at arm's length.

"Not so fast, my little princess. Don't you want to see what I have for you?"

"If the sahib wishes to show me, I will be very happy."

Prasad reached into the pocket of his jacket and brought out his package. He tore off the wrapping, revealing a small atomizer filled with amber liquid. He held it up for her to see.

"What is this, sahib?"

"Hold it to your nose. See how good it smells? Now,

take off your clothes and I'll show you how it works."

Aijana Bibi looked at Prasad with a questioning half smile, but she obeyed him. First, she undid the drawstring of her pyjamas and allowed them to fall slowly to the floor. Then she opened the buttons of her *kameez* and, as gracefully as she could, drew it slowly over her head. Like a child watching his birthday present being unwrapped, Prasad held his breath as her body was revealed. Aijana tossed the *kameez* onto the cushion and stood quietly, looking at Prasad.

Ram Lal drew in a deep breath and exhaled slowly. His organ swollen, he raptly contemplated the perfection of her breasts, her waist, her hips. An image passed through his mind, one that had escaped him on his previous visits. The girl was a *yakshi*, an incarnation of the goddesses in ancient Indian sculpture—broad-hipped, narrow-waisted, with large, high, rounded breasts. He had seen such a statue in the archaeological museum in Mathura.

"What about my gift, sahib?"

Startled out of his reverie, Prasad raised the atomizer and pointed it at Aijana Bibi.

"Raise your arms over your head and hold them there," he ordered. Then he delicately squeezed the bulb and sprayed perfume on her breasts.

"It's cold, sahib!" she squealed, crossing her arms over her chest. "But it smells so nice."

"Keep your arms over your head!" Ram Lal sprayed her armpits, her belly, her pubic hair, her bottom, her feet, and, finally, both sides of her neck behind the ears. The girl gasped at each spray but she kept her arms over her head.

"How do you like it, my *rani*?" Prasad asked. He hadn't suspected how strong the perfume would smell.

"It's nice, sahib. It makes me smell so nice. Here, let me do it to you."

Prasad lay down on the cushion and Aijana swiftly removed his clothes. He lay there with his organ erect and ready, while the girl practiced spraying the perfume. Then she took careful aim at his penis, but before she could spray it Prasad reached up and, laughing, pulled her down on top of him and squeezed her to his chest. The atomizer fell to the floor. Aijana Bibi spread her legs, slowly eased herself astride, and began to move her body up and down.

Ram Lal lay with his eyes closed. He reached for Aijana's breasts and cupped them with his hands as she cried out and thrust more powerfully. How well, oh how marvelously well she played her game of counterfeit lust, his little *rani*! He moaned and climaxed, gasping with pleasure. He pulled the girl down on his chest while she continued to move her body back and forth. When his organ subsided, she lay quietly.

Ram Lal groaned and opened his eyes. Aijana Bibi's head was on his chest; her eyes were closed. He inhaled her perfume, the cheap scent mingling with the sweetness of the coconut oil and the odor of their lovemaking. He reached his arms over Aijana to caress her bottom.

"Sahib?"

"What can I do for my little princess?"

"It's my turn to spray you with perfume." She reached down to the floor to retrieve the atomizer, but Ram Lal was too fast. He turned on his side, rolling Aijana off his chest onto the floor where she struggled and laughed as he wrestled away the atomizer.

"Ahah! Now I'll spray you again," he said menacingly. Crouching and covering herself with her arms, Aijana retreated to a corner. Prasad stalked her, moving the atomizer this way and that to penetrate her defenses.

"Wait!" Ram Lal said. "I'll let you spray me if you do one thing."

"What thing, sahib?"

"Tell me what Saxena Sahib told you when he came here last night."

"Who, sahib?" Aijana looked wary.

"You know, my princess. Don't try to fool me. The fat policeman who comes to see you. Does he bring you presents like I do?"

"No, sahib. But he'll beat me if I say anything." A worried look appeared in her face.

"Nonsense, my little *rani.*" Ram Lal's voice was soothing. "Did anything ever happen before? You can trust me. I'm in the government too, you know." Ram Lal stood tall. "I am president of the Municipal Committee. We give the license to Zakia Begum so you can stay in this nice house instead of a dirty room in some nasty alley." Did she understand what he was saying? Did she realize how dangerous he could be if she opposed him? He might not look very powerful, standing there naked. But one word to Zakia Begum and she'd be out on the street. And no other house would be foolish enough to take her in.

Ram Lal held the atomizer above his head and sprayed a small amount on his hair. He shuddered as if he were suffering. When Aijana laughed at him and dropped her arms, he grabbed her by the waist and carried her back to the cushion where he sat her on his lap and rubbed the atomizer up and down her back. Aijana stopped laughing and began to fondle his flaccid organ.

"Sahib?"

"Yes, my little *yakshi.* What do you want to tell me?"

"Saxena Sahib . . ."

"Yes?"

"He said that Pandit Nehru was coming to the university. Panditji will come for the ceremonies."

"What ceremonies, my love?"

"I don't know, sahib. Some prayers, maybe? Some festival? He just said ceremonies."

"Why is Saxena so concerned about Panditji?"

"He said he has to organize all the policemen to protect him. It's a big responsibility."

"Yes, it is a big responsibility. But everyone in Ramgarh loves Panditji. There's nothing to fear." Ram Lal's organ was growing under Aijana's ministrations.

"But he said that some of the Muslim students were traitors and *budmashes*. Are they traitors and roughnecks, sahib?"

"If all the Muslims in India were as sweet as you, my princess, we would never have been divided into two countries."

Aijana slipped off Ram Lal's lap and knelt between his legs. She took his engorged penis in her mouth and slowly moved her head back and forth. Ram Lal .lay back on the cushion, panting, turning his head from side to side. Aijana's head moved faster as Prasad heaved his pelvis to synchronize with her motion. He climaxed, reared up, grasped blindly at the girl's hair, and fell back with his arms spread wide. Then he bellowed with shock and curled into a fetal position as a triumphant Aijana Bibi sprayed him with the cold, atomized perfume.

17

"Please take your seat, Superintendent Sahib. I will intimate to the collector that you are here." The dapper clerk left off grooming his mustache and pointed to a well-worn cane chair in the corner of the outer office beneath a framed magazine photograph of Prime Minister Nehru. He rose, buttoned his *achkan*, and knocked softly at the door behind his desk. A buzzer sounded somewhere. The clerk cautiously opened the door, entered Bharat Chaudhri's office, and just as cautiously closed the door behind him.

Mohammed Abdul Karim carefully lowered himself into the chair, only to have the broken fibers of the woven rattan seat penetrate his trousers and stick into his buttocks. He quickly rose and took a look around the office. All the usual trappings: an old Imperial typewriter, several wooden filing cabinets, some rickety wooden chairs, a telephone. An old man squatted next to the wall, stacking bundles of tattered files tied with colored ribbon. Hanging from the ceiling was the *punkah*, a fan consisting of a long wooden beam with a rectangle of heavy cloth hanging from it. In the hot weather it would be made to swing back and forth by a man sitting outside on the veranda, pulling on a rope that passed through a hole in the wall.

The inner office door opened. Bharat Chaudhri was standing there, a welcoming smile gracing his cleanshaven, regular features, which were right out of the cinema advertisements. Smoke Char Minar! Drink Vimto!

"Sorry to keep you waiting, Karim. Come in and sit down." He handed the clerk a file folder. "Type this up in final form, Joshi, and bring it in for my signature."

Karim followed Chaudhri into the office, nearly stumbling when he tripped over a pile of files lying on the floor near the door.

"Take a pew, Superintendent. Smoke if you wish."

What did it mean, take a pew?

Chaudhri opened the polished brass buttons of his blazer, adjusted his tie, and sat down at his desk. He selected a pipe from the rack of briars on his desk and packed it carefully with tobacco from a tin of Senior Service Virginia Flake. He struck a match and carefully and methodically lighted the pipe, starting around the edge of the bowl and then burning inward to the center until the tobacco was glowing to his satisfaction.

"You're still standing, Karim? Sit down, sit down, old man. Ah! Now I see. Sorry, Karim. I meant to say chair. At Cambridge we would often say pew. That's what they call the seats in their churches, you know."

Karim settled into the large overstuffed wing chair facing Chaudhri, resting his neck and arms on its slightly soiled lace antimacassars. What with the smoke wreathing Chaudhri's head and the sunlight streaming through the window behind the collector's chair, he was unable to make out the expression on his face.

"It's nice and and comfortable, isn't it?" Chaudhri said with relish. "I really don't fancy those infernal teak chairs with their cane seats and lumpy cotton cushions. I brought this desk and swivel chair and that wing chair you're sitting in back with me when I returned from England. The transport and duty cost the earth, but it was worth it." He leaned forward across the desk. "You really cannot find a comfortable piece of furniture in this country, Karim." Chaudhri pounded the desk with his fist. "You really cannot!"

"It *is* very comfortable, Collector Sahib." Karim inhaled smoke from his Sepoy, enjoying the unaccustomed English luxury. With some hesitation he let his hand touch the fabric of the chair, feeling its hand-worked appliqué of roses and ferns. "You must be the first collector of Ramgarh District to have gone to Cambridge."

"The first *Indian* collector who has gone to Cambridge, Karim. The first *Indian* collector. But doubtless there were Englishmen before me who had. Look there, over the fireplace. Do you see that cricket bat with the names lettered on it? That was my bat when I played for Downing College. I was the first Indian to play for my college, Karim. I scored a century one time. Ah, those were great days, Karim. Great days!" Chaudhri closed his eyes for a moment.

"Well now, Karim," Chaudhri said, tapping his pipe on the edge of the ashtray, "what was it that you wanted to talk about?"

"The man who caught fire, sir . . . ," Karim began.

"Ah yes. The man who caught fire. Terrible. Terrible. Not to be believed. Not to be believed." Chaudhri leaned forward and looked Karim directly in the eye. "Not to be believed!"

"Yes, sir," Karim said. Was this a typical product of Cambridge University?

"Who was the man, by the way?"

"We don't know, sir. He died that night in hospital and the body has not been claimed. But I think he's the same man who set fire to my sleeper bogie in the railway yard."

"Ah yes. The railway bogie fire. Terrible! Terrible! You're a lucky man, Karim. Does this man's death close the case, then?"

"I think not, sir. I can't believe that he was working alone. Someone must have informed him that I was arriving by that train. And then there's that attempt to burn a building at the university. And why just when the new vice chancellor was being greeted? I'm sure there was a political motive behind it. It must be political." Karim paused. "Collector Sahib, can you suggest who in Ramgarh might want to damage the Muslim University?"

"Ah yes. The Muslim University." Chaudhri swiveled around and looked out of the window behind his desk. He sucked noisily on his pipe. "India is a secular country, wouldn't you agree, Karim? Not like Pakistan. *Not* like Pakistan. Sometimes I wonder how long we'll tolerate a Muslim university in Ramgarh and a Hindu university in Banaras."

"Sir . . ."

Chaudhri swiveled back to face Karim. "We're moving in the right direction, I think. Do you follow the Acts of Parliament, Karim? I thought not. Well, Act 63 of the Laws of 1951 removes the disqualification of non-Muslims from serving on the court of the Muslim University."

"Yes, sir, but . . ."

"It's just a first step, mind you, but it's in the right direction. Next we can open the Banaras court to non-Hindu members. Our public institutions must be secular in a secular state. Don't you agree, Karim?"

Karim squirmed in his overstuffed chair. He lighted another Sepoy. How could he get this man to stop rambling?

"Sir, Prime Minister Nehru will be visiting the university on the ninth of February to install the new vice chancellor. You have been informed of that, sir?"

"Yes, Karim. Yes, Karim." Chaudhri sounded testy. "I'm aware of that. I *am* aware of that." He tapped his pipe into the ashtray again and replaced it on the rack. "We are relying on you and your men to provide security for the P.M. Is that what you wanted to talk about?"

"Yes, sir, and . . ."

"I'm not a policeman, Karim. Security is your responsibility, not mine. What time is it?"

"What, sir? Oh. Ten past eleven, sir." Now what?

"Time for tea." Chaudhri pressed the button under his desk three times. "We call it 'elevenses' in England. Helps to break up the morning, you know."

The office door opened and Joshi padded in, holding a tray bearing a tea service of white china with a small blue flowered design. It had none of the chips and cracks Karim was used to in the service at police headquarters. Joshi served the tea and left the office as silently as he had entered it.

Karim drank quietly, watching Chaudhri's expression overspread with pleasure as he sipped his tea. Damn this man! He had to get him to talk seriously. Maybe a frontal attack would work.

"Collector Sahib," Karim began, "the resources of the Ramgarh Police will be seriously strained when the prime minister visits the university. We know that there are violent people in this city. We can't watch them all." Karim paused. Chaudhri delicately drained his cup and set it down. "Will you grant a Preventive Detention Order for a two-week period for certain individuals whom we feel might be planning a disturbance?"

"Ah, yes. Preventive detention. Hmmm. Preventive detention. A useful device, Karim. An exceedingly useful device. We can take people into custody before they commit an act of political violence." Chaudhri began to fill another pipe. Slowly and methodically he performed the same ritual as before. Karim watched impatiently, convinced he was stalling for time.

"Preventive detention, my dear Karim, is a very complicated matter, as you must know. We cannot go through the streets indiscriminately sweeping people up because we think they look like they might commit some criminal act. There must be names, evidence, testimony, documents, Karim." Chaudhri leaned over the desk, his eyes intently focused on Karim's. "Names! Evidence! Testimony! Documents! Who are these individuals? What evidence do you have against them?"

"Collector Sahib, do you know of Surendra Gupta, who is supposed to be the local head of the R.S.S.?"

"Gupta? Little Gupta the lawyer?" Chaudhri guffawed and leaned back in his chair. "The pleader who waits outside the Magistrate's Court to pick up his cases? Are you saying that this insignificant little insect is likely to commit political violence? My dear Karim, you surprise me. You really surprise me. What do you have against this nonentity?"

"Sir, I suspect that he gave the orders for the two petrol bombings. He is said to be head of the R.S.S., which is a banned organization."

"That's not much to go on, Karim. Not much to go on." Chaudhri swiveled around and looked out of the window. "Look there, Karim! Do you see him? It's Gupta! Do you see him sitting there in the garden in front of the court? See there? He's at that third little table from the flowerbed. He's the one without any clients."

Karim stood up and looked over Chaudhri's shoulder.

"I've not met him, sir. So that's what he looks like. Not very impressive, I agree. But Godse was not very impressive either, and he killed Gandhiji." Chaudhri was stalling. He had to get him to commit himself. One last try might do it.

"Collector Sahib, the prime minister is coming. If anything happens to him, we will all pay. You, me, the university, the town. I, for one, don't want to jeopardize my career."

Chaudhri stared at Gupta, sucking on his pipe and slowly rocking back and forth in his chair. The sound of Joshi's typewriter filtered through the door. Karim counted three rings of the bell that signaled the end of a line of type.

"Very well, Karim. You've made your point." Chaudhri swiveled around and faced Karim. "Get me the details. The evidence. The names. I will apply to the home secretary in Lucknow. He will ask the minister for the order." Chaudhri's voice and manner had changed. He was no longer the Cambridge graduate discoursing on Indian law and customs. He was the bureaucrat, acting to protect his rear. "What else do you want? Nothing? Good. On your way out tell Joshi I want him."

18

The police jeep dropped Karim off in the drive in front of his bungalow. He stepped onto the veranda and knocked on the door. His shoulders sagged with fatigue. Five fifteen. Still time for a nap before the dinner reception at Mirza's house this evening. Thank goodness.

"*Arrey*, Faiz Khan!" he called. What was keeping the old man? Finally there was a rattling sound and then the front door bolt was pulled aside.

"You are early this evening, *huzoor*."

"I'm going out to dinner tonight, Faiz Khan, so you won't have to cook for me. Did I forget to tell you this before I left this morning? Well, no matter. You may have my food. But you must do these things. Get out my new black *shervani* and polish my black shoes. I'll have my tea and my bath in an hour." Karim looked closely at the bearer. What was bothering the old man? "Is something the matter?"

"Superintendent Sahib, this letter came. In the morning post."

Karim took the proffered envelope from the bearer's gnarled brown hand. The stamp showed a steam locomotive and a green flag with the star and crescent of Islam. He turned it over and read the sender's name and address:

Lt. Col. Mohammed Bashir Khan
D/26 Ordnance Lines
Rawalpindi Cantonment
West Pakistan

The letter had been opened and crudely resealed. Karim grinned. What amateurs! Probably a Pakistani censor and then an Indian censor had had a go at the letter. Might as well not even seal the envelope if they were going to make such a mess of it.

Karim followed Faiz Khan through the sitting room and entered his bedroom. He put the letter on his dresser, took off his working uniform, and gave it to the bearer to brush and hang in the teakwood armoire. He went into the bathroom and washed his face and neck, returned to the bedroom, and lay down on the bed with the letter. The graceful curves of the Urdu script reminded him of the hours Bashir and he had struggled with chalk and slate in the shade of his father's *neem* tree, while the playful shouts of the other village boys resounded outside the compound wall.

January 9, 1952

Beloved Brother,

The news of your escape from death has made all of us feel very happy and grateful. Allah has protected you from your enemies.

Our honored mother and father have decided to make the *hajj* to Mecca next year so that they may give proper thanks to God for your safety.

My family are all healthy. Abda will give birth again in May. We hope that it will be a son this time. Aisha and Zakia are in the cantonment primary school. They are making good progress in their studies, especially in English.

My posting here seems to be secure for at least three years. The quarters are comfortable, and we have a pleasant garden. The previous occupant was an English major seconded to our ordnance corps, and he and his wife trained the servants well. We will be sorry to leave this place when my next transfer comes.

Mother and father are in fairly good health, considering their age. I wish I could say that they are content. They long to see you again. It has been nearly five years since they came from India, and mother especially is afraid that she will not see you before she dies.

Are you still satisfied with your decision to remain, Abdul? Has the attempt on your life not changed your mind? You know that you could make a decent career here if you decided to emigrate.

I hope that this letter finds you in good health and good spirits. May the blessings of Allah be upon you.

Your loving brother,
Bashir

Karim lay back on his pillow and wiped his eyes with the end of the pillowcase. Five years! And four years since Syeeda had died in childbirth. Oh Syeeda! Why had she been taken away from him? His shoulders shook and he buried his face in the pillow.

After a minute he opened his eyes. Above his head the white mosquito net hung in looping folds. Syeeda. How young and sweet and small she had been. Too young? Too small? She had been sick so often, she had been so exhausted as she plodded from room to room, heavy with child. But she had endured it all with a smile, hoping to give him a healthy son.

Then the pains had begun. He had held her hand as she lay on her *charpoy* wearing a pure white *kameez*, with her long black hair washed and oiled and her gold wedding bangles on her wrists.

The midwife had come. He had waited outside the house, chain-smoking Sepoys. One hour. Three hours. Seven hours. The birthing had been slow. Her cries had seemed to grow weaker. Had something gone wrong? Syeeda? Syeeda! He had run into the birthing room and found her lying on the floor in a pool of blood, with the midwife pushing on her belly.

"Sahib! Get the doctor!"

By the time the doctor had arrived, the baby's feet were exposed, but the body was trapped in the birth canal, held fast by the umbilical cord coiled around its neck. And Syeeda . . . Oh God! . . . dying in that pool of blood.

A horsefly buzzed in through the window and a green gecko on the wall came alert. But the fly quickly flew out again.

No more mourning, Karim thought. It had been Allah's will. He would not let himself get trapped by grieving about things that could not be changed. Mirza's dinner. Would Ellen Siddiqi be there, he wondered. He tried to nap.

19

"Here, Iqbal." Ellen held out one end of the six yards of silk. Yes, the gold embroidery struck a nice contrast with the dark green of the cloth. Just the thing for Acting Vice Chancellor Mirza's party. And the short-sleeved *choli* would leave her midriff bare. Ellen Siddiqi, the Bombay movie star! "Would you hold the end, please?" she said.

Iqbal slipped on his black shoes and stood up. "A *sari*, Ellen? You look much better in Muslim dress. *Kameez* and *shalvar*, maybe?"

"Don't you like me to wear Indian costume, dear? I thought you did. What's wrong with this beautiful *sari*?"

Iqbal looked into the wall mirror and fastened the collar of his black *shervani*. Catching Ellen's eye in the mirror, he said, "If you must know, Ellen, that *choli* is too revealing. Muslim women are very modest, Ellen. You know that. That tennis outfit of yours. It's bad enough. But that *choli* . . . really, Ellen."

"Iqbal, I had no idea you felt that way about my tennis dress." Ellen came over and embraced him and kissed him on the lips. "Poor Iqbal. You're jealous. I'm sorry. Hold me tight. Mmmmm." Ellen's hands slipped around Iqbal's waist and pulled him toward her.

"Please, Ellen. Not now. We're going to be late." Iqbal pushed her away and turned back to the mirror. Ellen stood there silent, biting her lip.

After a moment she continued dressing. If Iqbal was going to feel that way, she had better learn to put the *sari* on alone. She laid the *sari* on the bed and took one end of it to wrap around her waist. She tucked one corner into the waistband of her long petticoat and twirled around once so that the *sari* wrapped her fully. Then she tucked it in the waistband all around. So far, so good. Now for the hard part. If only she had learned this in her teens, like all those Indian women. She gathered the remainder of the cloth in large pleats in front, finally tucking the top of the pleats into her waistband and leaving about three yards free at the end. This she passed behind her and then diagonally across her chest and over her left shoulder. Done. Turning to Iqbal, she asked, "Do you remember this *sari*, Iqbal?"

"No. Should I?"

"You gave it to me in Minneapolis for my birthday."

Iqbal frowned. He looked around the room, avoiding her eyes. "Let's go, Ellen. The rickshaw's waiting. Here's your shawl."

Ellen had become good friends with Dr. Ibrahim Mirza in the eight months that he had acted as vice chancellor. And her friendship had helped him to deal with his grief at the death of his wife the previous year. Dr. Mirza was a kindly, outgoing man. The thought of him rattling around alone in that big official bungalow had saddened her. Iqbal hadn't seemed to mind very much when she had helped Mirza to organize receptions and garden parties for the faculty and visiting dignitaries. After all, what did a man know about such things? And that garden! Such gorgeous roses and cannas and cosmos. So she had ignored the staff club gossips and had done her bit to make the social side of Mirza's job easier. Anyway, it wasn't going to go on much longer. This new man Gilani. He probably had a wife. In any case, he didn't look like he was much interested in social activities.

With the tropical haste that Ellen always felt was a touch unseemly, the chill darkness of the North Indian winter had overtaken the last pink streaks of daylight as she and Iqbal arrived by rickshaw at the vice chancellor's lodge. To her surprise, a police jeep growled in at the same time, printing its tire tracks like pug marks in the crushed red brick of the drive. The jeep's passenger, wearing a black *shervani* and white trousers, dismounted and entered the cone of light at the portico. Ellen paused for a moment and then recognized this lean, taut man with the aquiline nose and grizzled mustache as her friend Superintendent Karim.

Karim came closer and *salaamed*. In spite of their similar dress, Karim could not have appeared more different from Iqbal. The hunter and the peasant, Ellen thought, recalling an anthropology course as she looked from Karim to her round-faced, paunchy husband. Something about Karim reminded her of Paul Anderson. Ellen shivered and pulled her shawl tighter around her shoulders.

"Superintendent Karim! Iqbal Sahib! Ellen! What a beautiful *sari*!" Ibrahim Mirza's hearty voice boomed out over the garden. He looked down on his guests from the veranda, his thick white hair covered by a gray karakul Muslim cap. When Ellen had climbed the three steps he took her hands in his and turned to Karim. "Have you met my favorite faculty wife?" Ellen glanced at Iqbal, whose eyes were narrowed.

"We have met, Doctor Mirza," Ellen said, while Karim nodded agreement. "Don't you remember? I introduced Mr.

Karim to you and Doctor Gilani at the parade."

"Ah yes. That tragic parade. Poor Doctor Gilani. What an introduction to our university. Has anything been found out, Superintendent Sahib?"

"Nothing for certain, Doctor Mirza. We're continuing to interview the students. It's possible there is a connection between Saturday's tragedy and the railway bogie fire on January first."

"That's interesting," Iqbal said. "Would that mean there's some kind of conspiracy to set these fires?"

"That poor fellow who was burned on Saturday died without regaining consciousness, Doctor Siddiqi, so we may never find out."

"Poor chap. A terrible way to die." Mirza's voice was softer than Ellen had ever heard it. "Well," he said, "there are more pleasant things to discuss this evening." He held aside the door curtain. "Come into the house. I've got a little surprise for you. A friend of mine came back from New Delhi yesterday and brought some Coca-Cola. We'll have it tonight in your honor. Sit down, everyone." Mirza's hearty laugh was muffled by the carpets, hangings, and overstuffed furniture of the reception room.

"How nice, Doctor Mirza. I haven't had a Coke for the longest time." Ellen handed her shawl to a white-uniformed bearer. "Have you ever tasted Coca-Cola, Mr. Karim?"

"I'm afraid not, Mrs. Siddiqi. Is it an alcoholic drink? We Muslims refrain from alcohol, you know."

"I'd like to have a rupee for every Muslim in India who has drunk alcohol," Iqbal snorted.

"It's completely nonalcoholic, Mr. Karim. You've had the bottles chilled, Doctor Mirza?"

"They've been in the ice since this morning, Ellen. We'll

open them when the other guests arrive. I've invited your friends Anwar Hussain and Wahid Sherif."

Despite herself, Ellen's glance betrayed her mixed feelings at hearing this news. Would the tone of the dinner party be set by Anwar's bitterness? She walked over to the fireplace and stared into the flames. She adjusted her *sari* on her shoulder and smoothed her hair into place.

"I'm so pleased, Doctor Mirza. Anwar's a dear boy but I wish he would get married and settle down. He seems so unhappy these days."

"His mother would agree with you completely, Ellen. Have you got someone in mind?" Mirza whispered conspiratorially. "She would have to be an exceptionally tolerant girl."

Ellen sat down in a chair facing Karim. He was watching her closely. Maybe too closely. Iqbal would not like it. Did he like her *sari*? "If this were Minneapolis, I could get him a date in five minutes."

"If this were Minneapolis," Mirza replied, "Anwar would be too frozen to do anything." Ellen and Iqbal burst out laughing.

"Central heating makes many things possible in winter, Doctor Sahib," Iqbal said with a wink.

A loud angry voice came through the door from the drive, followed by a servile whine and soothing, muffled tones. Ellen saw Karim tense up and look at Mirza to see if he was concerned by the unpleasant scene taking place outside. She knew it was Anwar, engaging in one of his usual altercations with a rickshaw *wallah*. Mirza rose and went out onto the veranda. Christ! What a way to begin an evening!

Mirza held aside the curtain and let Anwar Hussain and Wahid Sherif into the room.

"What nerve! That rickshaw *wallah* wanted a rupee to

bring us over here! A nighttime differential! Where does he think he is?" Anwar's anger over a pittance made him appear ridiculous, but Ellen had seen other middle-class Indians do the same thing.

"Superintendent Sahib, Iqbal Sahib, Ellen Begum. How pleasant, how delightful, to meet you on this lovely evening. The moon stands abashed by the honor of your character." Wahid Sherif greeted his fellow guests with an exaggerated courtly *salaam* as the flowery Persianized Urdu gushed from his lips. Ellen did not understand, but she knew Wahid was putting on one of his acts.

"Wahid Sahib," Mirza guffawed in English, "are you trying to recreate the Moghul court in Delhi? You're a hundred years too late, you know."

"Doctor Sahib, is it ever too late for courtesy and politeness between honorable gentlemen . . . and ladies?" Wahid replied, bowing in Ellen's direction.

"How gracious of you, Wahid," Ellen responded. "But haven't I read that ladies were kept secluded behind marble screens and silken curtains in the Moghul court?" She turned to Karim. "Isn't that so, Mr. Karim?"

"Madam?" he asked, startled by Ellen's question.

"Weren't the Moghul court ladies in *purdah*, Mr. Karim?"

Karim wiped his mustache nervously and said as if reciting in a classroom, "That was in accordance with Muslim tradition, madam." He turned to Mirza and asked for permission to smoke. Granted it, he lighted a Sepoy and inhaled hungrily. His face relaxed and smiling, he turned again to Ellen. "Being in *purdah*, madam, did not mean that they did not have the love and devotion of their husbands and families. Women had their sphere and men had their sphere. Women's beauty, madam, was not a commodity to be hawked in the bazaars and displayed in films."

"*Shabbash!*" Wahid and Iqbal said together. Ellen had met Wahid's wife. She was in *purdah* yet she was happy, taking care of her children and meeting other *purdah*-bound ladies in their homes.

"You sound very conservative, Mr. Karim," said Ellen. And a bit pompous too, she thought.

"My late wife was not in *purdah*, madam."

Ellen leaned closer to Karim. "Your late wife, Mr. Karim? I'm so sorry. Can you tell me what happened?"

While the other men chatted and joked in Urdu and English, Karim quietly told Ellen the story of his marriage and his wife's death. How sad it was. This poor lonely man could barely keep from crying. Ellen put her hand on Karim's and squeezed it.

The white-uniformed bearer appeared and placed trays of batter-dipped fried vegetable pieces on the coffee table. "Ellen," Mirza said, "try these *pakoras*. My cook makes the best *pakoras* in Ramgarh. You too, gentlemen. Eat while they're hot."

The bearer returned with bottles of Coca-Cola and glasses.

"Attention, everyone," Mirza said, clapping his hands. "To honor our American guest, we have an American drink, Coca-Cola!"

Ellen bit her lip as the bearer pried off the bottle caps and casually wiped the bottle openings with his bare hand.

"A toast!" Mirza proposed.

"To Superintendent Karim!" Ellen interjected. Mirza's face fell. "May Ramgarh be safe and peaceful while he is here."

"Thank you, Mrs. Siddiqi. Thank you, Doctor Mirza." Karim sipped the Coca-Cola and wrinkled his nose from the bubbles. "It's quite pleasant. Not as sweet as our Indian drinks."

"You have your work cut out for you in this place, Superintendent Sahib," Anwar said.

"Why is that, Anwar Sahib?"

"The Hindus are out to get us. Have you seen the newspapers?"

"What are you talking about, Anwar Sahib?" Mirza demanded.

"I'm talking about Urdu, Mirza Sahib. These Hindus! They'll drown us in Hindi. No more Urdu in the courts and the schools." Anwar looked directly at Karim. "They've taken away our property. They've put Hindus on the court of our university. And now they want to take away our language." Anwar spoke with ferocious intensity. The muscles of his jaw were throbbing. "They're out to destroy our community."

"But how can they possibly do that, Anwar?" Ellen asked. "There are fifty million Muslims in India." Poor Anwar. He was worse than ever.

"You're quite right, Ellen, about the number of Muslims in India," Mirza interjected. "But it's a geographical question as well as a linguistic one. There are fourteen official languages listed in the Constitution. Eleven are regional languages, plus Urdu, Sanskrit, and English. The Muslims, the Urdu speakers, are a minority in every region of India. We have no territorial basis any more, now that Pakistan exists. We are a permanent minority to India as a whole and in every one of the states and districts."

"So, when the U.P. state government proposes to eliminate English and substitute Hindi, they're striking at Urdu from behind," Iqbal said to Ellen.

"They're getting back at us for eight hundred years of Muslim rule in northern India, Superintendent Sahib," Anwar continued. "I'm positive that fire on Saturday was part of a plot against the university." Anwar's voice grew harsher. "I tell you we've got to fight fire with fire or we'll be wiped out as a community!"

Ellen looked at Karim. He seemed incredulous. His hand shook slightly as he lighted a cigarette.

"Anwar Sahib, forgive me, but I must disagree." Karim looked around at the others. Was he looking for moral support? "You have seen what violence does. I have seen what violence does. Tell me, has violence ever done any real good for anyone, Anwar Sahib? No, no. Wait before you answer, Anwar Sahib." He drew on his cigarette. "I've been a policeman for fourteen years, here in U.P. and in the army. Violence . . . it doesn't solve problems, it only makes them worse. Hasn't enough blood been spilled already? Hasn't enough property been destroyed? We Muslims are a small minority in India. How can we make progress unless we put our faith in God and in the law, Anwar Sahib?"

"Well said, Superintendent Sahib," Mirza said. "And now, our food is ready. Ellen, will you lead the way into the dining room?"

Not a moment too soon, Doctor Mirza, Ellen thought. The argument was nearly getting out of control. He had handled himself very well, Karim had, but she didn't think he had made much of a dent in Anwar's wall of hate. That's what Anwar was—a hater. Pleasant at times—but basically a hater.

"What a lovely table, Doctor Mirza," Ellen exclaimed as she passed through the curtained doorway into the dining room. Each place had been set with a polished brass *thali* tray and three brass bowls. Curries and yogurt filled the bowls, while in the center of each tray was a pile of *biryani*; she could already taste that flavorsome mixture of rice and spiced meat. And trays of toasted *chapatis* stood in the center of the table on either side of a large floral bouquet.

"I've heard rumors that you can eat with your fingers like a true Indian, Ellen. Tonight you shall show me." Mirza's booming laugh made Ellen smile at the challenge.

"We shall see, Doctor Mirza. I might not do it to your satisfaction."

"Sit down, everyone. There are place cards. Now, Ellen. Show me."

Ellen took a *chapati* from the tray with her right hand, tore off a small piece of it, and used it as a scoop to transfer a small amount of curry to her mouth.

"*Shabbash!*" Mirza's approval was echoed by the others.

"I have never before seen a European eat with anything but a knife and fork, Mrs. Siddiqi," Karim said from his seat opposite Ellen. "You do it quite well."

"All I had to do was get rid of my Western inhibitions, Mr. Karim. Actually, I enjoy it. Indian food tastes better when it's eaten with the fingers. When in Rome . . . , you know." Her foot touched Karim's. She pulled it back.

"My uncle, the former vice chancellor," Anwar said, "told me that when he was a student here, the English principal occasionally shared a meal in the hostel with the students. He would eat with his fingers. But uncle thought most of the English were more interested in getting Indians to use the knife and fork."

"Naturally," Wahid said. "The civilizing mission of the British."

"Of course. The white man's burden and all that," Anwar replied.

Ellen's sandal touched Karim's shoe again. She looked at him and silently moved her lips to say "sorry." Karim was looking at her intently, questioningly. Was he sending her a message? Was he saying to her: You are a beautiful, intelligent woman and I admire you very much? What was she getting into? Who was this man? Why was she attracted to him? Ellen blushed under Karim's gaze.

"The prime minister's visit, Superintendent Sahib," Mirza said. "How are the preparations going?"

"They are proceeding, Doctor Mirza. They are proceeding. Your campus map—very helpful, that. And your inauguration plan. We'll be bringing in some U.P. armed constabulary to help out the Ramgarh police." Karim lighted a cigarette. "I'll be going to New Delhi on Sunday to talk with the P.M.'s security people."

"Where do you stay when you go to New Delhi, Mr. Karim?" Ellen asked.

"The Khyber Hotel, Mrs. Siddiqi. It's a small hotel on Connaught Place. I could stay in the police lines, but I usually like to go to the cinema, and it's more convenient to be near Connaught Circus."

Well, well, well! So Karim was not entirely the aloof, efficient police officer. He liked to go to the cinema. How charming!

"Ellen, what do you think will happen in American politics this year?" Wahid inquired, breaking Ellen's reverie. She started, blushed, and tried to respond.

"I . . . I . . . don't really know, Wahid. I've been away too long."

"Many correspondents seem to think that Eisenhower can have the presidency if he wants it, but he hasn't said that he wants it," Wahid said.

"What about Truman?" Mirza asked. "Won't he try to run again?"

"American politics is a mystery to me," Anwar said. "How

can you run a country where the president can be of one party and the parliament be another?" The conversation looped from one topic to another until midnight.

"Doctor Sahib," Anwar announced, "we have kept you up too long. I, for one, wish to take my leave."

"Yes. Yes. Keeping you up too late. Work tomorrow." A *coda* of apologies, thank you's, lovely evening's, delicious dinner's.

"Let me drive you home in my jeep, Doctor Siddiqi. You won't easily get a rickshaw at this time of night." Karim stood on the veranda signaling his driver to bring the jeep to the portico.

"Isn't that nice of Mr. Karim, Iqbal. You and I can sit in the back."

"No, madam. It will be best for you to sit in the front with the driver. It's less bumpy there. Doctor Siddiqi and I will sit in the back."

The jeep's headlamps guided them out of the vice chancellor's lodge and onto the road leading to the faculty quarters. When they reached the Siddiqi's house, they found Alice in tears, holding a message hand printed in Hindi on rough paper. Schnitzel lay dead on the bedroom floor, his legs contorted, his lips drawn back from his teeth in an eternal grotesque smile.

20

Iqbal Siddiqi lay in the double bed, his head propped by pillows and his thighs supporting a mystery novel. From time to time he removed an arm from beneath the flowered quilt, flipped a page, and quickly returned it to the warmth. His eyes moved across the pages, indifferent to Ellen as she sat naked at her dressing table, brushing her hair. Her skin glowed from the warmth of her bath.

Ellen's bare feet touched a straw basket under her dressing table. Schnitzel's basket, where he had always slept. Tears returned to her eyes. Ellen missed Schnitzel as she would have missed a dear friend. Little Schnitzel, who had wakened her every morning with a touch of his cold nose and a wet lick of his tongue across her ear. Schnitzel had died near his box, his body grotesquely distorted as he had tried to reach it before the poison took his life.

Ellen shifted the brush to the other hand and continued. There had been the note Alice had found near the gate, but it had been in Hindi. What had it said? Schnitzel had been trained not to eat the occasional bit of garbage that found its way into the compound. Someone must have tempted him with poisoned meat offered by hand. But who? And why?

Iqbal had been of no help at all that night. He had stood around, looking unhappy and helpless, while Karim had taken charge of the situation. He had questioned Alice and had taken away Schnitzel's body and the note for laboratory analysis. He had been as shocked as they by the poisoning.

Ellen turned and looked at Iqbal, hoping to find some response in his eyes behind those eyeglasses that made him look so distinguished. He did not return her glance.

Ellen stood and looked at herself in the mirror. She was good to look at, wasn't she? Her waist slim, her hips nicely rounded, her breasts firm and well shaped. What was wrong with her? Even if Iqbal was sterile from the chemicals he handled, why didn't he even try any more?

"Put something on, Ellen! You'll catch your death of cold." Iqbal had let the book fall face down. He was looking at her now, but sternly.

Ellen put her blue flannel bathrobe over her shoulders. Iqbal had bought it for her because it matched her eyes. She dabbed her body with the perfume she had brought from the States. She stepped into her slippers and went over to the dresser where she kept her pyjamas. She paused and leaned over the dresser, rearranging its little collection of souvenirs from the trips they had taken. She stood there preoccupied, while behind her Iqbal continued to read. Her hands trembled slightly as they grasped the little wooden toys, brass bowls, and silver spoons. Then she bent over and opened her pyjama drawer. She began to take out a pair of warm flannel pyjamas, but suddenly she stopped and pushed the drawer closed with a bang. She turned and, with the robe billowing out to the side, moved to Iqbal's side of the bed.

Startled by the noise, Iqbal looked searchingly into Ellen's eyes. She stood over him with her robe open, her body exposed. Slowly, deliberately, Ellen put the novel on the night stand, removed Iqbal's glasses, eased aside the quilt, and sat down on the bed facing him.

Iqbal smiled and reached for Ellen's shoulders. She shrugged off the robe, leaned forward, and—her eyes closed—opened Iqbal's pyjama top and undid the draw-string of the bottom. She kissed Iqbal and rested against him, pressing her breasts against his chest.

Ellen's desire surged as she nestled into Iqbal's arms. She kissed him on the chin, the neck, the nipples. She moved her body so that she could kiss him on the stomach. Iqbal leaned forward and kissed her neck as she kissed his penis and fondled it with her hand. Their breathing became faster as she fondled and squeezed and kissed. Iqbal shoved the quilt aside entirely and reached between Ellen's legs to caress her.

Ellen became increasingly dismayed as Iqbal's penis failed to react. She shifted her body to lie astride Iqbal, kissing his face and chest and moving her now wet vulva rapidly over his penis. The bed creaked in rhythm with her movement.

Iqbal tried to respond. He kissed Ellen. He cupped her breasts in his hands and licked her swollen nipples. But his organ failed to stiffen.

Finally, panting, weary, Ellen lay down beside Iqbal and held him close. Iqbal held her tightly, whispering apologies into her ear, stroking her hair, kissing the tears from her cheeks. He turned out the light and they both fell into a restless sleep.

With the morning came chill, rainy weather. Ellen woke when Iqbal, who was taking his bath, accidentally knocked his dipper against the bucket of bath water. She went to the window, pulled aside the flowered curtain, and watched the rainwater fall from the spout on the roof. Then she moved to the bathroom and stood in the doorway, watching Iqbal shave.

"What are you thinking about, Ellen?" Iqbal asked, his face white with lather.

"I have to get my passport extended. It expires in about a month."

"Really? Don't they last for five years?"

"American passports last three years, but they can be extended."

"So what are you going to do?" Iqbal inquired, without seeming to think the matter was very important. He began to stroke the razor down the side of his face.

"I'll go to New Delhi on Sunday and take Alice with me for company. I'll do some shopping also. Can you have your dinners at the staff club?"

Iqbal drew the razor up under his chin. "I'll eat tinned food, if necessary. Or maybe I'll get some invitations. Where will you stay?"

"At the Imperial. Where I stayed last time I went to New Delhi." Ellen spoke in a quiet, subdued voice.

"Lucky you, Ellen," Iqbal said, trying to cheer her up. "The best hotel in New Delhi. How long will you stay?"

"A day. Maybe two. Depends on the embassy. You know those bureaucrats."

Iqbal finished his shave, washed the lather from his face, and toweled it dry. He turned to Ellen and said brightly, "It'll do you good to get away from Ramgarh. Stay a few extra days if you want to. Have yourself a good time."

21

The weary lorry driver, ready to stop for a cup of strong "hundred-mile" tea to fortify himself for the next leg of his nighttime run down the Grand Trunk Road, slowed only slightly when the small wooden tea shop appeared in the glare of his headlamps. There were no tables or benches on the packed dirt in front of the shop. No light showed. The wooden shutters were closed and locked. A faded film poster, pasted askew over the shutters, exhorted the public to come to the Picture Palace to see "Daag," starring Dilip Kumar and Nimmi. Dollops of mud thrown up by passing cars and lorries had splattered the actors' faces, even though the shop was set back from the road, with its rear close to a brick wall on which the name Pushpa Transport (Private) Ltd. was crudely painted. A few hundred yards down the road, intermittently visible through the gathering mist like a flashing harbor buoy, a swinging Caltex petrol sign reflected the light of a solitary street lamp. The disappointed lorry driver shifted gears, gunned his engine, and moved on through the night.

Inside the tea shop Surendra Gupta looked at his three colleagues slurping tea in the light of a paraffin lantern—his "hunting companions," as they would prefer the police to believe, though they were as likely to injure each other as to bag a bird on the wing. Gautam Sharma, the ascetic-looking Brahmin schoolmaster; Babu Ram, the richest and the fattest *paanwallah* in the city; and Man Singh, the burly, pugnacious owner of Pushpa Transport. They were the remnant of the Ramgarh R.S.S., sitting around a battered table among the cups, saucers, kettles, and other debris of the defunct tea shop.

Could he trust them? What Ram Lal Prasad had told him that morning would soon be known all over the town. But how he would *use* the information—ah, that could not be revealed until the proper time.

What an opportunity this was! It might never come again in his lifetime. Had Lord Shiva revealed his wishes by providing this opportunity? Would the elephant god Ganesh, the son of Shiva, whose statue looked benignly down on them from a shelf on the wall behind Sharma, smooth the way to success?

Babu Ram, the dealer in betel, spoke first. As usual, he brought the gossip that was coursing through Ramgarh's narrow streets and alleys. Wasn't his *paan* shop right at the corner of Mahatma Gandhi Road where the vegetable market was held every morning? Didn't nearly every customer exchange the latest gossip, whether he was buying a simple *paan* of betel leaf with ground lime paste and shredded areca nut or a spectacular creation with added tobacco, spices, and bits of silver foil?

"It's all around town by now, Man Singhji," Babu Ram said, laughing and shaking his jowls. "Your lorry and that foreign woman at the university. I hope it hasn't cost you too much to fix it up with Saxena."

"You stick to your *paan* and leave my business to me, Babu!" Man Singh's face wrapped itself around his hate. He pounded his fist on the table, shaking the cups and saucers. "I'll take care of that foreign bitch. She'll forget she was ever in that *tonga*, and no one else will testify against me."

Gupta felt his stomach squeeze into a knot. What kind of mess had Man Singh gotten into now? If there was anything they didn't need it was a policeman sticking his nose into their business. Remember when Man Singh had killed a man in an argument after a road accident and had put a knife in the dead man's hand and claimed self-defense? It had taken all of his time and ability to get the police to take a bribe and make no charges. He had no time for that foolishness now.

"What's this about a foreign woman, Man Singhji?" Gupta asked nervously. He leaned forward to adjust the lantern.

"It's nothing, Guptaji. The police say one of my lorries tipped over a *tonga*. Saxena wants a thousand for the *tonga* and two fifty for the horse, plus his usual *bakhsheesh*. A thousand for that old *tonga*? It was about to fall apart anyway. And that old nag? Hopeless! By now it's been ground up and roasted by the kabob sellers outside the Picture Palace." Man Singh leaned back with a broad smile under his gray handlebar mustache and held up his huge hands in front of him. "He says the passenger, that foreign woman, will identify my lorry. I told him to forget it. The foreigner will never identify my lorry." He winked. "I've given her a good scare."

Gupta's hands tightened into fists; his heart throbbed so hard he thought his companions could hear it. "Man Singhji, I beg you. Don't get involved with the police. We don't want them around. As your lawyer, listen to me. It's not very much money for you. Pay them and have done with it."

"Don't tell me how to run my business, Gupta!" Man

Singh shouted, rising and leaning over the table. Gupta recoiled, nearly falling backward. His shoulder brushed against a clay water jar, which fell to the brick floor and shattered. Babu Ram and Sharma looked open-mouthed at Man Singh. The silence in the dingy little room was electric.

"Gentlemen! Gentlemen!" Sharma's dry voice cut through the tension. "Keep your voices down. Remember, this shop is supposed to be empty. And remember also that we are all comrades in a holy cause. Let us be calm!"

Gupta sucked a lungful of air through his tightened lips. "Yes. Yes. You're correct, Man Singhji. It's none of my business." His heart was still pounding. The situation was not good. He needed Man Singh. He needed Man Singh's *lathiwallahs* and *goondas* for the time when it might be necessary to settle some scores with the enemies of the R.S.S. And he needed Man Singh's fleet of lorries, with their hard-drinking, hard-fighting drivers and cleaners, to move men to where they were needed.

"That's all right, then." Man Singh sat down and swayed back in his chair. "Give me another cup of tea, Sharma. I'm going outside to piss." He lurched out the back door of the shop.

Sharma and Babu looked at Gupta, their mouths open, their eyes questioning. What were they thinking? Were they as appalled as he was? Had he shown lack of leadership? He tried to measure his comrades, to judge their reaction. He needed them. He had to trust them, didn't he?

"Gentlemen," Gupta said when Man Singh returned, "let's get down to business. We have lots to talk about. The foundry business, Man Singhji. How is it progressing?"

"Have I ever failed to do what I said I would do, Guptaji?" Man Singh replied, wrapping his huge hands around his teacup. "First, I took the model apart. Then I gave separate pieces to four different lock founders, all good men and friends of mine. One of them is from my home village. Him I gave the trigger and hammer mechanism." Man Singh leaned forward and looked at his companions with a gleam in his eye. "I told them all it was for a new type of hinge. Even if they suspect what it's for, they don't know where the other parts are being made." Man Singh reached under his *dhoti*. "Here. Have a look." He laid a heavy metal object on the table.

Gupta, Sharma, and Babu Ram stared at the object. Was it really a gun? It was obviously not a police or military service revolver. What looked like a piece of iron pipe extended at nearly a right angle from just below the top of an oblong piece of gray metal. Gupta shivered. In the dim light of the lantern, the object seemed more menacing than he had expected. Face to face with the reality of the gun, Gupta struggled to keep his nerves under control.

Man Singh picked up the gun in his right hand. He held it confidently, turning it from side to side. "It's heavy," he said, "but not too heavy. If it was too light, it couldn't shoot straight."

Man Singh turned the gun slightly on its side and held it close to the lamp. With his left hand he pulled back a small knob. A trigger emerged from the handle and the barrel swiveled down. Gupta, Sharma, and Babu Ram watched intently. "The bullet goes in here," Man Singh said, pointing to a hole in the rear end of the barrel. He pressed the barrel back into place, pointed the gun at Gupta, and pulled the trigger.

Click!

Gupta reared back in shock and Man Singh laughed out loud. "You saw there was no bullet in the gun, Guptaji. Don't be so afraid. Haven't we all shot a pistol before?"

"Let me see the gun, Man Singhji," Sharma asked. He hefted the gun in his hand, squinted down the barrel, and operated the trigger mechanism. "How many of these do you have?"

"Only one, Sharmaji. We made nine, but only this one works. I think if we copy this one it will be better."

"It shoots only one bullet. You have to reload for every shot."

"You think I don't know that, Sharma?"

"Have you actually shot a bullet from this gun, Man Singhji?" Babu Ram asked.

"Yes, I tell you! Those police bullets fit this gun and it shoots."

"I believe you, Man Singhji," Gupta said in a soothing tone. "How fast are you making these guns?"

"We make one every three or four days. Then it takes a day for my machinist to fit it together. Let's say we average one a week." Man Singh looked around proudly. "In six months we'll have enough for a real *tamasha*." Babu Ram and Sharma guffawed.

Gupta waited until the laughter had died down. He removed his glasses and wiped them on a fold of his *dhoti*. "We can't wait six months, Man Singhji," he said in a soft voice.

The room fell silent. Man Singh sat back with his large hands gripping the edge of the table. Babu Ram's mouth was open, and his hand, which had been about to insert a *paan* between his reddened lips, was motionless in midair. Sharma's eyes were closed as if he were awaiting the executioner's ax. A slight jingling sound came from the teacups as Man Singh's hands shook the table.

"What do you mean, Guptaji?" Sharma finally asked.

"He's coming to Ramgarh on February ninth."

"Who is coming to Ramgarh on February ninth?"

"That scoundrel Nehru, of course!"

"Nehru? The prime minister?" Babu Ram asked.

"Who else, you . . . , you . . .!" Gupta fell into a fit of coughing as he fought to control his anger. He wiped his mouth with his handkerchief, took a deep breath, and said quietly, "Nehru will be coming to Ramgarh on February ninth to install the new vice chancellor at the Muslim University." He paused. "We will kill him then."

Silence again descended on the dimly lit room. Gupta's men sat transfixed by his words, like mice paralyzed in front of a cobra. "We will kill him then." The words seemed to echo off the wall. "We will kill him then."

Gupta's worst fears appeared to be justified. Where was the enthusiasm, where was the eagerness to begin the battle for *Hindu Raj*? The men looked at each other and then turned to Gupta.

"What are you talking about, Guptaji?" Babu asked. "Do you know what you're saying?" Beads of sweat appeared on his fat face, and he patted his forehead and jowls with his handkerchief. "We've made no preparations. We haven't notified other R.S.S. groups. You want us to act alone?"

"Don't you see, Babuji?" Gupta replied, his voice rising. "We're not alone. Thousands of R.S.S. men are on our side. Only we are the ones who have been chosen to be Rama's bow and arrow. This opportunity has been given to us by God." He looked to Sharma, on whose Brahmin's ability he relied to find in the scriptures the rationale for his proposals. "Sharma, am I not right?"

"You have a plan?" Sharma asked, his voice soft, dry, matter-of-fact.

"No. I have no specific plan. I don't know his itinerary, so I have no plan. When I find out where he'll be, I'll make a plan. It will be a good plan, and it will work." Gupta was emphatic. He tried to convey confidence, readiness for action, certainty of the outcome.

Sharma was silent, his eyes closed, his right hand gripping his pen so tightly Gupta thought it would snap into two pieces. A dog barked in the distance.

"Yes, Gupta, you're right!" Man Singh burst out. "We've been hiding in places like this for three years and we've gotten soft!" He waved the gun in the air. "Action! That's what we need!"

"Don't be a fool!" Sharma looked to Babu Ram for support. "If something good is to come out of this you need an organization, you need men, you need . . . ," Sharma gurgled as Man Singh's hands tightened around his throat.

"Sit down, Man Singhji!" Gupta shouted.

"No man calls me a fool, Guptaji," Man Singh said, relaxing his grip and returning to his seat. Sharma was panting and rubbing his throat.

"Let me explain," Gupta began.

Marshaling his arguments with all the logic and persuasiveness at his command, Gupta tried to show his companions that they had to do it alone. The more who knew about it, the greater the likelihood of leaks to the police. One leak and it would be all over. They would be in jail for the rest of their lives.

Once the deed was done, he argued, there would be chaos in the country. Many groups would be fighting to take over. But only the R.S.S. had the message that would arouse the Hindu masses to action. *Hindu Raj! Ram Raj!* Could meaningless phrases like democratic socialism, parliamentary democracy, or secular republic do anything but further confuse the illiterate Hindu masses? *Hindu Raj!* They would follow the men who shouted this rallying cry. There would be violence, disorder, killing. But the R.S.S would succeed because it would have the masses on its side.

The argument raged through the night. Cup after cup of tea was drunk. Babu Ram rejected Gupta's notion of not alerting the other R.S.S. groups. They needed to move swiftly to take over all of India. Sharma wanted to look at concrete plans before he would approve. Man Singh, supporting Gupta one moment, opposing him the next, was intrigued by the prospect of being a hero and a leader of India. Finally, when Gupta had answered all the objections and they heard the *muezzins* calling the Muslim faithful to their prayers in the cold, rainy dawn, they were convinced.

22

The Upper India Express rattled northwest toward Delhi, shrieking a warning at every level crossing. When the train had passed, the crossing guards would unchain the barrier poles and the bullock carts, lorries, and cars, which in many cases had been waiting for half an hour, would struggle across the tracks with an explosion of shouts and grinding gears. The railway embankment and the khaki-colored mud villages that dotted the intensively cultivated Ganges Plain were the only raised features in the flat landscape.

Ellen Siddiqi, sitting alone in a small, two-person first-class compartment, finished filing her nails and pushed her raincoat and handbag to the end of the leatherette bench seat. She opened the tiffin basket that Alice had packed for her. Thermos of tea, hard-boiled eggs, bread, an orange. She spread a paper napkin on her lap and peeled an egg. As she nibbled she watched the countryside slipping past her barred window, noting how a woman's brilliant *sari* would occasionally stand out from the pale green and gold of the wheat fields and the dull olive green of the ancient trees.

When her meal was finished she tossed the scraps out the window for the birds, rose and shook a few particles from her plaid skirt, and washed her hands and face in the water closet. Then she took out her compact and repaired her makeup. As she inspected her face in the mirror, Ellen thought of Karim. She knew he was in the second class bogie just behind hers. She had seen him in the turmoil of the Ramgarh station platform when she had left Iqbal and the coolie, who were trying to squeeze Alice and their luggage into the already packed third-class women's compartment.

Ellen returned to watching the countryside, daydreaming as the bogie rattled and swayed. She watched with disgust, her hand over her mouth, when the train passed hundreds of vultures flocking around a man who was skinning a dead cow. But soon she lay down on the seat, pillowed her head on her raincoat, and closed her eyes.

Ellen awakened when the Upper India Express pulled into Alipur around 4:30. She checked to see that the compartment door was locked and settled down at the window to enjoy the tumultuous platform scene. A crowd of passengers—some of them quite well dressed—was pushing and shoving into the third-class bogies near the end of the train. It was marvelous how thrifty even wealthy Indians were. You didn't buy a first-class ticket to Delhi from Alipur, even if you had to spend the hour's journey crammed into a filthy third-class compartment.

The food vendors concentrated their efforts on the long-distance passengers. There was the tea vendor, selling hot milky tea in throwaway red clay cups: "*Chai! Garam chai! Chai garam!*" A boy thrust a banana through Ellen's barred window: "*Kela! Kele! Ek anna ka do! Kele! Ek anna ka do!*" The *paan* and cigarette vendor: "*Paan bidi paan!* Cigarette! *Paan bidi bidi paan!*" The sellers of roasted chickpeas, kabobs, and freshly fried *poorees* squatted by their charcoal stoves, touting their wares and waving straw fans over them in a halfhearted attempt to keep away the flies.

A gnarled brown hand reached in through the window and clutched at Ellen's sleeve. "*Bakhsheesh*, memsahib," said a blind beggar, being led about by a small girl. His eye-sockets were empty holes; his voice was soft and entreating. "*Bakhsheesh*, memsahib," the beggar whined. Ellen recoiled in shock and disgust. Then she quickly recovered and reached into her purse for a coin.

"*Jao!* Go elsewhere, grandfather!" Ellen looked to see who had ordered the beggar away.

"Mr. Karim! How nice of you. I'm going to New Delhi also, as you see." Ellen struggled to keep her voice calm. She knew she was blushing. How lean and handsome he looked. She smoothed her hair into place, a habit that helped relieve her nervous tension.

"That beggar. I'm sorry he bothered you, Mrs. Siddiqi. They make railway journeys very unpleasant for Europeans." Karim took a small bite of his *pooree*. "It's best to ignore them, isn't it?"

"That's hard to do, Mr. Karim, but thanks. What's that you're eating? It looks delicious."

"Surely you have taken *pooree*, Mrs. Siddiqi. Wait, I will get one for you. Fresh from the hot oil. They're quite safe."

As Karim walked over to the *pooree* vendor, the train guard blew his whistle. Quickly he purchased a freshly fried *pooree* and walked toward Ellen's window, holding it out in his hand. Almost immediately a black bird swooped down and snatched the *pooree*. Karim stopped, looked at his empty hand, looked at Ellen, and burst out laughing. The engine's whistle sounded. Karim called out to Ellen, but his voice was drowned out by a blast of escaping steam. He jumped into his compartment as the train moved slowly along the platform.

The train had gone barely a few hundred yards when the engine whistled a warning, the brakes squealed, and the train shuddered to a stop. Ellen was thrown forward, and her tiffin basket fell onto the floor. What now? From the front of the train she heard the sound of an altercation and the braying of a donkey. The voices rose in volume and finally were silenced. She saw a gray donkey, with a load of bricks on its back, trot off the roadbed pursued by a young woman waving a stick. As the train started up and gained speed, Ellen saw the donkey pause to chew some leaves from a tree, so old and twisted and rotted that it seemed ready to fall. But it stood. Just like India, Ellen thought. In spite of what had been done to it, it survived.

Whistling and puffing, the Upper India Express rumbled across the Jumna River Bridge outside Delhi nearly on time at 5:30. Ellen opened her eyes and glanced down at the river on whose sandy banks the *dhobies* had spread their washing to dry. Two *dhobies*, probably anxious to finish before dark, were energetically beating pieces of cloth against smooth rocks set in the riverbed. Ellen felt she could almost hear the grunts of the washermen as they swung the garments through the air and the rhythmic slap of the wet fabric against the rocks. Then the train passed the Red Fort and entered the cavernous platform area of Delhi Station.

The noise was nearly unbearable. Shouting, cries of vendors, and announcements over the loudspeakers produced a cacophony that made Ellen wince. Even before the train came to a stop, her window was attacked by coolies who had caught sight of her white face. "Coolie, memsahib? Good coolie, memsahib?" Ellen sighed, put on her raincoat, and gathered up her handbag and tiffin basket. Screwing up her courage to face the ordeal of leaving the station, she unlocked her compartment door.

"May I help, Mrs. Siddiqi?"

Ellen looked up and saw Karim standing at the edge of the group of coolies, a small suitcase in his hand and a smile on his face. Thank goodness! "Oh, yes, thank you, Mr. Karim. In the women's compartment with Alice. My luggage." She smiled back with relief.

"*Achcha*. You," he said in Hindustani, pointing to a coolie whose face was marked by smallpox, "come with me!" He led the man toward the third-class bogies, leaving behind four grumbling coolies.

Ellen's coolie, with the suitcases and Alice's bedding roll balanced on his head, led Karim, Ellen, and Alice down the platform and over the pedestrian bridge to the barrier, where they surrendered their tickets to the guard. Then they passed through the crowded booking hall and emerged onto the station forecourt. The sun, setting in the southwest, glinted directly into their eyes so that they found it difficult to see where their coolie was taking them. All around them taxi drivers were touting for their business: "Big taxi, sahib! *Pukka* taxi, sahib!" But the coolie was oblivious. Ignoring the motley collection of Chevrolets, Vauxhalls, Morris Minors, and miscellaneous decrepit vehicles in the taxi line, he led them directly across from the station to a shiny Dodge sedan parked under a shed. He set his headload down on the ground, turned to Ellen with a broad smile, and said, "Best taxi, memsahib!" Ellen knew she had been snared.

Karim took care of the arrangements, seeing to it that the baggage was stowed in the boot, that the coolie was paid a fair price, and that the taxi's meter was turned on. Then he turned to Ellen and said, "I hope you enjoy your stay in Delhi, Mrs. Siddiqi."

"But Mr. Karim. You'll share my taxi, of course. I'll drop you at your hotel. Alice," she said to her maid, "you sit in front with the driver. Come on, Mr. Karim."

The taxi pulled out of its parking place under the shed, joined the stream of traffic headed east on Queens Road, and then turned south on Elgin Road, passing through the Esplanade below the Lahore Gate of the Red Fort. The lawns and gardens of the Esplanade were thronged with strollers enjoying the bracing air of the evening.

"You have seen the Red Fort, Mrs. Siddiqi?"

"Twice. Isn't it beautiful inside? More like a palace than a fort." Was Karim trying to do more than make small talk? Ellen was intrigued but so tired from the journey. If she could just close her eyes for a few minutes.

The taxi turned and headed toward the Delhi Gate, leading to New Delhi. The traffic slowed, as *tongas*, bicycles, and pedestrians joined the stream. Shops and stalls, restaurants and offices, lined the crowded street.

"Faiz Bazaar. Very busy place," Karim said. "Look there! Moti Mahal! You have taken food there? It's well known for *tandoori* preparations." He smiled at Ellen.

"*Tandoori* preparations, Mr. Karim?"

"Delhi specialty. Mostly chicken and fish but baked with spices in a large clay oven called a *tandoor*. You must try it, Mrs. Siddiqi."

"Do they serve them at the Imperial Hotel?"

"I doubt it. They have mostly English food there, isn't it?"

"I'm afraid so, Mr. Karim."

The taxi leaped forward as it passed through the Delhi Gate, crossed the expanse of open space south of the old city wall, and entered the Delhi-Mathura Road. Traffic was light, and the landscape suddenly changed from crowded bazaar to gardens, bungalows, and a cricket ground. They drove under a railway bridge and turned right. Some young women were playing volleyball in a garden

"Lady Irwin College," Karim said. He looked up at the sky. "It will be dark soon, Mrs. Siddiqi."

"What pictures are you going to see, Mr. Karim?" Ellen felt a bit embarrassed at not holding up her end of the conversation. "While you're in New Delhi."

"If I can get a booking, it will be *Jhansi-ki-Rani*, India's first color cinema. It's a story from 1857, about a queen who was a soldier. Do you like our Indian films, madam?"

"I've not seen any, Mr. Karim. I can't understand Hindi well enough, and my husband doesn't like to go to the Picture Palace in Ramgarh. He says it has bad pictures and too many fleas."

Karim chuckled. "Correct. Correct. Fleas are a problem at the Picture Palace. But it's a pity you haven't seen at least one. Mirrors of Indian society, these films." He peered out the window. "Ah, Barakhamba Road. It's not far. My hotel. Let me pay you for my ride."

"Absolutely not, Mr. Karim. You've been so helpful. I won't take anything from you. Just forget it. My treat."

"You're very kind, madam. You'll be at the Imperial? Not very far from the Khyber Hotel. *Arrey*, driver! Turn right on Connaught Circus. Khyber Hotel. Stop there."

"*Achcha*, sahib!"

The taxi turned right, into a quiet street on the outer ring of Connaught Place and came to a stop in front of a shop selling luggage and leather goods. The building was stucco, painted a warm tan some time ago but now stained with dirt and splashes of red spittle. A staircase on one side led to the upper floors, where a neon sign proclaimed Hotel Khyber! Comfortable Rooms, Modern Facilities!

"It's not the Imperial, but it suits my needs," Karim said, opening the door. "The driver will take you directly to the Imperial Hotel, Mrs. Siddiqi. Pay him just what the meter says, plus a small tip. I've taken his number and he knows that you're not to be cheated. Good night. Maybe we'll meet on the train back to Ramgarh."

Ellen held out her hand to Karim. He seemed surprised. He cautiously took her hand in his and shook it once.

"I hope so, Mr. Karim. Maybe we'll run into each other here in New Delhi. I might try to see that picture you mentioned."

It was a ride of less than ten minutes to the Imperial Hotel. The Dodge drove through the hotel gardens and then under the portico just as the lights were coming on. Coolies in khaki uniforms took the luggage from the boot while Ellen paid the driver. A tall, fiercely mustachioed commissionaire in white *achkan*, golden cummerbund, medal ribbons, and starched turban escorted her to the reception desk, where a smiling Anglo-Indian clerk gave her the register to sign.

"How nice to see you again, Mrs. Siddiqi. We've put a cot in the dressing room for your servant. Her meals will be served in the servants' hall. Will you have bed tea at the usual time?"

"Eight o'clock is early enough for me, Mr. Fernandes." Who wanted to be awakened at six by a bearer with tea and biscuits?

"Yes, madam. Bearer! Room 35. Dinner will be served as usual from eight to ten, Mrs. Siddiqi."

"Will the food be as usual, Mr. Fernandes?"

"Madam still has her sense of humor, I see. Here's the

menu card for this evening." Fernandes turned away to greet another guest.

Ellen read the card. Mulligatawny soup, roast mutton or chicken, chipped potatoes, peas, sardines on toast or devil on horseback, salad, chocolate gateau, Polson's coffee. The usual. Her shoulders sagged. With a sigh, she returned the menu card and trudged down the hall behind the bearer.

23

"Superintendent Karim, you are aware, of course, what the reaction of the Hindus will be if anything unfortunate happens at the Muslim University?" Deputy Inspector General of Police (C.I.D.) Rustom Cawasji Poonawalla leaned back in his chair, turning to one side and looking at the portrait of the prime minister on his office wall. Karim followed his glance, shivered slightly, and turned back to Poonawalla. The D.I.G.'s face was in profile. The nose was a typical Parsi nose. Its curvature and prominence made his own appear inconspicuous by comparison. If this man smokes cigarettes, Karim thought, he could certainly smoke them in a rainstorm.

As if in response to Karim's thought, Poonawalla reached into an ivory inlaid box on his desk and brought out a round tin of fifty State Express 555's. He broke the key off the bottom, inserted the end of the steel opening strip into it, and began to turn. The vacuum was broken with a hiss, and the sweet smell of fresh Virginia tobacco emerged from the tin. Both men lighted up and drew the smoke deep into their lungs.

"Wouldn't the reaction depend on who is responsible, sir?"

"No, Karim, it would not," Poonawalla said flatly, turning to face him. "The Hindu population will not make fine distinctions of that sort. A Muslim merchant a thousand miles away in Bombay will be held personally responsible by his Hindu competitor across the road for anything that happens at the Muslim University on nine February."

Karim coughed. And coughed again. The strong, acrid smoke seemed stuck in his lungs. He held his handkerchief over his mouth in embarrassment. But mixed with embarrassment was a momentary feeling, an insight he had not had before. It was as if a photographer's flash had briefly illuminated and clarified a scene and then darkness had covered it up. He had seen himself at the point of a gigantic inverted pyramid, struggling to keep it from pressing him into the ground.

Poonawalla rose from his chair and moved quickly to the sideboard under the prime minister's picture. He poured a glass of water from a brass carafe and brought it to Karim.

"Thank you, sir. I'm not used to this brand of cigarette." Karim's voice was weak. He panted as he sipped the water. "That's better."

"Relax, Karim." Poonawalla rested his hand on Karim's shoulder. "I'm aware of what you must be feeling. Communal violence is a terrible thing. But you're not the first district S.P. we've worked with." Poonawalla's voice was reassuring. "We'll give you all the support you need."

"Thank you, sir." He was right! No doubt about it, Poonawalla was right. He knew what the consequences would be. It would be terrible! These Parsis! Only a hundred thousand of them in all. Like a tiny island in a sea of Hindus and Muslims. Oh, they were smart! They had had what it took to survive and prosper for a thousand years.

Poonawalla returned to his chair, picked up the folder

of documents Karim had brought in, and began to leaf through them. Here and there he put his initials. Then he closed the folder and turned to Karim.

"Have you been fully briefed by my staff?"

"Yes, sir."

"Have they approved your preparations for the visit?"

"Yes, sir."

Poonawalla leaned back again in his chair. The three rows of ribbons on the breast of his uniform jacket summarized his professional life. Probably came into the police after an army career. Maybe passed over for lieutenant general or something. Or else his political sense failed him that one time.

"Is there anything you need that I can get you, Karim?"

"Would the prime minister wear a bulletproof vest, sir?"

"Not possible. Don't I wish it were. Won't hear of it. The political consequences would be unfortunate. Imagine! Panditji not trusting his own people, people he loves and who love him? If it became known—and it would be impossible to hide it—it might even *encourage* an assassination attempt. Sorry, Karim. No vest. Anything else?"

"No, sir."

"Very well. I'll sign . . . here," he scratched his name on the first page of the file, "and you sign . . . there." Karim leaned over the desk and added his signature. "Keep in touch, Karim. By telephone. Let my people know every few days how things are progressing."

"Yes, sir." Karim rose, saluted, and left the room with his file. He walked down the long corridor toward the main gate of the C.I.D. compound, past the offices and the uniformed peons and the bulletin boards of the central security staff. He reached the gate, squinted in the bright midday sun, and signed himself out. The gate closed behind him, and a feeling of both freedom and foreboding came over him. It was his responsibility now, no one else's. If anything happened, he would pay the price.

Ellen Siddiqi finished her passport business at Bahawalpur House, the American Embassy, around noon. She waited at the gate while the *chowkidar*, a uniformed Gurkha with a chestful of battle ribbons, hailed a taxi for her.

"Ellen Anderson! Ellen!" It was someone shrieking from a car that was drawing to a stop. "My God! What are you doing here? My God! This is incredible!"

Ellen peered into the large Ford station wagon and saw Mary Parker, a classmate from Minneapolis. "Mary Parker! What are *you* doing here? I thought you were in New York."

"Ellen! My God!" Mary shrieked again. "This is fantastic! Get in!" Ellen entered the rear of the car and kissed her friend. She was still the bright, petite woman with dark bangs and glasses that she remembered from the university.

"I'm Mary Phillips now, Ellen." She held out her left hand and displayed a wedding ring. "I met Gordon when I was in journalism school at Columbia. He's an economist. He got his Ph.D. He joined the Ford Foundation." Mary was still speaking in short, staccato bursts. "Been here three months."

"Do you like it here, Mary?"

"It's okay." She waved her hand to indicate the car. "Belongs to the foundation. House belongs to the foundation. Servants belong to the foundation." She looked wistfully at Ellen. "I was going to Connaught Circus. Lunch and some shopping. Come with me, Ellen."

Three hours later, after sandwiches and ice cream at the Kwality and shopping at the Central Cottage Industries Emporium, after telling each other about everything that had happened since they left Minneapolis, after describing their not-so-exciting lives in New Delhi and Ramgarh, Mary Phillips dropped Ellen off under the portico of the Imperial Hotel.

"Ellen, the foundation's having a big do tonight. For Kidwai, the agriculture minister. I'd love for you to come. You'll meet the Bowleses. Lots of other Americans. I'd love for you to meet Gordon."

"Well, I should go back to Ramgarh tonight if I can make the Calcutta Mail. Iqbal's all alone."

"One more day won't matter, Ellen. It'll be such fun to introduce you around. Please?"

"Well, let me think about it. What time and where?"

"Ford Foundation. Lodi Estate. Eight o'clock. Informal. See you."

Ellen put the strap of her new shopping bag over her shoulder, acknowledged the commissionaire's salute with a smile, and entered the lobby.

"Message for you, Mrs. Siddiqi," Fernandes the reception clerk said, handing her an envelope. Ellen tore it open.

Dear Mrs. Siddiqi,

I would be honoured if you would join me for a tandoori dinner and an Indian cinema this evening.

Can you meet me at seven o'clock at Hotel Khyber, Connaught Place?

Yours faithfully,
Karim

Ellen suddenly felt warm. She put her hand to her cheek.

"Is something the matter, Mrs. Siddiqi?" Fernandes asked.

"No. No. Just feeling a little warm, that's all." She wiped her forehead with her handkerchief.

"It was an Indian gentleman who left that note for you."

"Yes. I know." She blushed.

"He seemed a decent sort of fellow. I hope he isn't bothering you, madam." Fernandes seemed genuinely concerned. "We won't let him into the hotel again if you prefer not to see him."

Ellen took her room key. "It's okay, Mr. Fernandes. He's someone I know. Thanks." She walked slowly down the corridor to her room. Had it been so obvious? Even to Fernandes?

Ellen inserted her key into the lock. She stood for a moment with her hand on the doorknob, staring irresolutely at the polished brass numbers on the door. Then she straightened her back and entered her room.

Alice had laid out clean underwear and her blue dress on the bed and was filling the bath with water. Abstractedly Ellen let her help her undress and get into the tub. The deep warm water covered her, soothing her skin and nerve endings and cleansing away the dust of the street. She lay back with her eyes closed. It was heavenly. If only she could stay there forever.

Mohammed Abdul Karim puffed on his cigarette, drew in the comforting smoke and blew it up at the ceiling. The neon hotel sign outside the window shone through the curtain and cast a rosy light on the opposite wall. He glanced down at Ellen Siddiqi's blonde hair, which mingled with his own black and gray chest hair as she lay on him with her eyes closed and her left hand touching the two round scars on his arm. Their clothes, as if scattered by a violent wind, were thrown haphazardly on the chairs, the chest of drawers, and the floor. His undershirt hung from a drawerpull like a limp banner in the calm that follows the storm.

Karim felt relaxed for the first time since his meeting with Poonawalla. He drew again on his Sepoy and blew a smoke ring into the air. God, how marvelous! So many surprises. Her arrival at his hotel. Really! She had really come! Her delight at the *tandoori* chicken and the *naan* bread. Her enjoyment of the cinema show. And then . . .

What a woman she was. Such a wonderful lover, helping him to unbend, to overcome his fear and his awkwardness. Making him feel like a virile young man again.

Karim stubbed out the cigarette in the ashtray on his night table. Ellen stirred, groaned, opened her eyes, and smiled at him. She stretched her arms and rolled off his chest, making sweet humming sounds. She lay on her back next to Karim, her blue eyes sparkling, her blonde hair in disarray on her forehead.

Karim shifted his body, leaned on his elbow, and looked at Ellen.

Even in the half light he could see that she had such a different body from that of his wife. Such long, hairless legs, with strong athletic muscles from hours on the tennis court. His wife had probably never seen a tennis court in her sheltered, small-town Muslim girl's life. He brushed Ellen's hair from her face. How much more woman she was: as tall as he, as capable and independent as any man. He moved his hand down from Ellen's face to her breasts and caressed the white skin and pink nipples. His wife's had been dark brown, barely distinguishable from her skin. He leaned forward and took the nearest nipple in his mouth.

Ellen began to hum again. She took his hand and placed it between her legs. She took his penis in her own hand.

Karim stroked with care, his finger penetrating and caressing, caressing. His hand grasped and molded; his finger explored and stroked as Ellen had taught him to do. Ellen's hums changed to sighs as she felt his penis swell and stiffen as she massaged it gently.

Ellen's arm wrapped around Karim's shoulder and pulled him onto her body. She wrinkled her nose as his mustache tickled her earlobe. Karim slowly penetrated, reaching deep into Ellen, stretching, pushing, rubbing. Ellen's tongue probed deep into Karim's mouth, mirroring the action of his penis. Karim's thrusts were slow and deliberate at first. Ellen's powerful hips matched Karim thrust for thrust as their pace increased. Their hearts beat faster; their breath came in gasps. Suddenly Ellen gave a hoarse cry and her fingernails dug into Karim's back. He winced and paused, but it was too late. A surge of ineffable pleasure enveloped his loins. Ellen's legs wrapped around him and in ecstasy they fell over the precipice together.

24

Mohammed Abdul Karim slammed his foot on the brake pedal as the dark, brownish-gray water buffalo moved its massive bulk diagonally across the road into his jeep's path. The wheels locked, rubber squealed on concrete, the jeep spun around, and the passenger side hit the buffalo violently in the ribs. The animal stopped, turned its head to inspect its flank, flicked its tail against the flies, and then continued down the Grand Trunk Road as if nothing had happened.

Karim sat in the jeep, taking deep breaths and listening to the rapid pounding of his heart. He was lucky. He had known several police officers injured in collisions with water buffaloes. Just as now, the animal had plodded away unscathed.

The sound of the accident had drawn the customers away from the stalls and shops at the side of the road. A small crowd had gathered, and the road traffic had come to a halt. "Are you all right, sahib?" one of the men asked.

"*Thik hai.* All right," Karim replied, without really knowing if he was. The sixteen-mile ride back from Sitapur *chauki* had been on rutted, unpaved roads. His neck ached. His back ached. And . . . Oh! How his bottom ached! Colliding with that buffalo hadn't helped.

An insistent horn jarred Karim to full attention. His jeep was blocking the road and a lorry was waiting to pass. He put the jeep in gear and let out the clutch. The jeep began to move, but a squealing sound came from the impacted side. He stopped and found the front mudguard bent in and touching the tire.

Damn! He'd have to get that fixed straightaway. Pulling it out by hand helped a little; it didn't touch when the wheel was straight. At least he could drive to a petrol station and get a temporary repair. Good! There was the Caltex down the road.

Karim steered the jeep carefully the quarter mile to the Caltex station and off the paved road onto the station forecourt. A battered Vauxhall was perched over the grease pit.

"*Sat Sri Akal*, Superintendent Sahib," said Tej Pal Singh, smiling and touching his turban in welcome. He was sitting on the ground, filing a piece of metal that he held between his feet.

"*Sat Sri Akal*, Teja," Karim replied. "Where is your uncle?"

"Down here in the pit, Superintendent Sahib!" Smiling broadly, Harbans Singh emerged from beneath the Vauxhall, wiping his hands on a rag. "Welcome, Superintendent Sahib. Teja! Tea for the sahib! And bring a chair. Sit down, Superintendent. We're honored by your visit."

Karim accepted the chair and reached into his jacket pocket for a cigarette. Then thought better of it.

"I've been intending to come and visit you, sardarji, but . . . you know how it is when you take up a new posting. Uh . . . have a look at my mudguard, will you? I just collided with a buffalo." Karim laughed. "Naturally, the buffalo was unhurt."

"Naturally, sahib," said Harbans Singh gleefully. "If you survive a collision with one of them, you're one of the lucky few. Is this all the damage? You must have been driving slowly." He bent over the damaged mudguard. "*Achcha.* Nothing serious. I'll just bend it back a bit with this bar and you'll be able to drive. If you want it really fixed, you'll have to take it to a panel-beating shop. There, *thik hai.* That'll do it." Harbans Singh stood erect. "Now, how about that cup of tea?"

"How have you been feeling, sardarji?" Karim asked, after they were seated and sipping their tea.

"I'm feeling all right, Superintendent Sahib. It's been nearly a month and the marks are almost gone." The Sikh looked intently into Karim's eyes. Was he sending a message? Of gratitude? Of resentment? "I went to the District Hospital this past week for my last checkup."

A bullock cart carrying a load of paraffin tins lumbered slowly by on its way to the countryside. The driver twisted the bullocks' tails and shouted oaths at them.

"We think we know who set our bogie on fire, sardarji," Karim said, "but we can't do anything about him."

Harbans Singh recoiled slightly and looked skeptically at Karim. "Why not, sahib. Does he have political support or something?"

"Nothing like that. He's dead. Died of burns after he tried to burn down one of the university buildings."

"Ah, that man. I think I saw him, you know, sahib. When I went back for a change of dressing. Before he died. I think it was before he died. You couldn't really tell if he was alive or dead. Completely covered in bandages, with a tube into his mouth and drips into his arms. It reminded me of Cairo Military Hospital after El Alamein. Our tanks burned petrol, and when they . . ." Harbans Singh was silent for a moment. "So that was how it happened, sahib? Not a pleasant way to die."

"No, sardarji."

"Maybe it's better to die than to live, in some cases, Superintendent Sahib. There was another man in the hospital last week who also reminded me of the war. He'd lost his right hand and one eye and part of his face. He had told the doctors it was a pressure boiler explosion, but he told me that his pistol had blown apart when he fired it."

Karim put his cup and saucer down on the ground. He longed to have a cigarette in his nervous hand. "Did this man say where he had got the pistol, sardarji? They have to be registered, you know."

"He didn't say, sahib." Harbans Singh contemplated the leaves in the bottom of his cup. "It was probably unregistered."

"Sardarji, will you permit me to smoke?"

"Of course, sahib. The petrol pump is closed. There's no danger."

Karim lighted a Sepoy and inhaled deeply. He relaxed. Harbans Singh's story was disturbing. Pistols didn't usually explode when they were fired, unless they used bullets that were too strong for the gun. Injured men didn't usually lie to the doctors who were taking care of them. Who was this man? Where had he come from? Where had he worked? Whom had he associated with? If there was one unregistered pistol out there, maybe there were more. And what kind of doctors were they who couldn't tell the difference between an injury from a pistol explosion and one from a boiler explosion?

"Sardarji, this man. The one in the hospital. You know his name?"

"He called himself Ram Singh, sahib."

Karim sighed. Within a radius of ten miles of Ramgarh there were probably five thousand Ram Singhs.

"Have you heard any more talk about burning buildings?"

"No, sahib. That tea shop down the road where I heard it the other time—it's closed down. We go to a different one now. Although maybe the *chaiwallah* will open it up again. I've seen a light there at night from time to time." Harbans Singh scratched his beard.

"Where do you think they got the petrol for those fires, sardarji?"

"It could have been many places, sahib. There are two petrol stations on the G.T. Road; there are—"

"Yes, I've seen your Caltex and the Burmah-Shell near the police compound."

"—the private pumps that some of the transport firms have. Pushpa Transport, over there behind the tea shop, has one. They buy their petrol direct from the wholesaler. They save money that way, sahib."

"Would these petrol pumps sell a single gallon to someone who came by with a tin?"

"Of course, sahib. And also the petrol might have been siphoned. From a car or a lorry."

Karim was silent. The investigation had not moved forward since the burned man had died in the hospital. Maybe Saxena should get cracking and question the people who had access to petrol. Maybe they would have some bit of information that would identify the burned man.

"Some more tea, Superintendent Sahib?"

"No, thanks, sardarji. I must make a move. Let me know if you hear anything. *Sat Sri Akal*!"

"*Sat Sri Akal*, Superintendent Sahib!"

Karim's jeep started easily and he turned smoothly onto the Grand Trunk Road in the direction of the tea shop. Might as well have a look at it while he was in the area. He drove slowly alongside the shop and parked. The shutters were closed and the cinema advertisement was smeared with mud thrown up by passing lorries. He got out and walked around the shop. Nothing unusual. A strong smell of urine. Someone had pissed here recently. A door in the back at the top of a couple of wooden steps. He tried the door. Locked. He turned and found that he could just see over the brick wall into a compound. A couple of lorries being worked on, a small glassed-in office, a petrol pump, a sign that said Pushpa Transport. Over in the corner a workbench, with a man doing something with some steel parts while a burly, mustachioed man looked over his shoulder.

Pushpa Transport! Where had he run across that name before? Yes. They owned the lorry that had tipped over Ellen Siddiqi's *tonga*. Interesting.

Karim stepped down and took one last look at the tea shop. Not much to go on. Might as well get back and tell Saxena to inquire about the petrol tin. Saxena didn't seem to have made much progress in his investigation. Could he be holding back something?

As Karim drove off in his jeep, a Pushpa Transport driver, who had been watching him from the *paan* shop across the road, flipped his *bidi* into the dirt and walked slowly toward the compound. A police officer! Not merely a constable but an officer! Snooping around the tea shop. Looking over the wall. Man Singh would be very, very grateful to the man who gave him that little piece of information.

25

Warmed by the midday sun, Mohammed Abdul Karim pedaled his borrowed bicycle past the university's academic and administrative buildings and steered it down a tranquil, tree-lined street into the faculty residential area. Misgivings about his mission churned in his mind. Preoccupied, he rolled unseeingly by the large bungalows of the professors, with their carefully tended gardens; rattled past the small bungalows and semidetached houses allocated to the readers and senior lecturers; and was startled to find himself among the simple row houses of the lecturers and other low-level professional employees. Upset by his mistake, he turned around and looked for the lane leading to Iqbal Siddiqi's semidetached house. He was puffing and drops of sweat were collecting inside his collar by the time he reached Siddiqi's garden wall. He rapped on the door and waited, his heart pounding. He nervously smoothed his mustache. Had he made a mistake in coming here? What if . . . ?

"Come in, come in, Mr. Karim. I got your note." Ellen Siddiqi gave Karim a broad smile as she held the door wide open. "Please excuse me. Just got back from tennis. Haven't had a chance to change." Karim pushed his bicycle into the garden, leaned it against the wall, and followed Ellen up the path to the door of the house, admiring her bare legs and the swing of her hips under the short tennis skirt. Briefly a warning signal flashed somewhere in the primal core of his brain. White woman. European woman. Watch out! But his rational mind, his policeman's mind, prevailed against both the fear and the longing that had ridden with him from his house, that were alongside him now behind Ellen as the sunshine glinted on her hair.

Ellen swung the door closed behind them and stood with her back to it. "Alice has gone home to her family for a wedding. You'll have American coffee? I'll make it." Karim turned to her. There was an expression on her face that he had not seen before. "Oh, Karim!" She rushed forward, siezed his head, and pulled his face down to hers for a kiss.

Karim tensed. But Ellen's lips pressed urgently against his, and slowly he relaxed and wrapped his arms around her. Her body was warm and moist from tennis, with a scent of sweat only partly masked by perfume. Ellen nuzzled her cheek against his. "There's nobody here," she whispered. "I've waited for you to come." Karim squeezed her to him and then held her away.

"Mrs. Siddiqi, I . . ."

"Ellen! I'm not Mrs. Siddiqi when we're alone!" She smiled mischievously. "And what shall I call you, O Great Superintendent? Are you Abdul to your friends? Or Karim? Tell me, my mysterious oriental lover!" Ellen chuckled and held him close. "How shall I speak your name?"

"Abdul."

"That's a nice name. What does it mean?"

"Servant. Servant of God." Karim grinned. "What does Ellen mean?"

"Ellen is also Helen. It means light."

Karim fondled Ellen's hair. He was struck by the contrast between his brown hand and her blonde hair. "Most appropriate. When I think of you I think also of your light hair."

"Have you thought of me often?" Ellen played with his tie.

"Every day. Even when I should be thinking of other things. Of my work. But mostly when I'm alone."

"How do you think of me?" Ellen asked with a smile. She patted her hair into place.

"Shall I tell you? I'm embarrassed."

"Please. Tell me." Her blue eyes seemed to sparkle.

"I think of you in the Khyber Hotel." Karim could barely keep from laughing.

"Is that all?" Ellen demanded, drawing back. "Is that so embarrassing?"

"I think of you without any clothes on."

Ellen's laugh filled the room. "Now *that's* embarrassing. But it should be more embarrassing for me." She stopped laughing. "Funny, though, I don't feel embarrassed."

"How do you feel?" Karim said.

"Like having a cup of coffee. Come on. Let's go into the kitchen. We can talk while I make it."

Ellen led Karim through the living and dining rooms, with their colorful curtains, to the kitchen. "I'm not used to puttering around in here," she laughed, waving at the starkly simple equipment. "Tonight I'll be making my first meal on the *chula*," she said, pointing to the small coal-fired clay stove on the floor. "Thank goodness for canned food."

Ellen filled a bowl with water from a pottery water jar, inserted a small immersion heater, and plugged the cord into a wall outlet. "It'll take five minutes, Abdul. Uh . . . you came about the *tonga* driver?"

"Well, Ellen, as I told you at the parade, the driver and the owner of the lorry have been found." Karim dug in his pockets for cigarettes. "They live here in Ramgarh. We've charged them on the basis of your identification of the lorry."

"And I know I was right about that!" Ellen interjected. Karim smiled. How many Indians would have given the *tongawallah* a moment's thought?

"Of course. Uh, may I smoke?"

"Better not," Ellen said, shaking her head. "Iqbal . . ."

"I see. Well, my deputy has finally persuaded the lorry owner to compensate the *tonga* driver, if you decline to testify and the charges are dropped. He'll give a thousand rupees for a new *tonga* and two hundred fifty for a new horse."

"And what about pain and suffering?" Ellen demanded, her eyes flashing. "And the money he could have made since the accident?"

"And what about your pain and suffering?" Karim nodded. Ellen was silent. She leaned back against the sink and folded her arms across her chest.

"Is it enough?" she asked, after a moment.

"It's enough for a horse and *tonga*. But there will be no judgment and compensation award for anything else without a trial." Karim took a deep breath. "It depends on you, Ellen. What do you want to do?"

Ellen shrugged. "I don't know." She turned to pour the now boiling water into two cups and to measure out the instant coffee and the powdered milk and sugar. She clinked the cups onto a tray and added a plate of sweet biscuits. "Let's have the coffee in the living room."

Ellen sat down on the sofa next to Karim and abstractedly stirred her coffee. Then she set the cup on the coffee table and smoothed her white skirt down over her legs. "What should I do, Abdul?" she asked.

"It's your decision, Ellen. I can't tell you what to do. But I can tell you this," Karim added. "We're dealing with a man who is likely to take some desperate actions. He is probably responsible for poisoning your dog."

"Schnitzel? He killed Schnitzel? Oh my God!" Ellen's eyes filled with tears. "Why didn't you tell me, Abdul?"

"Ellen, there was not enough evidence to prove it. And I wanted to spare you." Karim put his hand on Ellen's. "I'm sorry, Ellen." They sat quietly, the silence broken only by the distant cry of a vegetable peddler.

"Well," Ellen said, "what's done is done. We can't bring back poor Schnitzel."

"There is also this, Ellen." Karim sipped his coffee. A cigarette would have been so delicious now. "The lorry owner will be defended by a lawyer. I'm a lawyer myself, Ellen. In the army I prosecuted deserters and thieves. I know what those fellows can do. Motions, postponements, false witness, legal tricks. Who knows how long. And you'll have to be available to testify."

"Iqbal would blow his top," Ellen said. Karim was silent. "I wouldn't like it either. Will he pay the money right away?" Karim nodded. Ellen drained her cup and set it down.

"Okay," she said with finality, "drop the charges. If you're sure he'll pay, I won't testify." She touched Karim's arm and smiled at him as if to show that he had lifted a burden from her shoulders.

"I'll take care of it," Karim said, rising to leave. Ellen rose also and put her hands on Karim's shoulders, nervously rubbing his superintendent's insignia between her fingers. Karim looked down at her face. His eyes looked into her eyes.

"Don't go," Ellen said. "We have two hours before Iqbal comes home." Karim took Ellen in his arms and held her close to him, so close he could feel his swelling organ pressing against her. He released her and they looked again into each other's eyes, the unspoken desire hanging in the room like a mist. Ellen's hands fumbled with Karim's trousers.

"Ellen, I . . . ," he whispered.

"No talking, Abdul. Not a word. Just relax. I'll take care of everything."

"No, Ellen. We must not do this in Iqbal's house." Karim slipped his arms around her waist and held her close.

"Oh, Abdul! My sweet Abdul. What's the matter?"

Karim released her and they sat together on the sofa. Ellen straightened her skirt.

"Ellen . . ." Karim looked around the room, searching for the right words. "Ellen, I don't know what to say. I don't know how to speak of such things in English. English I use for my work. Urdu is my personal language. You must help me." He took hold of her hands. "I have great affection for you. It's the correct word, isn't it? Affection?

"But you're a foreigner, a European, a non-Muslim. Do you know what we call non-Muslims, Ellen? *Kaffirs*! Infidels! I should avoid any contact with you." He paused. "But you're not like those English memsahibs who made us feel like dirty beggar children. I'm not afraid to come to your house and be alone with you, although it is dangerous for both of us." Ellen leaned over and kissed him. "No! No! I'm not finished," Karim said, drawing back. "You're different. But you're a married woman. You have a husband who must love you and—"

"Some marriage!" Ellen broke in. "Iqbal . . . Iqbal was so different back in Minneapolis. I want children, Abdul. And I want to feel like a wife, not just a piece of property!" She wiped her eyes.

"But you belong to his family, do you not? In your marriage contract—the one your father signed—you were taken in as a member of the Siddiqi family?" Ellen laughed out loud. "I'm sorry, Ellen," Karim said. "I did not mean to joke."

"Oh, Abdul," Ellen chuckled. "I know you're not joking. You're dead serious. I'm sorry."

"But what are you laughing at?"

"The marriage contract. Iqbal and I have no marriage contract! We had a civil marriage in front of a justice of the peace." Ellen rested her head on Karim's shoulder. "There were no Muslim priests in Minneapolis, and Iqbal wouldn't have a Protestant ceremony. So we went to city hall for a civil marriage."

"Couldn't you have had a Muslim marriage when you came to India?"

"I suppose so. But Iqbal's father died while we were on our way over. Then Iqbal returned to the university. So we never got around to it."

"I see," Karim said thoughtfully. "So by Muslim law you may not be fully married." He rubbed his cheek and turned to Ellen. "If you're not married by Muslim law you could . . ." He turned away.

"Could what, Abdul?" Ellen took his chin in her hand and turned his face toward her. He looked at her but he did not see her. He saw the face of his dead wife, with her soft brown eyes and her black hair parted in the middle and her brown face with the red *tikka* on her forehead.

"You could marry me and be my *begum*. We would have a family. Boys, girls, lots of children. You would have a good house. We would have a fine life together."

"What did you say, Abdul?"

Karim looked vacantly at Ellen. His jaw hung down. He had been speaking in Urdu.

What a lonely, joyless life he had been leading! Karim covered his face with his hands as his self-control fell apart. His shoulders shook; his grief poured out in tears and sobs.

"Abdul, poor Abdul," Ellen murmured, slipping her arm around his shoulders. She pulled his head down and held it against her bosom, gently stroking the gray-streaked black hair. Karim's sobs diminished. He sat up, blew his nose, and wiped away the tears.

"I'm sorry, Ellen," he said.

"It's good to cry sometimes. For men too. You feel better afterward."

"Yes, I feel better." He paused and looked away. "I must go now. Back to work." He turned back to Ellen, tears again filling his eyes. "What shall I do, Ellen? I'm so unhappy without you."

"I know, Abdul. I'm unhappy too. I feel trapped." Ellen wiped her own eyes and stood up. "We need time to think, Abdul. We need time to decide what we want to do." She took his hands in hers, pulled him up, and put his arms around her. "I've been married twice, Abdul." Karim started. "Yes, Iqbal's my second husband. If a woman is divorced twice, people wonder about her."

Ellen moved back a step, grasped Karim's arms, and held him away from her. "Go back to your office," she said. "Think about your future. Let me think about mine."

26

"How is the investigation going, Saxenaji?" Karim took a long pull on his second cigarette of the day, inhaling deeply, and blew the smoke up toward the ceiling, where it joined the dust that had been there for decades. He glanced with distaste across his desk at Deputy Superintendent Saxena, who sat before him with eyes bloodshot and swollen, needing a shave and smelling of liquor. How could the man stand to look at himself in the mirror? What could be going on that he had let himself fall apart this way? What if the inspector general suddenly dropped in?

"Slowly, Superintendent Sahib." Saxena's normally harsh voice was tempered by a whine. Self-pity, perhaps? Or was it one of the effects of last night's carousal. "We've been keeping an eye on Gupta. He's not done anything out of the ordinary. Or seen anyone. Just his usual clientele of thieves and *goondas*." Saxena picked up the saucer of tea that lay on the desk before him and drained it. He gasped with satisfaction and wiped his mouth with his sleeve. "We've found no new physical evidence since the suitcase up at the university. No one has claimed the burned man's body. By the way," he said, exploring his ear with his little finger, "the hospital people are keeping it packed in ice, but they don't think it'll last much longer. What do you think we should do about it?"

Karim sipped his tea, watching Saxena's eyes as the deputy waited for instructions. How had this man reached his position? Didn't he know the first thing about police work?

"Considering the circumstances," Karim replied, "I don't think anyone will come forward, unless it's a relative. But we have to make a reasonable effort to identify the man." He took another puff of his cigarette. "Why don't you do one thing," he said, stubbing it out in the ashtray. "Have about a hundred notices printed and post them in the city. In the cantonment also. You know. The date and time of the fire, time of death, the man's measurements—the usual. Give it a week. If no one comes forward, I'll ask the district magistrate to issue an order for the cremation of the remains." Simple, straightforward police procedure. Strictly according to regulations. Any assistant subinspector could have thought of it.

"It's a messy business, Superintendent Sahib," Saxena said with a wry smile. He took out a handkerchief, blew his nose, inspected the results, and put the handkerchief away.

"Anything else?" Karim asked. Anything at all would be welcome. "What about the suitcase?"

"The suitcase? Oh, we got nowhere with that. We took it around to the luggage dealers and they all identified it as a type that hasn't been made for at least ten years. But no one could say if they had sold it themselves." Saxena scratched under one arm. "Maybe it was stolen somewhere."

"Right," Karim said. "What if it was? Is there a *chor bazaar* in Ramgarh, where the thieves peddle their stuff?"

"Not exactly a *chor bazaar,* but probably much of the

stuff is stolen. I mean the Saturday market on the Grand Trunk Road near the Delhi Gate. Do you . . . ."

"Send two men in plain clothes next Saturday. Have them take the suitcase and go around to all the peddlers and ask them who they might have sold it to." Karim paused and pondered, rubbing his mustache. "They shouldn't deny that they're policemen, but they must make sure the peddlers understand what we want." He took out his fountain pen and played with it. "What we want is who the peddler sold it to, and when. Not where he got it, not whether it's stolen. Just who he sold it to. Understand? And when."

Saxena smiled. "It's no use, Superintendent Sahib. These people won't tell us anything. They're more afraid of the *goondas* and the *dadas* than of us. Give me an hour with each of them and I'll have the information for you." Saxena leaned back in his chair, clenched a fist, and flexed his right arm.

"But will it be the truth, Saxena? And will it stand up in court? I've seen enough testimony thrown out for lack of corroboration." Karim leaned forward across the desk, pointing his pen at Saxena. "I've got a better way, Saxena. Tell your men to say that the seller's name will be kept secret and that there will be a reward of five hundred rupees if his information results in a conviction. Understand? We attract the fly with sugar, not pepper."

"Yes, sir."

"Misra!" Karim called to his head constable. "More tea, please." He lit up another cigarette. "Anything else, Saxena? No new evidence at all?"

"Not yet, Superintendent Sahib." A puzzled look appeared in Saxena's eyes.

"What about the two petrol tins? You know, the one from the railway yard and the other one from the university. Have you taken them around to all the petrol pumps for identification?" Misra entered with fresh teacups and removed the empty ones from Karim's desk. "Close the door when you go out, Misra."

"They're both badly burned, sahib. How can they be identified?"

Karim leaned forward in his chair, barely able to keep his fists from pounding the desk. He arranged his papers into orderly piles while he thought about his answer.

"You surprise me, Saxena. You really do. You're not serious, are you? What's happened to all your training and experience?"

"What are you talking about?" Saxena demanded, scowling. His eyes burned into Karim's, hostile, challenging.

"Do you seriously mean to imply that no information can be got from those tins just because they're badly burned?"

"Well, I suppose we could take them around. The petrol dealers might be able to identify them. Maybe they could tell us who bought petrol by the tin." Saxena cleared his throat and wiped his nose again with his handkerchief. "Maybe . . ."

"Maybe you'd better get on it straightaway, Saxena, before their memories get too hazy. And go to *all* the petrol pumps. Some lorry operators and factories have their own pumps. And while you're asking, check for any safety violations. You understand what I'm saying?"

"Yes, Superintendent Sahib." Saxena grinned and relaxed.

"One more thing. This investigation must be speeded up. There's too much at stake here." Karim paused, pondering how best to inform Saxena of his decision, finally deciding to come straight out with it. "I'm taking over, Saxena. From now on report to me every morning for instructions."

Saxena's hands clenched into fists, and he quickly lowered them out of Karim's sight. "But Superintendent Sahib," he whined, "you explicitly gave me the railway bogie fire. It took place before you took charge of the district, and it's rightly my responsibility."

"You've had a month, Saxena, and where have you got to? Those petrol tins. Why should I have to tell you what to do with them? And the suitcase. Do you see what I mean?" Karim rearranged the papers on his desk and moved his telephone away from the edge. "Now understand this, Saxenaji," he continued in a milder tone, "I'm not going to announce to the world that I'm taking over. You'll continue to work on the case. But you'll follow my instructions and you'll report to me every day. Understood? Right. Now get cracking on those two projects."

Saxena rose and pulled down his rumpled uniform jacket. He started toward the door, stopped, turned to Karim as if to say something, and then turned back to the door and left the room. Karim heard him curse at a hapless constable as he clumped into his own office.

With a sigh Karim lit another cigarette and turned to the pile of reports on his desk. Saxena was gone, but the acrid odor of his body still pervaded the room.

Superintendent Karim drove his jeep through the gate in the wall enclosing the cluster of one-story buildings that served as the Ramgarh District Hospital and parked under a tree. He took his briefcase from the seat and walked up a red dirt driveway toward the main building, stepping carefully between knots of people sitting on the ground, talking, eating, and playing with small children. He waved away the peddlers of empty glass bottles and vials. What an absurdity, he thought. The outmoded infusions, decoctions, embrocations, and tinctures that the government provided would be contaminated as soon as the pharmacist dispensed them.

Reaching the veranda he threaded his way through a wretched crowd of patients—dull-eyed mothers with lethargic children at the breast, heavily bandaged sufferers with head or limb swathed in dirty cotton, feeble old men and women waiting to be cared for. He wrinkled his nose against the smells of antiseptic, unwashed bodies, and dried blood.

"*Arrey, chaukidar*!" he called to an old watchman wearing a white turban and a green sash. "Where is Doctor Lalchand's office?" The *chaukidar* raised his hand to smooth his handlebar mustache, squinted at Karim's uniform through aged eyes, and gestured that Karim should follow him. They entered the building and stepped carefully down a corridor even more densely packed and noisy than the veranda. Patients were waiting in irregular queues to enter two examining rooms, one for men with a male doctor and another for women and children with a female doctor. They leaned against the walls, adding their personal contributions to the dirt and hair oil that soiled the peeling whitewash.

At the end of the corridor the *chaukidar* opened the door to a rear veranda and led Karim to the right. When the door closed behind them the tap of a typewriter and the murmur of educated voices replaced the noise of the corridor. The man held open a printed curtain and gestured Karim to enter a small outer office, where a male typist took his name and asked him to sit.

"Doctor Lalchand is with a patient, Superintendent Sahib. He'll be coming just now."

A pleasant office, Karim thought. Nice curtains. Red flowers in a vase. Looks like a woman's touch. Orderly. No mounds of files in the corners, gathering dust. A diploma on the wall from Grant Medical College in Bombay. An image flashed into Karim's mind of his young wife, dying in agony far from a hospital. Then his wife was replaced by Ellen Siddiqi, standing naked in the corner and beckoning to him. Karim rested his briefcase on his lap and stared at the diploma, but Ellen's image would not go away.

"Superintendent Karim! Good afternoon, good afternoon!" Dr. Lalchand bustled in, wearing a white coat with a stethoscope and other medical paraphernalia in the pockets. The man had to practice real medicine, Karim thought, in addition to running the hospital and coping with the paper work. "Sorry to keep you waiting. Emergency. A rabid dog bit one of our peons. He came here straightaway, thank God. His neighbors killed the dog." Lalchand wiped his cleanshaven cheeks with a handkerchief. "I've given him the first antirabies injection. Nasty business, Superintendent Sahib. A long needle into the abdomen." Karim winced. "Fourteen times, no less." Lalchand brightened. "So how are you keeping?"

"Very well, Doctor Sahib. I'm staying away from dogs." Both men chuckled. "About the body of that burned man. We're posting notices. If we don't get some information in about a week, we'll get an order to take it off your hands."

"Good," Lalchand said. "As the weather gets warmer we'll begin to have trouble with it. And ice is expensive." He winked.

"And, uh, Doctor Sahib, these records," Karim opened his briefcase and pulled out a file, "the ones you sent me yesterday . . ."

"Have you found them useful? This man—Ram Singh he calls himself—seems to be something of a mystery. Have you checked his . . ."

"Uh, Doctor Sahib, perhaps we could continue our talk in private?"

"Oh! Of course. Sorry. Just step into my office here."

Lalchand grinned. "Top secret stuff, eh?" He led the way into his private office.

Twenty minutes later Karim and Lalchand emerged from the office and stepped out onto the veranda. "I'm going to Building Three, Kaushal," Lalchand called back to his clerk. "Come on, Superintendent Sahib. It's the surgical ward, just over there in the corner of the compound."

Building Three was also a one-storied structure with a veranda. The two men were met by the sister-in-charge, a tall Anglo-Indian woman with a massive bosom, wearing a white cap. She reminded Karim of the fishing boats he had seen in Bombay Harbor during the war.

"Has the explosion patient been moved to a private room, Sister Amelia?" Lalchand inquired. That tone, Karim thought. A man telling his banker that his payment would be late. Karim smiled cordially at her, knowing that in her own domain the sister-in-charge had the power of a maharajah. Sister Amelia nodded majestically to Lalchand and Karim and convoyed them down the veranda to a small room at the corner of the building.

"Wake up, Ram Singh!" Sister Amelia commanded. "You have visitors!" With a firm but gentle movement she raised the patient's head and chest so that he could see Karim and Lalchand. Karim could barely avoid recoiling when the man's body was raised. The head was almost totally bandaged; only the left eye and part of the mouth were visible. The heavily bandaged right forearm was strapped across the man's chest, but it was truncated, reaching only to the breastbone. A yellow intravenous fluid dripped into his left forearm, while another yellow fluid dripped out of him into a bottle hanging on the side of the bed. Horrible! Yet there was a man under those layers of cotton. In pain. Clinging to life.

Dr. Lalchand was less moved by the patient's plight.

"Well now," he said in a loud voice. "You have a visitor. Your first visitor, isn't it? Have you no family? This is Superintendent Karim from the police. He wants to ask you some questions. Can you hear me?" Dr. Lalchand bent over and put his ear to the man's mouth. "He says he can't hear me. Nonsense! You were talking with the nurses at noontime! You can hear me perfectly." The man's eye closed. "No so fast, young man!" Rising and turning to Karim, the doctor shook his head and muttered, "We can ask, but that won't make him answer. Maybe it will be better if you give me the questions and I'll ask them. It also might be safer to keep you away from direct contact with him."

Karim took a deep breath, wishing that he had been puffing on a Sepoy. "Ask him those questions we discussed, Doctor Sahib," he said.

"*What is your name?*" the doctor said and held his ear to the man's mouth. "Ram Singh, he says, Superintendent Sahib."

"*Where do you live? Mohalla . . . ?* Ah, *Mohalla* Loharia—the blacksmiths.

"*And who is your employer?* Shiv Narayan, superintendent at the sugar mill.

"*How did this accident take place?* He says a boiler exploded while he was mending it. Let him rest for a minute, Superintendent. Sister Amelia, will you look after him please, while we go out on the veranda."

"Well, what do you think?" Lalchand asked, as they lighted cigarettes. "His answers are consistent with his previous statements."

"Consistent, Doctor Sahib, but false. There was no explosion at the sugar mill," Karim said quietly. "Shiv Narayan has no employee named Ram Singh. No one living in *Mohalla* Loharia has verified this man's story." He paused, drew on his cigarette, and looked out across the compound. "Doctor Sahib, I think . . . I mean, I have good reason to believe this man was engaged in illegal acts involving an unregistered pistol." He turned back to the doctor. "What about my asking the questions? Is it safe?"

"Hmm. Well, I don't know. Maybe if you wear a clean white coat over your uniform it will be all right." Lalchand looked into the room. "Sister, please have an orderly bring the white coat from my office. It's hanging on a hook. We'll look after the patient."

A groaning man was carried into the ward on a stretcher by two orderlies. His clothes and shoes were piled around his body. "Hit by a lorry this morning," Lalchand said. "Broken ribs and an arm. He'll survive."

"What chance does Ram Singh have, Doctor Sahib?"

"Less than fifty percent, I'd say. Infection. That's our biggest worry in cases like this." Lalchand shrugged. "There's a landowner's son in there with a compound fracture of the leg. Broken bones were coming out through the skin. His father brought penicillin from the market and the leg is healing nicely." He smiled wryly. "This man here has to make do with sulfas. You see how well our government looks after its people?" Karim smiled also. "Those powder burns," Lalchand went on, "the ones mentioned in the records. They're questionable. We have no pathologist to make a positive identification, and I couldn't swear it was *not* a pressure boiler explosion." He turned away from Karim and looked at the sparse grass of the hospital compound. "You know, even if he lives he may suffer from brain damage."

"Brain damage? What kind?"

"Well, I can't say. We have no neurologist here. It depends on how much the blood vessels and the brain itself are damaged. He may not be able to walk or to speak as well as he did. You can't predict these things."

"Poor fellow," Karim said. The injuries were far worse than any penalty the law might impose. And what if he were innocent? What if he were just boasting about the pistol? Some men would do that.

Karim pulled absent-mindedly at his mustache. After a moment he said, "Doctor Sahib, I'm in a quandary. If I press this man too hard, his life might be in danger. But if he really did have an unregistered pistol, the community may be in danger. There may be who knows how many other illegal pistols in Ramgarh, ready to be used for some crime. Do you see my problem?"

"I see your problem. But I'm a doctor, not a policeman. I have to make medical judgments. Here's your white coat now. I'm going to give you five minutes with him, no more. Let's go in now."

Karim leaned over the bed and put his mouth close to the patient's head. "I am the superintendent of police," he said in a loud voice. "Your name is not Ram Singh and you don't work in the sugar mill. What is your name?" He put his ear close to the man's mouth. There was no answer.

"Where did you get that pistol that exploded in your hand? Hey? Answer me! The pistol! Where did you get it? Who gave it to you?" Again there was no answer.

"Easy, Superintendent. He can't take much more," the doctor reminded Karim.

"Listen to me now," Karim nearly shouted. "We know you had an unregistered pistol. If you get out of this hospital, we're going to arrest you and charge you with illegal possession. Understand? Illegal possession! Three years in prison! Do you hear me? If you tell me all about it we can try to get you off. You understand me?"

Again the man refused or was unable to answer. Karim

straightened up and looked at Dr. Lalchand.

"That's all, Superintendent. Come back in a week or so. Maybe he'll be a little better then."

Karim's shoulders slumped and his legs dragged as he found his way back to the jeep. How many pistols were out there in the narrow lanes and crowded tenements of the city, waiting to be used by violent men? How many such men would be waiting in the crowd when the prime minister came to Ramgarh in less than two weeks?

27

"No, sahib! Please! No!"

Deputy Superintendent Mohan Saxena tightened his grip on Aijana Bibi's thick black hair and pulled her head back. Her arms, tightly fastened behind her with his leather belt, twisted helplessly. Their naked bodies were locked together by his powerful right arm holding her to him.

"Drink! Drink, I said!" He forced the mouth of a bottle of fiery country rum between her lips and against her clenched teeth. He tipped the bottle and rum spilled out between her teeth into her throat. More ran down her chin and between her breasts. Aijana choked and coughed and screamed.

"You bitch! I'll show you who's in charge around here!" Saxena yelled. He gave Aijana a stinging blow on the cheek with the flat of his hand. Aijana stopped screaming, gasped, and began to wail, tears streaming from her eyes. "Shut up! Shut up, I said!" Saxena threw Aijana face down on the white mattress and took another large swill of rum.

"Shut up, you whore!" Saxena shouted as Aijana continued to wail into the mattress. He stood over her, struggling to keep his balance, fighting to control the murderous fury that had come close to boiling over since Karim's arrival.

His penis hung soft and limp beneath a belly that was running to fat. He swayed and took another swallow of liquor, emptying the bottle. He cursed and threw it to the corner of the room, where it shattered on the floor.

Saxena turned to look at Aijana. She lay on her stomach with her hips supported by the end of one of the bolsters, which had fallen across the mattress in their convulsive intercourse earlier in the evening. Aijana had been better than ever. She had made his body squirm and his heart pound with pleasure. What a girl! And what a fool he'd been, boasting about leading the P.M.'s motorcade in from Nawabganj. Maybe the rum would make her forget what he had said. If only she would stop that infernal wailing.

With bloodshot eyes Saxena saw Aijana's wrists twisting inside the leather loops that restrained them. He saw the swelling roundness of her bottom, thrust into prominence by the bolster. He kneeled down beside her.

"Are you going to be quiet? No? Then I'll give you something to yell about!" Saxena raised his hand and gave Aijana a burning spank on the bottom. She screamed. Placing his left hand on her neck to hold her down, he gave her six more blows. Aijana screamed louder than ever, thrashing wildly to escape the blows.

"Who's there?" Saxena demanded in answer to an insistent tapping on the door.

"It's Zakia Begum, sahib. Is everything all right?" Her voice was soft and plaintive. Aijana Bibi stopped wailing and lay quietly on the mattress. Marks from Saxena's hand began to appear on her bottom.

"Leave me alone, woman! I'll call you when I want you." Saxena turned to Aijana. His penis now stood erect and swollen, a monstrous organ that he cradled in his hand as he watched Aijana tremble in anticipation of the next blow.

"Did I hurt my little Aijana Bibi?" Saxena crooned, while

he stroked and kneaded the girl's burning bottom. "Are you going to be a good girl and not make so much noise, my little one?"

"Yes, sahib," she answered in a weak and breathless voice. Saxena lifted her hips, pushed the bolster aside, and turned Aijana onto her back. She groaned as her body pressed down on her bound wrists. She spread her legs to accept Saxena's huge organ inside her.

"Sahib, please untie my hands. It hurts too much," Aijana pleaded. "I'm sorry I screamed so much. I won't do it any more."

"That's my good girl. If you want me to come to you, you have to do what I like. Here, let me lift you up." Saxena pulled Aijana into an upright position, keeping her impaled on his penis. He reached behind her and removed the belt from her wrists. Aijana stretched her arms with relief and wrapped them around Saxena's neck. Shifting her legs to support herself, she began to bounce up and down on Saxena's organ. "That's good! I like that. You've not done that before. Good. Good. Good. Good. Aaaaaaah!" A powerful spasm shook Saxena and he fell forward, pinning Aijana beneath him. He lay there, silent, still.

Aijana Bibi gasped under Saxena's weight. "Sahib?" she whispered into his ear. There was no answer. Managing to push Saxena's legs aside, she extricated herself from beneath him. She stood up and wiped herself with a towel from the shelf near the door.

"Are you sleeping, sahib?" Aijana looked at Saxena's face, which was half buried in the white mattress cover. She knelt down to look more closely and, with difficulty, turned his head toward her. She bent her head down to call his name, and she noticed that there was no breath.

Aijana jumped up, her hands over her mouth, her eyes wide. She stood there for a full minute as if paralyzed by the sight of Saxena's body. Suddenly she turned, unbolted the door, and ran screaming down the corridor.

"What are you doing here, girl?" Zakia Begum demanded when Aijana Bibi burst totally naked through the printed curtain into the waiting room. "Get back into your room with the sahib. Do you want to be punished?"

"Mem . . . mem . . . memsahib!"

Zakia turned to the customer waiting in the cane chair. "Sometimes you wonder where young people learn their manners these days. Look at this one. No decency or modesty at all."

"Memsahib! Come quickly!"

Zakia Begum followed Aijana Bibi down the corridor, muttering imprecations at the waywardness of young people. She entered the room and stopped short. Saxena was lying as Aijana had left him.

"Saxena Sahib?"

"I think he's dead, memsahib," Aijana whispered.

Zakia uttered a hoarse cry, then quickly covered her mouth with the end of her sari. She looked wildly around the room. "I'll be ruined! This is terrible! I'll be ruined! I'll be ruined!"

Aijana told her what had happened. "What shall we do, memsahib?" Zakia chewed the end of her sari. She walked around the room pulling at her hair, shaking her fists. Then she stopped, smiled, and turned to Aijana.

"Get dressed, girl. Don't touch anything." Zakia returned to the waiting room.

"I'm so sorry for the disturbance, Bhargava Sahib," she said to the customer. "Just a minor matter. The electric heater failed to work in Aijana's room and the child was getting a chill. But the excitement seems to have brought on her menses a day early. I'm sorry. I know you were waiting for her tonight."

"That's all right. I'll have another girl."

"Bhargava Sahib, you and I are old friends, isn't it? Well, I'm afraid I'll have to close early just this one time." Zakia Begum sat down next to Bhargava and stroked the sleeve of his jacket. "I know you've been waiting and I hate to disappoint you." Her voice was soft and intimate. "Come tomorrow night and you can have another girl without any charge. All night if you wish."

Bhargava looked carefully at Zakia Begum. Her eyes, rimmed with kohl, pleaded with him. Something must be going on. He had never known her to close up with a customer waiting or to offer one of her girls free of charge.

"Well, all right. Save Hamida for me. I'll be here tomorrow at nine."

As Bhargava went down the stairs, Zakia Begum rushed to the kitchen where she found her *chokra*, the teenage son of a long-departed prostitute, who helped the cook and did all the chores, asleep on a mat.

She shook him awake.

"Latif, wake up! I want you to take this chit." She scribbled a short message on a piece of paper. "Run quickly to Ram Lal Prasad's bungalow. You know it, don't you? Good. This is very important. He must come at once, alone. Understand? Now go!" Zakia went back to the waiting room and sat in the chair by the window, looking out at the dark and narrow street.

Fifteen minutes later Ram Lal Prasad climbed the stairs to Zakia Begum's floor, panting slightly at the familiar exertion. She met him at the top, her finger over her lips. She let him in, locked the door, and turned off the light at the bottom of the stairs.

"Sahib," she whispered, "you are good to help an old woman who needs your advice. Come into the waiting room and have a sweet."

"Don't give me any sweets, woman! Just tell me why you called me over here at this hour!"

"Sahib, you are president of the Municipal Committee. You know how to handle these things."

"What things, for God's sake?"

"Sahib, Deputy Superintendent Saxena is in Aijana Bibi's room . . . dead."

"What do you mean, dead? Who killed him?"

"He just died, sahib. He was with Aijana and he just died."

"Let me see." Prasad dashed down the corridor to Aijana's room. Hamida and Abda, Zakia's other girls, were standing in the corner, whispering to each other. Aijana Bibi sat on the floor against the wall, crying softly.

Prasad felt for Saxena's pulse. The body was beginning to get cold. His mind raced. He had heard of things like this happening in moments of extreme passion. What did they call it? Stroke? Apoplexy? Heart attack? Yes, that's what it probably was. He wanted nothing to do with this business. But he didn't want Aijana Bibi to get into trouble, maybe go to jail, perhaps be sent to a shelter in some place far away. He looked at Aijana, squatting against the wall in the corner, tears draining down her cheeks.

"It wasn't your fault, my princess. A heart attack. Saxena Sahib had a heart attack." Prasad went over to Aijana, squatted down, and took her tear-stained face in his hands. "You're not to blame, my child." He stood up and pondered the situation.

"Very well," Prasad said. "Take a towel and a little water and wipe Saxena's genitals. Turn him over first. Here, we have to do it together, he's heavy. Good. Now, let's get him dressed. Where are his vest and underpants? I'll put them on him.

"Now then, where are his clothes? Ah. First his trousers. Now his socks and shoes. Good. Now his shirt and tie. That's good. He's beginning to look more presentable. Where's his jacket?"

"Here are his jacket and pistol, sahib," Zakia Begum said.

"Let me look in the pockets first." Identification card. Twenty-two rupees. Some change. Pen and pencil. Notebook. What was this? *Achcha?* Prasad opened an envelope and removed a typewritten document. Preventive detention order number 257, effective at 6:00 A.M. on January 31, 1952. Here's the name. Gupta! He looked at Saxena, lying on the mattress with his eyes open. Must have been preparing to serve the order and stopped off for a romp on his way. He returned the document to its envelope and put it in the jacket pocket.

"Sit him up, Zakia. Let's put his jacket on him. You girls lend a hand. Now the cap. Good. Now, where's your *chokra*? We need him to get the body out of here and down into the street."

Using a staw mat to slide the body, Prasad and the boy pulled Saxena down the corridor to the top of the stairs. Then the body was turned around and slowly lowered feet first to the bottom of the dark staircase. When they reached street level Prasad opened the door and looked out. Raucous laughter came from a brothel down the street, but there was no one walking or standing nearby. They pulled Saxena into the street and moved him to a shadowed area near the competing brothel. Then they extracted the mat from under the body and dashed back to Zakia Begum's doorway.

"Take this mat up to memsahib, *chokra*," Prasad ordered, "and tell her that I'll come by tomorrow to see her." Meanwhile, Prasad thought, he had to visit a friend in *Mohalla* Kanungoyan.

28

Karim picked up his telephone. "Doctor Sahib. How are you? Yes. It's been a violent month, hasn't it? Yes. What have you found out about Saxena?" Karim took a pencil and began to make notes. "No foul play? Really? Syphilis. Syphilis? Contagious? I wonder if he knew he had it? I see. How do you spell that? When would you put the time of death? I see." Karim looked through his office doorway and saw Head Constable Misra within earshot. "One moment, Doctor Sahib. Misra!" Karim called. "Run over to the *godown* room and fetch me some new notebooks. *Achcha*, Doctor Sahib, let me repeat to you what I've noted down. Cause of death: coronary thrombosis. Underlying conditions: advanced cardiovascular syphilis and atherosclerosis. No sign of any foul play. Probable time of death near midnight. What's that? Louder, please, Doctor Sahib. That bad, eh. At any time. I wonder when he had his last physical examination. Very well, Doctor Sahib. You'll send me the official report? Thank you, sir. Yes. Goodbye, Doctor Sahib."

Karim laid the telephone in its cradle and leaned back in his chair. So Saxena had just dropped dead in his tracks. In *Mohalla* Tavaif in front of a house of prostitution. Well, that explained the syphilis. He sighed. Thank God there was no need for a murder investigation. Where was that new packet of Sepoys?

But why had Saxena been in front of a whorehouse when he was supposed to be picking up Gupta for preventive detention? What had happened to his revolver? And how had Gupta found out about the PDO in time to go underground? Was there a connection? Saxena. Was he an R.S.S. sympathizer? What about the others? How many of his officers had been holding back because he was a Muslim? Karim felt his armpits beginning to sweat. He opened his jacket and loosened his shirt collar. He drew on his cigarette, but the smoke tasted like manure. He stubbed out the cigarette in the ashtray and sat with his hands on his desk, clenching them into fists so tightly that they trembled.

Gupta. Where could he have gone? Someone must be sheltering him. Yet he couldn't stay out of sight forever. He had to come up. And when he did, he'd be picked up.

Unless . . . he was wearing a disguise. He would have a good chance to slip right past them in the right disguise. Oh God! Let him be found quickly!

After a moment he stood up, wiped his face with his handkerchief, and stepped over to his office window. The grass in the police compound needed cutting. A *bhishti* was spraying the dirt footpaths with water from a goatskin bag. An off-duty policeman, in shorts, undershirt, and sneakers, walked past the window carrying a soccer ball under his arm. Misra returned from the *godown.* Everything seemed peaceful. But Karim had a sense of foreboding that struck him like a hard blow to the stomach.

"Telephone, Superintendent Sahib. Subinspector Pathak from the *tahsil chauki.*"

"Yes, Pathak," Karim said into the telephone. "What is it?"

"It's terrible, sahib! You must come quickly!" Pathak sounded in panic. His breath made a great hissing noise over the telephone.

"Pathak, calm down! What is terrible? Tell me at once!"

"Sahib! Sahib! Someone has thrown a dead pig into the *Jama Masjid* during the Sabbath service! I can't handle it, sahib! I . . . I . . . Help me, sahib!"

"Wait there, Pathak!" Karim shouted into the telephone, but Pathak had rung off.

"Misra, my jeep, *ek dum*! Where is Inspector Hafiz-ur-Rehman?"

"In court, sir. The bus stand robbery. He's testifying."

"Send a jeep to collect him. I want him to meet me at the *Jama Masjid* as soon as possible. Emergency!" Karim buttoned up his uniform and strapped his holstered pistol around his waist. There was no time to lose. If word of this atrocious desecration of the great Friday mosque were to spread unchecked through the Muslim *mohallas* of the city, if the rumormongers and the young Muslim *budmashes* heard a distorted and exaggerated story, a communal riot would be inevitable. And with it, injury and death. Could two Muslim policemen stop it in time?

Karim's driver turned on the siren as they dashed through the gate and onto the Grand Trunk Road. Traffic was light. The Muslim merchants and workers were at home, while the Hindus were still taking their afternoon naps. The jeep turned into Mahatma Gandhi Road and began the long ascent to the *Jama Masjid*, whose white domes shone majestically in the winter sunlight.

Karim gripped the windscreen frame with both hands. How like his headlong ride down the Grand Trunk Road only a month before, when his hands had been shackled. Most of the shops on M.G. Road were shuttered. But these were mostly Hindu-owned businesses. The real danger lay in the Muslim *mohallas*, in those narrow twisting alleys and courtyards where the young Muslims might be collecting clubs and bricks and preparing to march.

The jeep squealed to a stop in front of the *Jama Masjid*. A policeman was standing guard at the entrance. Karim kicked off his shoes and raced through the gate into the rectangular outer court, where he found Pathak surrounded by about a dozen elderly men, all remonstrating with him in loud voices. Their bearded faces and waving arms were only inches from his face. Pathak seemed nearly in tears.

"Pathak!" Karim called. "Where is the *imam*?"

"Superintendent Sahib! You're here! Gentlemen!" he cried to his tormentors. "The superintendent of police is here. Superintendent Karim, a Muslim like you. Everything will be all right. Just calm down and everything will be put right."

It was now Karim who was surrounded by the old men. "Take me to the *imam*, my brothers!" he demanded. Clutching hands pulled him to a corner of the court and pointed to the carcass of a dark gray boar, the kind that was usually found rooting in the garbage piles and drains of the Untouchable *mohallas*.

"Pathak!"

"Yes, Superintendent Sahib!"

"Go across the road to the *chauki* and get the sweeper. Have him come back with you and remove this carcass *ek dum*. Have him dispose of it."

"Yes, sir!" Pathak shouted, relief shining in his face.

"Now, brothers, take me to the *imam*," Karim repeated. Muttering and waving their arms, the old Muslims led him into the *maksoura*, the hall of prayer, where Karim found the *imam* sitting on the marble floor reading the Holy

Koran. He was a pale, gaunt, bearded old man, wearing spectacles and dressed in a robe and turban of white wool. He's already dressed in mourning for the lost purity of the mosque, Karim thought.

He sat down on the floor in front of the *imam* and waited. The old men retreated until they were barely within earshot and sat down themselves, a cluster of beards, turbans, and skullcaps moving this way and that as they grumbled to each other. The *imam* continued to read and stroke his beard. After about ten minutes he closed the Koran, removed his glasses, and raised his eyes to Karim. The eyes were filmed by age and cataracts, but their expression was shrewd. The man was no fanatic.

"*Imam* Sahib, I am Mohammed Abdul Karim Khan, superintendent of police for Ramgarh District." The *imam* said nothing. "May I speak with you about the sacrilege that has taken place?"

"This holy place has been profaned, my son," the *imam* said after a moment. He sounded sad rather than resentful. A good sign.

"It was a provocation, *Imam* Sahib. It was political, not religious. There are people in this city who seek to provoke violence between the Muslim and Hindu communities. They are bad people. Shall we allow ourselves to fall into their trap?" The *imam* was silent. Sweat dripped down Karim's body under his winter uniform jacket. He struggled to keep his voice calm and earnest.

"*Imam* Sahib, the Hindu and Muslim communities in Ramgarh have been at peace for a long time. But there are some who would make political capital out of violence, disorder, and death—the death of Muslim women and children, of old Muslims and very young Muslims, people who can't defend themselves."

"What do you propose, my son?" the *imam* said. Thank God! He was listening! The *imam* was listening!

"*Imam* Sahib, let the police find the culprits and bring them to punishment under the law. Let the Muslims remain at peace with their Hindu neighbors. Let them not allow a few *budmashes* to provoke them to senseless violence." Karim took a deep breath. "*Imam* Sahib, will you tell these men here to go into the *mohallas* and spread the word?"

The *imam* stroked his beard and looked carefully at Karim. Then he reached for Karim's shoulders with both hands, pulled his face closer, and peered into his eyes. Karim tried to swallow, but his throat was paralyzed. The seconds passed as if they were eons.

"You are right, my son. You speak the truth. I will talk to these men. But what about the others? The men here are only the remnant. There were others who went away before you came."

Karim's shoulders slumped. The mosque had suddenly become his tomb. Probably the most bitter men had left the mosque and gone to their *mohallas*, eager to rouse the young Muslims and get revenge.

"Send them out as quickly as you can, *Imam* Sahib. Let them bring your message to the Muslim people." Karim thought fast. How could the *imam's* message be gotten to the largest number of Muslims? How could enough uncertainty be spread so that violent men would think before they acted? What was that scheme those Americans in Lucknow were using to teach reading? Each one teach one? Yes. That was it.

"*Imam* Sahib," Karim continued, "tell each man to get two others to take your message to two others, and so on, and so on—like the branches of a tree. This way the message will reach the greatest number in the shortest time."

"Praise be to God, my son! I will do it!" the *imam* said.

"Another cup, Karim?"

"No, thanks, Collector Sahib."

Bharat Chaudhri delicately placed his teacup and saucer in the serving tray on his desk. He selected a pipe and carefully packed it from a newly opened tin of Senior Service Virginia Flake. Karim offered him his box of matches, but Chaudhri waved them away and struck his own. Karim lighted a cigarette and waited while the collector set fire to the tobacco. When it was burning well Chaudhri brushed some bits of ash from his tweed jacket, squeezed the creases of his gray flannel trousers between his thumb and forefinger, and settled back in his chair.

"Now then, Karim, what was it that brought you to my office without even making an appointment?"

Karim looked intently at Chaudhri, hoping to impress him with the gravity of his visit. "Collector Sahib," he said, "I have serious news to give you. The *Jama Masjid* in the old city. You know it?"

"Of course, Karim." Chaudhri swiveled to the left, his pipe between his teeth and his fingertips touching in front of his face. "It's a reasonably decent example of the late Moghul style. There's an interesting use of brick in the—"

"Collector Sahib, this afternoon, during the *khutba* service, someone threw a dead pig into the outer court of the mosque."

"—bases of the minarets. The prayer niche has . . . What did you say, Karim?"

"I said, sir, that a dead pig was thrown into the outer court of the mosque during the Sabbath service this afternoon."

Chaudhri swiveled around and stared at Karim. "But that's disgraceful, Karim!" His reaction seemed genuine. He hadn't appeared so distressed since he had agreed to apply for the preventive detention order for Gupta. He sucked noisily on his pipe and blew out clouds of smoke. "What do you make of it? Who would do such a dastardly thing?"

"I've wondered about that myself, sir. It could only be someone who wants to start trouble between the communities. But I've had no intelligence about any group or conspiracy."

"A dangerous situation, Karim! Dangerous! The mind boggles, Karim! The mind boggles! What have you done about it?"

"I've left a Muslim police inspector at the mosque to reassure anyone who comes there. And the *imam* has agreed to oppose any retaliation by the Muslims." Karim described how the *imam*'s message would be spread through the Muslim *mohallas*. "I don't think there will be any trouble today, sir. It's the Sabbath. But there's sufficient danger that I have to request you to issue a ban on gatherings and processions starting tomorrow."

"You have it, Karim! You have it!" Chaudhri pressed the button under his desk. Joshi appeared. "Joshi! Type up an order for Ramgarh City—"

"And Cantonment, sir," Karim interjected.

"—and Cantonment. All unauthorized gatherings of more than five persons and all processions, except weddings and funerals, are banned indefinitely, starting from eight o'clock tomorrow morning. You know the form. Then give it to me for signature and take it to the printer. I want the order distributed and posted tonight."

"If the printer will deliver them to my office, I'll see to the distribution and posting, sir."

"Now then, Karim," Chaudhri said, tapping his pipe into

the ashtray, "I have a little question for you. What about our friend Gupta, who so easily managed to escape preventive detention?"

Karim crossed his legs and lighted another cigarette. The collector's sarcasm was justified. He himself would have been more than unhappy if a suspect had evaded arrest after all that paper work and those telephone calls to Lucknow.

"It's very unfortunate, sir. We're looking for him. We're watching his house and his friends. It's strange how he apparently found out about the PDO in time to go underground."

"A leak, Karim! A leak! There must have been a leak somewhere. One can't trust anyone these days. By the way, have you seen this?" Chaudhri reached into his desk drawer, extracted a crudely printed leaflet, and passed it across to Karim. The leaflet was printed in Hindi, but it dealt with the Muslim University. The Muslim University was a hotbed of treason! The Muslim University must become a secular institution and admit fifty percent Hindu students! The Muslim University must adopt Hindi as its medium of instruction! The new vice chancellor must secularize the Muslim University!

Karim shivered. His hands trembled as he held the leaflet. The circumstantial evidence was there. The fire at the university. The missing case of pistol ammunition. The man in the hospital with his hand blown off. Gupta gone underground. And now the pig in the mosque and these leaflets, which were directed at the Muslim students even though they were in Hindi.

"Do you see it now, Collector Sahib? It all fits together. Someone is trying to stir up communal violence." Karim stubbed out his cigarette, stood up, and paced back and forth. "The prime minister," he said. "Someone out there wants to embarrass him with a communal riot. Are they trying to scare him so he won't come? But that's ridiculous. If anything, a communal riot would make him more likely to come. Then why?"

"Are you thinking what I'm thinking, Karim?"

"What are you thinking, Collector Sahib?"

"It's a plot." Chaudhri spoke softly, with none of his usual animation. "Someone is trying to make sure the P.M. does come to the university so they can kill him."

"But if that happens, it will be the Muslims who'll be blamed, sir. And that's ridiculous also! Nehru is the best friend of the Muslims. No Muslim would try to kill Nehru!"

"I know that, Karim, and you know that. But do the Hindu masses know that, Karim? Do the Hindu masses know that?"

Karim shivered. That pyramid. There it was again. Pressing him down. The Hindu population would not make fine distinctions, Poonawalla had said.

"Collector Sahib, the situation is dangerous. Something must be done."

"What do you have in mind, Karim? What do you have in mind? And remember, it must be done quickly. The installation ceremony is only one week away!"

29

The angry words flowed over the crowd of students like breakers crashing on a bouldered shore. One after another, smooth young faces leaned over the lectern and black-clad arms waved as the speakers vented their feelings in impassioned Urdu about the desecration of the *Jama Masjid*. The Muslim University Union building was packed with enraged students. The chairs in the assembly room had been folded, and everyone stood so that more could crowd in. The smell of four hundred young men in black *shervanis* was enough to wrinkle the painted noses of the bearded patriarchs whose portraits hung on the walls of the stately white room.

On the dais in front, the speakers eagerly waited their turn to inflame the audience to more wrath. On either side there was a kind of cheerleader, a student who led the shouts of anger and the slogans that were picked up and chanted by the crowd. The more skillful speakers conducted the audience like an orchestra, extracting crescendos of cheers or jeers at the appropriate moment.

Anwar Hussain stood in the crowd, near the side of the room not far from the portrait of his uncle, former Vice Chancellor Liaquat Hussain Khan. From time to time he smiled, particularly when the crowd of students burst into an angry roar. Wait until they heard what he had to say. Then they would be ready for some action!

The group of students waiting to speak got smaller. Anwar pushed forward until he was near the dais. When the last speaker had finished, the president of the union came to the lectern and raised his arms to quiet the crowd.

"Fellow Ramgarh students!" the president shouted, when the noise had diminished to a murmur. "It is time for us to take action! It is time for us to express our anger and revulsion to the authorities!" He reached into his inside pocket and pulled out a sheet of paper. "I have in my hands the text of a resolution to be given to the district magistrate, demanding that the culprits be apprehended and punished, that Muslim mosques, shrines, cemeteries, and other religious monuments be protected against desecration, and that shops and offices be closed for one day as an act of contrition!"

"Mr. President! Mr. President!" Anwar Hussain shouted. "Mr. President, may I speak?" He waved the papers that he had brought to the meeting. "Before you vote on the resolution, I must tell you of other terrible things!"

The president looked down at Anwar and a smile brightened his round face. He raised his arms to quiet the crowd. "Fellow students, your attention please! Please! Fellow students!" The noise finally abated. "Fellow students, a former honorary secretary of the union is asking to speak. I have the honor to present to you a Ramgarh old boy and a member of the founding family of this university, Anwar Hussain of Ramgarh." Applause rippled through the audience as Anwar climbed up to the lectern, but there was not much enthusiasm behind it. These students were not fools, Anwar thought. If he was just another speaker for that toothless resolution, they had had enough.

Anwar stood alone at the lectern, his hawklike eyes staring out over the crowd. The students' muttering slowly ceased and they waited expectantly for his words.

"Students of the Muslim University," Anwar said softly. He was barely audible in the back of the hall and the students strained to hear him. "Your religion has been attacked. The sacred *Jama Masjid* has been desecrated. Do you know who has committed this atrocious act? What will the police and the district magistrate say to you? They will say that it was committed by a person or persons unknown."

Grumbling broke out in several parts of the hall. Let them grumble, Anwar thought. No need to rush things. He'd have them eating out of his hand in a few moments.

Anwar's voice grew louder. "But *we* know who desecrated our mosque," he continued. "Did the *Christians* desecrate our mosque?" A few Noes were shouted. "Did the *Parsis* desecrate our mosque?" More Noes were shouted out. "Did the *Buddhists* desecrate our mosque?" This time the entire audience shouted "No!" in unison as Anwar's direction became clear.

The president of the union whispered to some of the other students on the dais. He turned to the audience and searched it with a worried look on his face.

Anwar paused. The crowd was silent, the tension was palpable as they waited expectantly for his next question. He looked from side to side. Now was the time. Now! "Did the *Hindus* desecrate our mosque?" A roar of Yeses surged through the hall. The fervor of the *jihad*, the holy war, was visible in the students' faces.

The president of the union came to the lectern and stood beside Anwar Hussain, his arms raised to quiet the crowd.

"The vote! I call for the vote! The resolution!" Any more of this inflammatory rhetoric and the university would be in deep trouble with the authorities.

Anwar Hussain raised his hand with his papers and waved them in the air. "There are more terrible things going on, my brothers," he shouted. "You must hear me out!"

"The vote!" cried the president. A wave of Noes shouted him down.

"Students of the Muslim University!" Anwar's voice trembled. The crowd was hushed, waiting for more. The president retreated from the lectern. "It is not only that they have desecrated our sacred mosque. Now they are attacking our university!" He waved a paper in his hand and threw copies into the audience. "This is what they are saying about our university. They are saying that it is a hotbed of treason! They are saying that it must become a secular university and become fifty percent Hindu! They are saying that the medium of instruction in the Muslim University must be—not English, not our beautiful, cultured Urdu—they are saying it must be common Hindi!"

The crowd was silent, stunned. Then a tremendous roar burst out. Anwar smiled. The time for action had come. He raised his arms. "Muslims!" he called. "Our religion, our language, and our university are in mortal danger. Let the black flags of protest be unfurled! Let the Muslims assemble at the *Jama Masjid* and make their demands known to all of India! *Urdu zindabad! Hindi murdabad!* Long live Urdu! Death to Hindi!"

The cheering crowd surged forward. A group of students reached up and pulled Anwar Hussain onto their shoulders and began to carry him around the room. The crowd picked up the slogans and the assembly hall resounded with their shouts.

Anwar's bearers carried him out the door and into the university grounds, where students who had not been able to get into the union learned from others what he had said and took up the cry of the slogans. Within minutes black flags had appeared and a disorderly procession had formed, moving in the direction of the old city with Anwar at its head.

30

Mohammed Abdul Karim shivered, coughed, and pulled his dressing gown tighter around his thin body. He laid his newspaper on the table, stubbed out his cigarette, and prepared to attack the omelet that Faiz Khan had just set in front of him. Whatever might be said about his ability to keep the house clean and tidy, there was no denying that Faiz Khan was a first-class cook. His omelets were superb. Karim had once watched him as he beat the whites until they were stiff and fluffy and then folded in the yolks. When the mixture had been fried in ghee with onions and green chilies, it came out golden yellow, light, and delicious. Karim broke off a wedge of toast, covered it with a slice of omelet, and placed the savory combination in his mouth. *Shabbash* Faiz Khan! He'd done it again.

He chewed slowly, sensuously, relishing the precious minutes of freedom and relaxation he permitted himself on weekend mornings. The spicy taste of the omelet reminded him of the days when his wife had served him his breakfast and watched him eat, talking about her activities, her friends, her concerns for the baby growing inside her.

He turned again to the *Times of India*. On page three was a brief announcement that Prime Minister Nehru would visit Ramgarh in a week. He wondered if Gupta had access to a newspaper in his hiding place. Nothing yet about the *Jama Masjid* incident. Maybe he'd been lucky. Maybe it would pass with no real trouble. He took another bite of the omelet.

Faiz Khan shuffled in from the kitchen and placed two fresh slices of toast on the table. As he raised the pot to pour another cup of coffee, there was a loud pounding on the front door. Startled, the old man set the pot down with a crash, spilling coffee on the tablecloth. He stepped to the front door and slid open the bolt. Muthu Singh, the head constable in charge of the university police *chauki*, pushed past Faiz Khan into the room. He was sweating and breathing heavily.

"Well, Muthu Singh," Karim said, "you're in a hurry this morning. What's the problem?"

"Superintendent Sahib! I came as fast as I could," he panted. "The students! They're marching up University Road toward the city! They have black flags and they're shouting slogans!" Muthu Singh wiped his forehead with his sleeve.

"What are they shouting?" Karim remained calm.

"Something about Urdu and Hindi, sahib. And the university. And the *Jama Masjid.*" A muscle in Muthu Singh's face twitched uncontrollably. "It's a forbidden procession, Superintendent Sahib! I spoke to the leaders, but they refused to disperse."

"Did you recognize any of the leaders?" Karim asked, taking the last bit of omelet.

"No, sahib. But one of them seemed older than the rest." Muthu Singh extracted a rag from his pocket and wiped his neck. He had started to breathe more easily.

"How many students are there, Muthu Singh? Just give me an estimate."

"It looked like over a thousand, Superintendent Sahib."

"I wonder what they think they're up to," Karim said, rising from the table. Muthu Singh's estimate would be far too high, as was usual in situations like this one. But time was short. This procession had to be headed off before it got into serious trouble. He had to alert Om Prakash to get a couple of dozen men ready with *lathis* and steel helmets. Then they would have to disperse these students and arrest the leaders. And he would probably be well advised to get the P.M.'s security on the phone. Damn this whole business!

Karim paused at the living room door and turned to the head constable. "You did well to come to me immediately, Muthu Singh. I'm going to give you a *chit* for Subinspector Om Prakash. You'll get on your bicycle and take it to headquarters straightaway." Muthu Singh nodded his head vigorously. "But sit down and have a cup of coffee while I get it ready."

Muthu Singh smiled gratefully and accepted a cup from Faiz Khan. Karim envied him. The head constable no longer need worry. He had passed on the burden of dealing with the situation to higher authority.

31

Ellen Siddiqi asked her rickshaw *wallah* to wait on Mahatma Gandhi Road in front of Modern Tailors. She removed her sandals and entered the shop, carrying her package. It was the new *sari* she had bought in New Delhi, a pale green cotton with a border design of deeper green. Nothing very fancy or expensive but just the thing to have the *darzi* make into an everyday dress that Alice could wash and iron easily.

"Ah, memsahib! Good morning," the smiling Muslim proprietor said, stroking his hennaed beard. He sat cross-legged on the white sheet that covered the floor of his shop, stitching buttonholes on a white silk wedding *shervani*. In the rear of the shop, under the dim light of an unshaded bulb, two more tailors were rocking the treadles of their sewing machines. Ellen sat down on a folding chair, her back against a wall of shelves laden with boxes of buttons, rolls of ribbon and lace, and bolts of cloth.

"You bring *sari*, memsahib?" The tailor unwrapped Ellen's *sari* and spread it out on the sheet. "Beautiful! Beautiful *sari*, memsahib. We make very fine frock for you from this *sari*." The tailor ran his hand over the material, feeling its weight and texture. "Rashid!" he called to the younger of the two tailors. "Fetch tea for memsahib!"

"No tea, thank you, Mr. Hamid." Ellen reached into her shopping bag. "I've brought this picture from a magazine. Could you copy this dress?" The tailor waggled his head affirmatively. "But instead of long sleeves make the sleeves come to just above the elbow. And make the skirt shorter, because I'll be wearing sandals, not high heels." Ellen carefully pointed to the places she wanted changed.

"*Thik hai*, memsahib. Where you want this fancy part to go?"

"Is there enough to put it around the bottom of the skirt and on the collar and sleeves?" This followed the design in the illustration, but the *sari* was little more than a yard wide so that there were only about two yards of border.

"We try, memsahib. Now we measure." Hamid rose and took a tape measure from the shelf. "Rashid! Write down!"

"What's that noise, Mr. Hamid?"

"Noise, memsahib?"

"That shouting. It seems to be from down the street. Don't you hear it?"

"Ah, yes. I hear now. Nothing, memsahib. New cinema show, maybe? Ready, memsahib?"

Ellen stood quietly while Hamid measured her bust, waist, hips, arms, neck, and height, calling out the numbers in Urdu to Rashid. He asked how deep she wanted the neck opening to be, if she wanted a pocket, what kind of lining, what kind of buttons. He touched her as he would have touched a wounded hummingbird. Hamid was aware, Ellen knew, that the slightest hint of impropriety would make her take her business to one of his many competitors. Any of them would be delighted to sew a dress for her for less than five dollars.

Was that the sound of a siren in the distance? And that shouting noise. It seemed louder.

"You come next week for fitting, memsahib?" Hamid

asked as he completed the measuring. "You come Wednesday?"

"*Achcha*, Mr. Hamid. Until Wednesday, then." She raised her hand to her forehead. "*Salaam aleikum*." The Muslim greeting.

"*Aleikum salaam*, memsahib," Hamid responded, beaming with pleasure.

Ellen stepped out of the tailor shop into the warm sunshine of Mahatma Gandhi Road. As she replaced her sandals she noticed a *tonga* racing down the street. It was carrying two young men with shaved heads, who were shaking their fists and apparently shouting slogans.

International Electrical Stores, where Ellen wanted to buy some fresh batteries for her flashlights, was also on Mahatma Gandhi Road but farther down from the old city's core, closer to the railway station. She gestured to the rickshaw *wallah* to follow her as she window-shopped her way down the narrow, sloping street. Strangely, Mahatma Gandhi Road was practically empty, with none of its usual Saturday morning bustle. Ellen looked at the displays of Western goods this part of the road featured: radios, electrical goods, books, furniture, automobile parts. It was comforting to see the trade names she had grown up with—Ford, General Electric, Motorola, Lux. But the unusual quiet, the narrowness of the street, the nearly unbroken line of buildings on both sides—it was strange, like walking through a trench.

Ellen paused to look at a display of books and was nearly knocked over by a young man who rushed out of an alley and ran down the street. Looking after him she saw a crowd of black-clad men milling in the street near the Grand Trunk Road intersection, about a quarter mile away. Their dress resembled the *shervanis* she had seen the students wear. She could see black flags being waved and now could hear distinctly that slogans were being shouted in a rhythmic cadence. It didn't look like the typical procession advertising a new film program at the Picture Palace.

"Memsahib! No go, memsahib!" Ellen's rickshaw *wallah* called out from behind her. She turned and found that he had stopped a few yards back and was gesturing to her not to proceed. "Finish, memsahib! No go!" The man seemed apprehensive about something. But she had to have those batteries in case the electricity went off again, as it had last night. So she paid off the rickshaw man and continued alone.

The crowd was closer now and the noise was louder. She could see a group of men in khaki uniforms behind the crowd. Ellen reached the electrical shop, went inside, and purchased her batteries.

"Go home, memsahib," the proprietor urged her. "We are closing now. There will be trouble." As soon as Ellen left the shop he began to roll down the steel shutter that protected his glass display window.

The black flag procession had moved up Mahatma Gandhi Road by now, and Ellen could make out the features of the marchers. They were obviously students from the Muslim University. What were they up to? All that noise and shouting and waving of banners. My God! Was that Anwar Hussain at the head of the procession?

Ellen watched in horror as a diminutive Hindu shopkeeper ran out into the street and pleaded with the marchers. A shower of stones shattered his window and a black-clad youth pushed him roughly down. Wherever there was an open shop the window was similarly smashed.

Anwar was close enough for Ellen to make him out clearly, but he had not seen her, sheltered as she was in a doorway.

Now the procession came abreast of Ellen's doorway.

Rocks, bricks, and bottles began to fall on the marchers, thrown from the roofs of buildings along the road. Her heart pounded. The sweat of fear stained her clothes. She looked up and saw young men on the roofs shouting at the marchers, throwing missiles, and scurrying from roof to roof. From time to time a student would scream in pain when he was hit. Some of them were bleeding. Their companions would help them to the shelter of a doorway. The students tried to throw the brickbats and bottles back at the men on the roofs, but still the missiles fell on them. Hemmed in by buildings on each side, and with the khaki-clad police closing in behind them, the procession struggled slowly up the narrow street.

She had to get out of there. But where could she go? She knew nothing of the maze of alleys that lay behind Mahatma Gandhi Road. Oh God! Where could she go?

"Ellen!" It was Anwar, standing in the middle of the road. It was amazing how she saw him so clearly—his nose, his eyes, even the hairs of his beard. Was that exaltation in his face? "What are you doing here? Go away!" he shouted. "You'll get hurt!" As Anwar started toward her Ellen saw a brick falling through the air, but it was as if she were watching a movie in slow motion. The brick struck Anwar on the side of the head, bounced off his shoulder, and shattered on the pavement. Anwar dropped to the ground and lay motionless, surrounded by students who seemed unable to help him. Ellen rushed to his side, kneeled down, and cradled his head in her arms. Ellen sobbed, her eyes nearly blinded by tears.

The procession began to move from the rear. The students in front were pushed by those in the back. The shouting of slogans changed to cries of fear and pain. Ellen stood up and tried to see down the street. Helmeted policemen had charged the procession from the rear and were beating the students with steel-tipped bamboo *lathis*. The students began to run up the road to escape the police. Those in the front of the procession, unaware at first of what was happening, were pressed forward or pushed aside by the students running from the rear. Bricks and bottles continued to fall on them from the nearby roofs. The noise of shouts and screams filled the narrow road and echoed between the buildings.

Ellen and some students had just managed to drag Anwar's body to the side of the street when the main wave of students surged forward. Ellen was suddenly knocked aside. Her sandal caught in a loose paving stone, and she fell into an open drain at the side of the road. She lay there, dazed, looking up at the legs of the running students. The filthy, smelly drainage soaked into her clothes. Whimpering like a puppy, her face streaked by tears, barely able to see, Ellen struggled out of the drain. She staggered to a narrow opening between two shops and slipped away from the nightmare of Mahatma Gandhi Road.

32

Saturday, February 9, 1952

A drop of sweat rolled down Surendra Gupta's face and lodged in the corner of his mouth. He licked away the salty drop and looked at his watch. It was time for his morning tea. Tea! What wouldn't he give for a cup of tea. He sank to his knees, painfully aware of the tension in his leg muscles and the weight of the revolver in his pocket. He carefully lifted the curtain that covered the small window and stole another glance at the peaceful Nawabganj street below.

Everything was ready. He had prepared himself for this day of glory by taking a ritual bath, having his head shaved except for the tuft at the back, and making an offering at the temple of Lord Shiva, the father of Ganesh, the God Who Overcomes Obstacles. Man Singh's driver was waiting by his stolen lorry, ready to move it into the path of Nehru's car and then disappear. In a nearby alley, next to the cloth shop, Man Singh himself was waiting with another stolen lorry, waiting to drive it into the Grand Trunk Road behind the prime minister's car and abandon it. When Nehru got out to see why his way was blocked and to greet the bystanders, Gupta would pick him off like a duck rising from a marsh.

Then, in the ensuing chaos, Gupta would quickly escape over the roofs to join Man Singh, drive back to Ramgarh, and organize the rising. Babu Ram and Sharma had thousands of leaflets ready. They would use Ram Lal's telephone to send word to R.S.S. men all over India. It would be the moment for *Hindu Raj* and *Ram Raj*; yes, Hindu Rule and the Rule of God.

Gupta wiped his eyeglasses and his forehead for the fifteenth time with his damp handkerchief. He opened his woolen jacket and flapped its two sides to get some air to his sweat-soaked *kurta*. He looked at his watch once more. Soon it would be time.

Gupta took the police service revolver out of his pocket and laid it on the floor beside him. Those homemade pistols were no good for this kind of work. No accuracy. This job required careful aim, a cool head, and the revolver that Ram Lal Prasad had taken from Saxena's body.

What a fool that Ram Lal was! He had asked only one hundred rupees for Saxena's gun. He could have gotten at least five hundred at the *chor bazaar*. The jungle was full of *dacoits* who would sell their mothers for a good police revolver.

Gupta's right leg began to ache. No! Not a cramp! Not now! He scrambled to his feet and hobbled around the small room, squeezing the muscle of his thigh. The cramp slowly subsided. He took the chair from the back wall and moved it to the window. The brief exercise made him feel more relaxed and confident.

What was that? A siren? Was he coming now? No, just the braying of a donkey somewhere in the distance. Wait! It *was* a siren. He's coming. Where's the revolver? Good. He moved the curtain aside slightly and rested the revolver on the window sill to steady it.

"The lorry! Damn that man. Why is he still smoking that blasted *bidi*? Can't he hear the damn siren? Ah, there he goes. Just in time. They're coming now. What's that woman doing in the road? Get out of the way, damn you!" Gupta's jaw dropped. My God! He was talking to himself, nearly shouting! He needed to concentrate.

The siren grew louder. A jeep with four policemen aboard rounded the bend in the road. At that moment the woman decided to cross. The jeep driver shouted and wrenched his steering wheel. The jeep spun around, coming to rest against the lorry that was blocking the way. A second jeep rounded the bend and braked to a shuddering stop. Then came a black Buick sedan, which squealed to a halt, barely avoiding a collision.

"Come on, Man Singh! Your turn now. Get that lorry moving," Gupta urged. He heard the grinding sound of an ancient starter from the alley down the road. The engine caught, turned over a few times, and died. "For God's sake, Man Singh! Get that blasted lorry started!" The engine caught and died again. "Damn you, Man Singh! Damn that blasted lorry!" Then the engine caught, roared twice, and the lorry reluctantly crawled into the main road and stopped behind the Buick. Man Singh jumped out and bolted back into the alley.

There was a moment of silence as each man in the motorcade checked himself for injuries. Then the shouting began. A small crowd of men and boys and barking dogs gathered by the roadside. The policemen in the lead jeep pounded on the lorry with their batons, shouting for the driver to get it out of the way.

Gupta aimed his revolver at the black Buick sedan, just a dozen yards below. The hammer was drawn back, the safety was off, his left hand supported his trembling right wrist.

"Come on, you scoundrel," he growled. "Get out, damn you! Just step out of the car, you Muslim lover!"

The two officers of the security guard conferred. A front window of the sedan was rolled down halfway, and the Sikh driver beckoned to the officers. They approached the Buick and one of them bent down and spoke to the passenger in the back seat. The other scanned the buildings that lined the road. Gupta pulled the revolver back from the window sill. Then he saw the Buick's window close and the officers move away from the car.

"Get out, you swine! Get out! Get out!" Gupta pleaded. The bastard wasn't going to get out of the car. Every picture in the newspapers, every newsreel at the Picture Palace, had shown Nehru getting out of his car to meet the people. Why not now? Why now did he have to stay in his car?

The senior officer shouted a command to the policemen. Joined by some of the bystanders, they pushed the blocking lorry to the side of the road. The spectators broke into a cheer. The dogs barked. In a minute the jeeps were turned around and loaded. The officer shouted another command and waved his stick. The motorcade moved with increasing speed, its sirens wailing, down the narrow road in the direction of Ramgarh.

Tears welled up in Gupta's eyes. His shoulders drooped, his shaven head hung down. A violent convulsion shook his body as he realized that he had failed. After a few moments he put the revolver in his pocket and stood up. Then he took the gun out and looked at it. The hammer was still cocked. The dark, satin steel was so cool, so clean. He took the barrel into his mouth. It tasted of oil. His finger slowly tightened around the trigger.

Then he paused and took the gun from his mouth. With

fierce intensity he uncocked the hammer, set the safety, and shoved the revolver into his pocket. He wiped his eyes, glanced at his watch, straightened his jacket, and hurried out of the room.

33

Saturday, February 9, 1952

Mohammed Abdul Karim drew on his cigarette, inhaling deeply as he looked out over the crowd that filled the Muslim University cricket ground. He was standing on the top row of the grandstand, dressed in his best uniform with his service ribbons pinned over his breast pocket. His hair was freshly cut, his cheeks closely shaved, his mustache neatly trimmed.

Everything seemed to be ready. Hafiz-ur-Rehman and Om Prakash were there at either end of the rostrum. He could see squads of Provincial Armed Constabulary, with loaded rifles, stationed at the four corners of the cricket ground. Plainclothes men, some wearing the student uniform of black *shervani*, white pants, and fur cap, were circulating among the nearly two thousand students milling about on the field. Nehru's personal bodyguard would be responsible for close protection. Now it was up to Allah.

Seated on chairs in the center was the faculty, many dressed in colorful robes representing universities in Europe and America. Ellen Siddiqi was there also, wearing *kameez* and *shalvar*. Behind the faculty was the roped-off *zenana* section, where the *purdah* ladies sat wearing the black *burqas* that covered them from head to ankle. And way in the back, almost hidden behind the students, were the hundreds—mostly Hindus—who had come out from Ramgarh City to receive *darshan* from the prime minister's presence. Gupta might be among them, Karim thought.

He walked over to Hafiz-ur-Rehman.

"The crowd seems very quiet, Superintendent Sahib," Hafiz said. "I don't understand it. A new vice chancellor. It's supposed to be a happy occasion, isn't it?"

"It is, Hafiz Sahib. But maybe . . . maybe they're still in shock from last week. Two killed? Thirty or forty hurt? Curfew every night? It's enough to take the joy out of any occasion." Karim looked out at the crowd. "Well, if it keeps them peaceful for a while let 'em stay in shock. They'll recover soon enough."

Hafiz grinned. "What about Gupta, sir? Anything new?"

"Not a word, Hafiz. Not even a rumor. He's been gone for over a week. We've been watching everyone he had anything to do with. We've had men at the railway station, the bus stand, the octroi posts—nothing."

"It's uncanny, sir. This is not Bombay, this is a small town. We should have picked him up by now."

Karim stamped out his cigarette. "And if he has anything political in mind, today's the day. By the way, Hafiz, have you alerted the men here that Gupta may be wearing a disguise?"

Hafiz-ur-Rehman stared at Karim. "My God! A disguise! Why didn't I think of it before? My God, sir. I don't know what to say."

Karim took off his cap and rubbed his forehead with his handkerchief. There it was again, that pyramid with its point pressing him into the ground. Fighting to keep from rebuking Hafiz-ur-Rehman, he lighted another Sepoy. His hands shook as he held the match to the cigarette.

"Get Om Prakash over here," Karim ordered. Hafiz-ur-

Rehman beckoned to the young officer, who trotted up and saluted.

"It's Gupta," Karim said. "He may be wearing some kind of disguise. We might not be able to recognize him. What do you think?" His hands continued to tremble.

"That's true, sir," Om Prakash said. "We should have thought of that. What should we do?"

"What sort of disguises might be available in Ramgarh?" Karim asked.

"There's no local theater here," Hafiz-ur-Rehman answered. "No one I know of who would be able to do a professional job. There's a wigmaker on Mahatma Gandhi Road. Could he make a false beard, I wonder?"

"What about dark glasses, like a film star?" Om Prakash suggested brightly.

Karim pulled at his mustache. "*Achcha*," he said. "There's no time to lose. Om Prakash, go out onto the field and tell them. Gupta may be disguised. Tell every uniformed policeman. Tell them to watch out for anything unusual. You know? A false beard or mustache, dark glasses, er . . . , a limp, a cane, a crutch. Any such person should identify himself." He paused to light another Sepoy. "Hafiz Sahib, you do this also. Speak to one of the plainclothes men. Just one, mind you. Have the plainclothes men tell each other. This way we might hide the identities of most of them. Understood? I'll get back to my post." He felt a little calmer now that he had taken some action.

Karim resumed his vigil on top of the grandstand. Damn those loudspeaker men! Those screeches would drive even a deaf man crazy! He could see Ellen sitting in the faculty section. Maybe she'd . . . *Purdah* ladies! What about the *purdah* ladies! Gupta would be short enough to pass for one if he hid under a *burqa*. But how . . . ? What could . . . ?

Ellen! Would she help? Moving slowly so as not to attract undue attention, Karim walked to the faculty section where Ellen was sitting next to Wahid Sherif. As Karim approached, Wahid frowned, said something to Ellen, and left his chair.

"Good morning, Mrs. Siddiqi," Karim said, saluting. "How have you been keeping?"

"Mr. Karim. How nice. You've got your hands full this morning. Won't you sit down?"

"I have no wish to take Doctor Wahid Sherif's chair," Karim said.

"Sit down for a moment."

"Ellen, I must talk to you," Karim whispered.

"Wahid's very upset. It's Anwar Hussain. He's dead, you know. Wahid holds you responsible." Ellen looked away. "I saw him die, Abdul. I was there." She turned back to Karim. "But it's not your fault. I've tried to reason with him, but it's no use. He won't listen."

"What's done is done. I'm sorry. But listen. Matter of urgency. I must speak to you. Please." He grasped her elbow. "We are looking for this man. A dangerous man. He may be in disguise. Will you help us?"

Ellen looked him sharply in the eye. "Of course. But what can I do? I'm a foreigner."

"Ellen, just go to the ladies' section and look around. Look at the *purdah* ladies. The man may be wearing a *burqa*. If you notice anything unusual, make a signal to me. You know? Large feet. Large hands. Broad shoulders. Er . . . smell like a man. You know. Can you do it?"

"It's exciting. Like the movies." Ellen giggled. "Don't tell my husband."

"I assure you, Ellen. It is of the gravest importance. But please. Only observe and signal. Do not approach anyone yourself. Will you help?"

"Of course, Abdul. What kind of signal?"

"*Achcha*. Yes . . . put your hand behind your ear like an old person. You know? Like an old man who is deaf."

"Wish me luck, Abdul." Ellen patted her hair into place and strolled over to the ladies' section. Karim watched her slim figure moving beneath the hand-loomed cloth of her *kameez*.

That's done, he thought. But if she did find Gupta, then what? If she made a mistake . . . ? If only they had some women in the police. He lighted another cigarette. A train whistled in the distance. The Upper India Express? He looked at his watch. Too early.

The sound of sirens brought everyone to their feet. The sound rose and fell, grew louder, and then diminished to silence. The prime minister's motorcade appeared at the gate of the cricket ground. Jawaharlal Nehru, slim, erect, smiling, left the black Buick sedan and, flanked by his assistant and two security officers, approached the welcoming party. Acting Vice Chancellor Ibrahim Mirza, his white hair contrasting with the deep green of his academic gown, greeted the prime minister with the Muslim *salaam aleikum*. Nehru, a Hindu, responded with *aleikum salaam*, a gesture that brought smiles to the faces of the welcoming party.

Rhythmic shouts rose from a group of students waiting not far from the entrance. *Urdu zindabad! Hindi murdabad! Urdu zindabad! Hindi murdabad!* Damn! Karim thought. Not again! Not another demonstration! Didn't these people have any sense? Couldn't they leave it until the ceremony was over and Nehru had gone? Good God! Look at him! He's going over to those students! Oh, General Poonawalla, why didn't you tell me he behaved like this? Look at him! They're all around him!

Followed by news cameramen the prime minister

plunged into the crowd of students, talking, listening, shaking hands, waving, flashing his captivating smile. Twice he placed his hand on a young man's shoulder and gave him his full attention. The shouting died down and was replaced by laughing and cheering. No wonder he's prime minister, Karim thought. Who could resist him?

But this was dangerous. No one could predict what a crowd might do, especially when those on the edge want something that's in the center. Karim jumped off the grandstand and hurried over to the thronging students.

The prime minister stopped shaking hands, said something to the students, and began to move back toward the welcoming party. The cameramen ran ahead, pausing to turn back for pictures. Nehru suddenly changed direction and headed straight for Karim. My God! He's coming toward me, Karim thought. He's coming toward me! I'd better get out of the way.

"Superintendent Karim?" Nehru asked in English. He held out his hand. "Poonawalla told me you'd be in charge here." Karim trembled. The sensitive features, the warm smile, the cultivated accent were overwhelming. He saluted but Nehru wanted to shake hands. "It's a big responsibility, Superintendent. I want you to know how much I appreciate your work." Speechless, Karim stood and watched the prime minister continue his walk to the platform, where he took his seat flanked by Mirza and Dr. Gilani, the vice chancellor-designate.

Karim pulled himself together and returned to his post at the top of the grandstand. It had been a scary ten minutes, but the prime minister was probably out of danger for the time being. But he must still leave this cricket ground. Only a month before a man had died horribly here.

Ibrahim Mirza rose and approached the microphone

warily, as if it were a tall poisonous plant. He looked out at the audience and back at the prime minister. Taking courage, he grasped the microphone stand and shouted, "Ladies and gentlemen!" A loud screech assailed the audience as the blast of sound echoed off the walls of the mosque across the field. A sound technician jumped up to the platform and instructed Dr. Mirza how to speak into the microphone. The prime minister made a joke and Dr. Mirza approached the microphone again.

"Ladies and gentlemen," he said in English, "the installation ceremonies for the new vice chancellor of the Muslim University will now commence." There were a few cheers from the students and the audience became quiet. Dr. Mirza's handsome face beamed at them.

"The Muslim University has just passed through a difficult period," Mirza continued. "Between the university and the city of Ramgarh there has been bad feeling. There has been tragedy." He turned to glance at the prime minister. "But this . . . this installation . . . is a time of renewal, a time to bind up the wounds of the past, a time to bring all of the communities together." Mirza smiled at the audience, as if pleased at how well his rhetoric was translating from the words on his manuscript to the sounds that came out of the loudspeakers. "Our first speaker will be the member of parliament for Ramgarh, Congress Party worker Thakur Lal Bahadur Anand." He turned to a short, fat man dressed in white homespun cotton. "Thakurji?"

A faint cheer broke from the townspeople at the back of the audience, as the politician rose laboriously to his feet and came to the microphone. He waved acknowledgment and then turned to the university audience with a stern look on his face. It was a time of reconciliation, he said, speaking in Hindi. The appointment of a new vice chancellor should signal a change in the relations between the university and the town. Cooperation, not confrontation, should be the key word. The member of parliament droned on. The audience sat inert, as if in a trance, and allowed the rhetoric to flow over them like vapor.

Karim was hungering for a cigarette. Politicians, he mused, it took them half an hour just to get warmed up. What a bore this little man was. Was this his representative in parliament? Was this what democracy produced?

Wait! What was that he said? The rights of minority communities must be protected but not at the expense of the rights of the majority? The fool! What was he trying to do, start another communal riot? My God!

Murmurs of disapproval rustled through the audience. Then shouts from a few students: *Urdu zindabad! Hindi murdabad!* A frown appeared on the prime minister's face. Fortunately, before the situation could deteriorate further, Thakur Lal Bahadur Anand abruptly returned to his seat. Karim breathed more easily. He looked out over the audience; there was no sign of any disturbance. He caught Ellen's eye. She shook her head.

Now it was time for the high point of the ceremonies, the introduction of the prime minister and the inauguration of Dr. Gilani.

Dr. Mirza began. He reviewed the prime minister's role in securing India's independence from the British. He discussed, one by one, his many incarcerations in British jails during the struggle. He called on the spirit of Mahatma Gandhi. He praised at length the prime minister's concern for the rights and welfare of the Muslims of India. Finally, with the audience squirming and shuffling their feet, he concluded his introduction by leading the prime minister to the microphone and embracing him. The university audience clapped with well-mannered enthusiasm. But from the townspeople in the back of the crowd there came wild cheering.

Karim tensed. Nehru was alone at the microphone. He stood with his head bowed, his palms pressed together, and acknowledged the applause. Karim glanced left and right. Hafiz and Prakash seemed alert. He scanned the audience. Nothing. He looked at Ellen. Nothing.

Nehru began to speak in the faultless accent he had learned at Harrow, where two of his English classmates had been future rulers of India. The audience settled down. Those who knew English followed the prime minister's words attentively. The others gazed at his face and basked in the *darshan* of his presence.

Karim kept his eyes on the audience, carefully watching the students, the townspeople, and the *purdah* ladies. Ellen Siddiqi made another gesture of futility. If Gupta was hidden under a *burqa* he'd been able to fool her. Or maybe he was in the group of townspeople. There were some *purdah* ladies there too. Prime Minister Sahib, please let it be a short speech. Do the installation and go back to where you will be safe from madmen.

The prime minister's speech was concrete, down-to-earth. He focused on the role the university should play in preparing Muslims to participate fully in national life. He called on the Muslims to think of themselves first of all as Indian citizens in a secular India. He said that Muslim religion and culture could continue to thrive in India, that Muslim graduates need not run away to Pakistan to find a career. The faculty and the administrators smiled benignly at Nehru's well-chosen words of exhortation and reassurance.

Karim suddenly twisted his head to the left. A small

black-clad figure—a *purdah* lady—was approaching the prime minister from the direction of the gate. But was it a *purdah* lady? Or was it Gupta? Karim jumped down from the grandstand. Would he be in time? He drew his revolver and called to Hafiz-ur-Rehman to join him. By the time they reached the *purdah* lady she was within easy pistol range of the prime minister. The woman stopped. The nearby spectators stared. Nehru paused and watched them.

"Stand where you are!" Karim ordered, speaking in Urdu and holding his hand up. "Do not approach the prime minister!" What would he do now? He couldn't order this person to raise the black veil that concealed the face. If it were an orthodox Muslim woman the male members of her family would be outraged. Riots might break out.

Karim stood there, hesitating. His finger tightened around the trigger of his gun. Then a genuine female voice said, "I have only a *chitty* for Panditji, sahib. A letter about my son in the prison." An authentic female arm, with rings on the fingers and bangles on the wrist, held out a small envelope with Nehru's name written on it in the careful Urdu of a professional scribe. A vision of his own mother flashed through Karim's mind. He put the revolver back in its holster.

"Give me the letter, mother. I will see that Panditji gets it. Now you go back to your place." Karim watched while the small figure disappeared into the crowd. He returned to his position, hoping that the incident had not unduly disturbed the prime minister.

Nehru brought his speech to a close with some complimentary words about Dr. Gilani. He expressed his confidence that Dr. Gilani, an old boy of the Muslim University, was the man who would lead it into a bright future. Then, without waiting to acknowledge the applause, he called Dr.

Gilani to his side and invested him with the ceremonial shawl of office, a scarf of green silk heavily appliquéd with silver and gold designs.

The installation was over. Thank God it had gone well so far. Now he had to get the prime minister safely to his car and back on the Grand Trunk Road to New Delhi. When Nehru was safely out of Ramgarh District and the inverted pyramid was no longer on his shoulders, he would go back to his bungalow, have a warm bath and one of Faiz Khan's chicken curries, and sleep for twenty-four hours.

The prime minister finished shaking hands with the platform dignitaries and began to make his way to the gate. Karim, Hafiz-ur-Rehman, and Om Prakash moved closer to him, taking their stations between Nehru and the surging, cheering crowd of students and townspeople. Karim gestured to the Provincial Armed Constabulary officer near the gate to send his troopers to surround the prime minister. This was no time to relax. Anything could happen.

Suddenly an altercation broke out. It seemed to come from the group of students that had shouted slogans loudest and most often. "Stop shoving! Get away from me!" Karim looked to the source of the shouting. It involved a dozen or more fur-capped, *shervani*-clad students. The shouting grew louder, more strident. A few other students were nervously tittering and laughing at them, but Karim sensed that the crowd's mood had abruptly changed from relaxed friendliness to anger.

Nehru continued to move slowly toward the gate, shaking hands, chatting, smiling, waving to well-wishers. His bodyguards stood close behind him, warily eyeing the hands and arms that were thrust toward him out of the unruly crowd.

"Hafiz Sahib, I'm going to have a look over there," Karim

shouted, pointing to the source of the argument. He began to push his way through the surging crowd of students. As he moved, most of the students turned toward him. Angry voices assailed him. "Murderer!" "Killer of Muslims!" "Traitor!" Good, Karim thought, as he pushed on. Let them be angry at me rather than at the prime minister. Just let him be out of here before anything happens.

He was no more than fifty feet from the scene of the altercation when a clear space suddenly opened up. It revealed a small man wearing Muslim clothes and steel-rimmed glasses. Other students were pushing him from side to side and shouting obscenities. Karim wondered how to deal with the situation.

Then it happened. One of the students hit the man on the side of the head and his fur cap fell to the ground. And from the back of his recently shaved head there grew the pigtail of an orthodox Hindu.

"Gupta!" Karim shouted. "Gupta! Surendra Gupta!" He broke into a run, pulling his revolver from its holster. "You're under arrest!"

The man turned to face Karim. It was indeed Surendra Gupta. His reddened lips were stretched wide, revealing clenched teeth, and he had a pistol pointed at Karim. There was a shot. A stunning hammer blow struck Karim's right chest. The force of the bullet spun him around and knocked him to the ground.

The students stood there, immobilized by fear and shock. Gupta, pistol in hand, ran toward the prime minister, now clearly isolated from the hushed crowd. Gupta shouted, "*Hindu Raj!*" The guards fumbled at their holsters as Gupta came closer. "*Hindu Raj! Ram Raj!*"

Another shot rang out. Gupta gasped and pitched forward, his pistol falling away from his hand. Karim let his smoking revolver rest on the ground. He laid his head on his arm and spat a dollop of blood from his mouth. The pain began to surge. The students' trousers seemed to dissolve into a white blur. He was so tired. If only his wife would massage his back, he would have a good sleep.

34

The following article appeared in *The Statesman*, New Delhi, on April 21, 1952.

"Ramgarh (from our Special Correspondent)—The trial of the three men implicated in the attempted assassination of the prime minister in February at the Muslim University is scheduled to commence tomorrow at the Ramgarh Magistrates Court. Gautam Sharma, a teacher, Man Singh, a lorry owner, and Babu Ram, a merchant, all of Ramgarh City, have been charged with violations of the Indian Penal Code. They include conspiracy to commit murder, attempted murder, conspiracy to commit treason, treason, conspiracy to commit sedition, sedition, unlicensed manufacture of lethal weapons, and theft of property. Police officials have indicated that more than enough evidence and testimony are available to ensure the conviction of the defendants. If convicted, they face penalties of death or life imprisonment.

"More than twenty journalists have come to Ramgarh to cover the trial, including reporters from newspapers and magazines in Bombay, New Delhi, and

Calcutta. Press attention to the case has been described by lawyers and judges here as 'sensational.' One senior judge was quoted as saying that the case has become a 'circus.' Mr. Bharat Chaudhri, B.A.(Cantab.), I.C.S., who will preside, has declined to comment on the case.

"It is known that the three defendants and the deceased assassin were members of the banned organization Rashtriya Swayamsevak Sangh. No one that this correspondent spoke to has suggested that the attempted assassination was any more than a local action by the four Ramgarh men.

"Mr. Ram Lal Prasad, a prominent manufacturer who is the president of the Municipal Committee and leader of the Ramgarh branch of the Hindu Mahasabha, has expressed the sorrow and outrage of the people of Ramgarh at the terrible events of February 9 at the university. Mr. Prasad told this correspondent that, in his opinion, the alleged actions of these men did not reflect the feelings of the people of Ramgarh. The town has had a reputation in the business community, he said, as a relatively peaceful place with good labour relations and good relations between the communities. He said that Ramgarh's people are nonviolent people, who welcome merchants and manufacturers of all communities to set up businesses in the town."

EPILOGUE

It was the hot season. It was that three-month period between the end of winter and the bursting of the monsoon rains, between the vernal equinox and the summer solstice, when the sun's vertical rays crept day by day northward from the equator, finally to reach the tropic of Cancer in Central India.

It was the time of the *loo*, the hot blast of wind that gusted from the desert of Rajasthan, searing Ramgarh like a flame, shriveling the leaves and parching the animals and the people. The farmers plowed their fields at night. The city folk remained indoors from late morning until early evening, splashing water on the *tatties*, the straw mats that were hung over doors and windows to cool the air.

Mohammed Abdul Karim squirmed in his wheelchair as the hospital orderly pushed him through the barrier onto the platform at Ramgarh Station. He wiped the perspiration from his forehead and neck. The fresh, clean uniform he had put on at the hospital was already blotched with sweat. He ached with weariness. It was only over Dr. Lalchand's strenuous objections that he had been able to leave the hospital at all.

The platform was an oven filled with dust. Heat radiated down from the corrugated iron roof, and windblown dust coursed through the shed. Karim shielded his eyes with his hand. Could he see her in this dust storm?

"First-class waiting room," Karim said to the orderly. They moved slowly down the platform, past sleeping coolies and panting pye dogs. Outside the waiting room Karim adjusted his jacket and cap. "Here's a rupee, Shukla," he said. "Push me into the room, then go and have your tiffin. Come and collect me when the train leaves."

Ellen and Iqbal Siddiqi, Wahid Sherif, and Ibrahim Mirza were sitting in the center of the darkened room under the ceiling fan. What dejection on the men's faces. And this gloomy waiting room. God, it looked depressing! The men stood up when he entered.

"Mr. Karim!" Ellen exclaimed. "You're out of the hospital!" By contrast with the sweat-stained men she looked cool and almost glowing in a pale green dress with a darker green design around the bottom. How good she looked in Western dress, he thought. But had she put on a bit of weight?

"I . . . I . . . ," Karim stammered. There it was again, that feeling that had first affected him at the N.C.C. parade and had overcome him in New Delhi. He paused and took a breath. His chest ached. "I heard you were going away, Mrs. Siddiqi. To America. I came to wish you good journey." He looked away from Ellen. "Doctor Siddiqi. Doctor Mirza. Doctor Sherif."

"I'm delighted to see that you're better, Superintendent Sahib," Mirza boomed. Iqbal and Wahid looked uncomfortable. Were they angry at Karim's intrusion into their private ceremony?

"I'm going home to visit my family, Mr. Karim. It was nice of you to come out in this heat to see me off. I must say, you do look like you're making a good recovery. Don't you think so, Iqbal?"

"Very good recovery," Iqbal growled. Did Iqbal give a damn if he recovered or not?

"We're all in your debt, Superintendent Sahib. For killing that madman. If Nehru had been shot at the university, we Muslims would be in deep trouble." Mirza brightened. "When do you receive your decoration?"

"When I am able to travel, I will go to New Delhi." Should he tell them how Ellen had helped him at the installation? Better not. It would only make Iqbal more unpleasant. "Will you be away for a very long time, Mrs. Siddiqi?"

"Probably about six months. It will take me nearly a month and a half to get home. Three weeks from Bombay to England and a week to New York. I'm taking the *Victoria* from Bombay. It's an Italian ship. Air conditioned, thank goodness." Ellen made a mock gesture of wiping her brow. "I'll be landing at Naples. Then the train to Calais and the boat to England. I'll take the *United States* to New York," she went on. "My first taste of America in almost three years."

Why was Ellen going into such detail about her trip home? What was she trying to say? Karim wiped his face. Didn't she know that all he cared about was when was she coming back?

The platform bell began to ring, announcing the arrival of the Upper India Express. The men looked at Ellen, fixing her image in their minds. Ellen looked at each one in turn. No one spoke.

"Perhaps we three should wait outside on the platform while Ellen and Iqbal say goodbye," Mirza finally said with an embarrassed smile. Wahid Sherif grunted agreement, and

Mirza pushed Karim through the door as the train steamed slowly alongside the platform. A coolie appeared, carrying a holdall and two suitcases that Karim recognized as Ellen's. Wahid Sherif went off with the coolie to find Ellen's reserved seat.

Karim leaned back in his chair. He was barely able to lift his handkerchief to his face. He could taste the dust in his mouth. Sweat dripped down under the bandage on his chest. The arriving and departing passengers were like wraiths in this dust-filled air.

"How are things at the university, Doctor Sahib?" Karim asked, just to pass the time. "No more fires, I hope."

"The students are on holiday right now, Superintendent Sahib. Things are quiet. Doctor Gilani has taken charge. I am playing billiards at the staff club." Mirza smiled down at Karim. "Do you play? When you are better you must come and play as my guest. You will enjoy it." Karim nodded gratefully. At this moment the last thing he could think of was a game of billiards.

From somewhere down the platform a pye dog's agonized yelp was heard just as Ellen and Iqbal came out of the waiting room. "That's a sound I'd like to forget," Ellen said. She held out her hand to Karim. Iqbal stood behind her, watching intently.

"Have a good journey, Mrs. Siddiqi," Karim said. "Come back soon." He held her hand in his. His grip was firm. Did he feel an answering squeeze? Ellen looked at him intently. What was she trying to tell him? Did she realize what her leaving was doing to him?

Karim's orderly appeared, grasped the handles of the wheelchair, and waited for instructions.

"Take good care of yourself, Mr. Karim. Get better very soon." Ellen smiled. "I'll send you a postcard from Minneapolis." She turned away and started for her compartment, accompanied by Iqbal and Mirza.

Meaningless words, Karim thought. Strictly an ordinary farewell. But what was there in her voice, in her inflection, in her handshake, in the way she had looked at him?

"Back to the hospital," Karim said to his orderly. The guard blew his whistle just as they reached the barrier. "Wait," Karim said. "Turn me around." He sat and watched while the train pulled slowly out of the station. Would she ever come back, he wondered.